Promise to Return

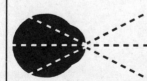

This Large Print Book carries the
Seal of Approval of N.A.V.H.

Promise to Return

Elizabeth Byler Younts

THORNDIKE PRESS
A part of Gale, Cengage Learning

GALE
CENGAGE Learning·

Farmington Hills, Mich • San Francisco • New York • Waterville, Maine
Meriden, Conn • Mason, Ohio • Chicago

GALE
CENGAGE Learning®

Copyright © 2013 by Elizabeth Ruth Younts.
Promise of Sunrise Series #1
Thorndike Press, a part of Gale, Cengage Learning.

Thorndike Press® Large Print Christian Romance.
The text of this Large Print edition is unabridged.
Other aspects of the book may vary from the original edition.
Set in 16 pt. Plantin.

LIBRARY OF CONGRESS CATALOGING-IN-PUBLICATION DATA

Younts, Elizabeth Byler.
    Promise to return / by Elizabeth Byler Younts.
        pages ; cm. — (Promise of sunrise series ; #1) (Thorndike Press large print Christian romance)
    ISBN 978-1-4104-6567-2 (hardcover) — ISBN 1-4104-6567-5 (hardcover)
    1. Amish—Fiction. 2. World War, 1939-1945—Conscientious objectors—Fiction. 3. Large type books. I. Title.
PS3625.O983P76 2014
813'.6—dc23   2013042909

Published in 2014 by arrangement with Howard Books, a division of Simon & Schuster, Inc.

Printed in the United States of America
1 2 3 4 5 6 7 18 17 16 15 14

For Davis, you're my hero

And for all the U.S. military, past and present, and your families, I salute you

ACKNOWLEDGMENTS

To my God and Creator, who first gave me the desire and chance tell stories. Without You, Lover of my Soul, none of this would be possible.

To my husband, Davis, a major in the Air Force JAG Corps. As I wrote this book during your deployment, your dedication to your mission and our freedom inspired me. We were over 6,000 miles apart, but your heart and support were so close to me the whole time. I love you more than words can say.

To my daughters, Felicity and Mercy. Such light you both bring to my life. I am so privileged to be your mama. You two are the brightest stars in my universe.

To Natasha Kern, the most amazing agent a writer could ever ask for. I cannot put into words how thankful I am for you. You aren't just an outstanding agent but also a truly phenomenal person. I am so happy to be working with you.

To my editors at Howard Books, Becky Nesbitt, Beth Adams, and Amanda Demastus. Thank you for taking a chance on a new writer. Wow! I am absolutely thrilled to be working with each of you.

To my mom and dad, Joe and Esther (Coblentz) Byler. Your excitement and support were integral. Living with you both during the deployment and the writing of this book made all the difference in the world. You were a constant resource about the Amish lifestyle and never stopped believing in me no matter my circumstances. I'm just so thankful to be your daughter.

To my siblings, Emmalene, Johannes, Joseph, and Brandalyn. What can I say to express my joy that I am related to such amazing people? Wow, I'm lucky! Thank you for loving and supporting this peculiar middle child.

To the "Pitt Crew," Allison Pittman and Raquel Martinez. Two great writers but, most important, dear friends who have seen me through thick and thin. I am so exceedingly blessed by you both.

Thank you to my Amish family; to my grandma, Mammie Lydia, one of my personal heroines, to my many aunts and uncles, and to my over one hundred first cousins. The life you live inspires me. I am so blessed to be part of a family with such a rich heritage, strong convictions, and all around amazing people.

I also want to thank several others who have been such an encouragement to me: CWG in San Antonio, where I was given my wings to fly; the wonderful military wives of my No Perfect Girls Allowed group, where I was given hope when I felt hopeless; Becky Stanton and April Gardener, whose expertise helped make this book better; Rachel Hauck with *My Book Therapy,* whose brainstorming session with me made all the difference; and Holly Varni, a dear friend whom God wanted me to meet.

AMISH PRAYER

We pray for the governments and rulers of the nations, especially of those lands where Thy children are. Do not permit them to shed innocent blood, but inspire them to rule according to Thy will . . .

May they at all times promote the good and discourage and repress the evil, so that we who fear Thy name may lead quiet and peaceful lives here on earth. Amen.

A Devoted Christian's Prayer Book
PATHWAY PUBLISHERS

CHAPTER 1

November 1943

The scent of cherry pie and warm taffy tickled Miriam Coblentz's nose. Her hands slipped through the soft taffy she was pulling. She and her partner, Eli Brenneman, were working over the soft, shiny candy ahead of the other teams. All those years of kneading dough, milking cows, and scrubbing the wooden slats on the floor with a brush had made her hands strong. Unfortunately, every other girl in the lineup next to her had the same upbringing, so she had no advantage.

She looked left and right and watched as several of the girls and boys that were partnered up would occasionally steal an innocent kiss as they leaned forward, folding and stretching the taffy. When she turned back to Eli Brenneman, she caught the twinkle in his eyes and she set her jaw.

"Don't even think about it," she scolded

him playfully.

"You know you want to." He winked at her.

His tenor voice danced in the air like laundry on a line in a lazy breeze. She wouldn't let it wrap around her enough to touch her heart, even though she felt weakened in the moment. Her heart skipped a beat when the face of her boyfriend, Henry Mast, broke into her mind. He was far away at a Civilian Public Service camp, serving out his draft with hundreds of other conscientious objectors. She hadn't seen him in over six months.

"What I want is to win." She bit her lower lip and smiled at Eli.

She began pulling with more vigor. Next to her stood her best friend and cousin, Ida May. This was the last Singing Ida May would attend before she married Jesse. Since Singings were only for the unmarried in the community, how would it be to attend them without her? Ida May and Miriam had been attending them together since they were sixteen and talking about them for years before. They'd already said goodbye to the others in their tight group of friends and Miriam would be the last one left. She hated being one of the oldest spinster girls in their Amish community. All the other unmarried girls couldn't be called girls any longer. They were in their late twenties or older and didn't even attend the Singings. Their chances at marriage were left to the occasional widower or visitor. At least Miriam had a boyfriend, despite their separation.

The taffy toughened in her hands. She and Eli were almost finished. She smiled as she worked faster, wanting to win. Eli's white-blond hair, dampened with sweat, set off his deep-set blue eyes. He gave her a crooked smile, as though he knew taffy was not the only pull she was feeling that night.

She felt eyes on her. A few people down from Eli stood Sylvia Mast, Henry's sister. Her gaze narrowed in on Miriam. Miriam inhaled and held her breath for a long moment. Sylvia wanted to be paired with Eli, along with half the other girls, but he always chose Miriam. Should Miriam have told him *no*? She already had a boyfriend. She and Eli had gone out a few times before Henry asked her to date, but it was years ago and unimportant. Was it wrong of her to enjoy her friendship with Eli, taking him away from all the eligible girls? Apparently, Sylvia thought so. She tensed her jaw before she finally turned away, relieving Miriam.

The sunset through the window fell across

the row of arms, making the darkening taffy glisten against the orange hues. *Pull. Pull. Pull.* Why did she want to push instead? The chatter among the other couples picked up as there were several ready to claim their win. *Pull. Pull.* Her fingers were fatigued and every pull wearied her joints. *Pull.* It would be easier to just give up. Her muscles had worked hard enough. Small beads of sweat formed at her forehead around her *kapp. Pull. Pull.* Her teeth clenched. *Pull.*

"Miriam." Eli gestured toward the taffy. "Look."

Her arms stopped moving as she examined the taffy. It had started out shiny and crystal clear and now it was a hazy, golden color.

"We're done!" she called out as she and Eli held up their taffy.

Miriam's sister Fannie, who was hosting the Singing, waddled over, holding her back as her large belly led her through the small crowd of young people still pulling taffy. She declared Miriam and Eli the winners. She patted Miriam on the arm.

"Looks like you and Eli are good together." She lifted her eyebrows.

"Nah, Fannie, don't say that." Miriam pretended to pinch her sister's arm, giggling at her. Miriam was the youngest and only unmarried sibling in her family. She had

16

grown accustomed to her older brothers and sisters chiding her about getting married. Though they all knew that she and Henry had had to postpone their wedding when he was drafted, she knew they just wanted to see her happy and moving on with her life. It made for a difficult choice. Waiting until Henry's service was fulfilled to marry made her *ungeduldich,* impatient, but she was determined to have the life she longed for, and that included Henry.

She looked to see if Eli had heard Fannie, and his wink and nod told her that he had. He squared his wide shoulders, towering over all the boys in the lineup. A movement behind him, through the window, suddenly caught her attention. A slow swagger, an easy footfall, hands in pockets, hat tilted to the side.

Henry?

Henry!

She gasped. How was it even possible? His camp in Hagerstown, Maryland was over three hundred miles away from her small Delaware town, Sunrise. He hadn't written to her about having any leave time.

She pushed the taffy into Eli's arms and grabbed a towel to wipe her greasy hands, dropping the towel on her way out the door. Her legs couldn't carry her fast enough. She stepped down the stairs and ran down the small hill, meeting Henry in the drive. He pulled her into the shadow of the house's awning and into his arms.

She cried. She nestled deep into his chest, her head just below his shoulder as she breathed him in. How was it possible that after all these months, the scent of his bar soap and the slightest bit of cologne was still so familiar? She felt his hat fall and his warm breath and mouth against her ear, her neck, and, finally on her lips. She returned his passionate kiss, letting all the frustrations of waiting and longing fall away.

When they released for a moment she looked into his dark eyes. He had been worth the wait. She brushed her hand through the side of his black hair, shorter than the other Amish boys'. Her heart pounded a little harder, wondering what people would say about his shorn hair. Would he be challenged over it, even given his special circumstances? Her mother's debilitating cataracts would be to her advantage for once, but her father would be critical of Henry. She peered over his shoulder, seeing the warm yellow glow from the windows of the *daudy haus.* The grandpa house, across the driveway, was where she lived with her aging parents. She could

18

almost hear their hickory rocking chairs creak against the floorboards. While it was tradition for one of the older siblings to build a small home on their property for their elderly parents, it had never felt like home to Miriam. Fanny's house had been the home of her youth, she missed living there. She was supposed to live in the *daudy haus* that Fanny had built for their parents only temporarily, but now, after several years, she'd felt herself aging as she waited for Henry.

"Why didn't you tell me you were coming?" She returned her gaze to Henry, then took his hand and began leading him toward her sister's house.

"Wait, not yet." He pulled her back into his arms and peered into her gray eyes.

"Everyone will want to see you, and you haven't told me how it is that you're even here," she pressed. "Not that I'm complaining, but if I'd known, I would've made sure to make a lemon meringue pie for you, and cinnamon rolls, and whatever else you would have wanted."

"Miriam, Miriam." His silky, deep voice enveloped her, running smoothly over her face and hands, warming them against the cold November air. "Slow down. Let me just see you and have you to myself for a few moments. I've missed you."

At his words, her heart felt as smooth and warm as the taffy inside the house. His soft, easy speech mirrored the quiet and private Henry she had fallen in love with years earlier. While he had all the friends he ever could ask for, he often desired to be with only her. It was what drew her to him from the beginning. He was so different from the loud and rowdy boys that filled their community. His serious and thoughtful ways had always intrigued her.

"I wanted to surprise you." He traced a finger along her jawline.

She began to shiver from the inside out. The cold and the thrill of Henry's arrival caused a physical reaction she couldn't have anticipated. He rubbed his hands against her arms, warming her, then took off his coat to wrap around her.

"Your suspenders. Where are they?" She looked around his back, finding the essential piece of clothing hanging loosely down his backside. "And your shirt — your collar is folded down." She put her hands on her hips. "Are you trying to be fancy now that you've been with all those Mennonites at the camp?"

"The shirts you and my *mem* sent with me are so worn through, they are not worth wearing unless I'm working. I had to buy a shirt off of one of the boys at the camp." Henry's eyes veered from her own, concerning Miriam.

"So it is a Mennonite shirt?"

"No." He pulled up his suspenders.

Miriam didn't budge her gaze as she patiently waited for answers. Henry's shoulders sagged and he sighed.

"It was a boy from Ohio. They don't wear stand-up collars like us. Don't be upset. I have some shirts at home and can change as soon as I get there." He cupped her face, his smile nearly dripping onto her set jaw. She softened at his touch. His love was palpable, and she wanted to carry it as close to her heart as she could.

"How long are you home?"

"Four days." Henry's jaw tightened, and his eyes wandered from her face again.

"That's not too bad." She pulled his coat around her more tightly, fending off the shudders that still wracked her. "Last time you only had two days."

The light of the fading sun caught Henry's eyes just right. Was it the shining of their joy that emerged from his eyes? He sniffed and diverted his face from her. A tremor burned through her stomach and heart.

Something was wrong.

21

Was the camp extending his two-year service? Had some other girl caught his eye, someone who served their food or cleaned the barracks? Many of them weren't even Amish.

"What's wrong?" Her voice was insistent.

"Henry Mast, is that you, my boy?" Miriam's neighbor Nancy Poole called over as she left Miriam's front door. Nancy had been the district's most dedicated driver and all-around helper. Miriam enjoyed her charming and enthusiastic manner, and though the Amish community only needed a driver for an occasional errand into town and emergencies, she still greatly preferred Nancy to any other driver.

"Hello," Henry said, waving.

"Hello, Miriam. I was just over to see your mother for some tea," Nancy said, out of breath from the short walk. Her large frame was clothed in a housedress and coat.

"I'm sure Mother enjoyed that." Miriam's mother, Rosemary, and Nancy were so different, opposites even, and their friendship consisted mostly of Nancy talking and Rosemary listening.

"All done with the camp life, are you?" Nancy's eyes bounced between the two.

"I'm just home on leave," Henry answered. "Are your boys well?" He took

22

Miriam's hand and pulled her closer to him.

Miriam felt the heat rise in her face. She wasn't accustomed to any affection expressed in front of others.

"Yes, we hear from them every few weeks. So far, so good," she sighed and the three were silent for a short spell. "Well, then, enjoy your visit. So glad you're well and happy. And if there's ever anything you need, you know where to find me."

They said their goodbyes and watched her walk away for several long moments.

"She's a good woman," Henry commented.

"Yes," Miriam said quickly so they could return to their earlier conversation. "And now, tell me more about this Ohio clothing and what's been happening at the camp."

"We should go inside; we have plenty of time to talk later."

"I thought you wanted us to be alone?" He was avoiding her question. She knew it.

"Are my sisters here?"

Miriam nodded.

"I should go say hello." He picked up his hat, returning it to his head, then put an arm around her waist and led her to the house. Miriam noticed the taffy pull was long over, and several of the girls quickly moved away from the windows when they saw them coming.

As they got to the door, she removed his coat.

"Here, put this back on." She handed him the plain Amish coat, hoping it would hide his Ohio shirt collar. "And keep your hat on."

"Are you that worried about how I look?"

"Aren't you?"

"No, I'm not. I'm the same Henry I have always been." She expected to hear irritation in his voice but there was none. He even smiled at her as he put his arms on her shoulders, looking at her intensely. Both made her feel his warmth. "I guess being at the camp has taught me how what we look like on the outside isn't the most important thing."

Miriam was taken off guard by his comment but steered it back to her concern over his shirt. He didn't need any extra negative attention right now.

Usually, Miriam could handle change, but Henry had changed because of the camp. It frightened her. She could only hope it was for the better, though his hair and shirt did concern her. Before he left, the community saw him as one of the most loyal boys in the district and even had hopes of him becoming a preacher. Had that loyalty changed as easily as his appearance?

The vivid memory of her sister Kathryn walking out the door for the last time, breaking their hearts and blemishing the family, dashed through her mind. No, she couldn't bring any more shame to her family with Henry's new ways. She couldn't think of anything worse. Once Henry returned for good he would have to go back to how he used to be, his look, his seriousness, his love for the church. They both had to remain faithful in all ways. Surely, the old Henry she'd fallen in love with was not so severely changed. She hoped.

"For me? Please?" She handed him the coat.

He slipped it on and winked at her. She pulled him close for a kiss. She touched his face, letting her fingertips graze the line of his jaw. She stroked his face several more times, enjoying the feeling of his closeness and the smoothness of his skin. He had been shaving more often at the camp, instead of growing out his beard as the boys usually did when they got baptized. What would people say?

The door opened, silhouetting a large, square-shouldered figure just inside the door frame.

"Eli!" The best friends shook hands vigorously.

"Henry Mast. Welcome back." Eli returned a wide grin as they released their grip on each other.

Miriam saw a sharpness behind Eli's eyes, however, and his voice was softly laced with annoyance. It reminded her of their time in school when he congratulated Henry for winning a foot race when it was clear he was angry for losing. Was he upset that Henry was visiting?

"What brings you here? Afraid Miriam might fall for me?"

His words hung heavy in the air. Miriam glared at him, not knowing what to say. Why was he acting this way? They had spent more time together at the Singings, sure, and he'd driven her home on occasion when it was too far for her to walk, but those weren't dates. She was committed to Henry.

"What, you can't take a joke?" Eli tipped Henry's hat off of his head.

Henry's laugh was the only one that rang genuine as he picked up his hat. He must have believed Eli was joking. She forced hers out like the bleat of a goat, and Eli's was just as unnatural. She wanted to be mad at Eli for what he'd said, but couldn't. They'd been friends too long, and he was the only one out of her close group of friends who was at a standstill in his life, just like her. She was waiting for Henry's return. Though Eli hadn't made it clear to her what he was waiting on, it seemed clear to everyone else. Miriam ignored his whispers because she enjoyed being around her friend.

They entered the house and continued through the mudroom and into the kitchen, where Henry was greeted with handshakes and hearty welcomes. Henry stiffly hugged his sisters, Sylvia and Rachel. She watched as he explained how long he'd be home.

"Don't tell *Mem* and *Dat* that I'm home — I want to surprise them," he said. The girls agreed, and he moved on to say hello to the rest of the group of young people.

Miriam watched him, satisfied that he was home. When the kitchen grew uncomfortably warm and a rim of sweat formed around his brow, she felt guilty for asking him to keep his hat and coat on.

"Go ahead. I know it's hot in here," she whispered in his ear. He immediately obliged, handing her his hat and coat to put away. She hoped that since the excitement of his sudden appearance had passed and couples were beginning to pair up for their drive home, no one would notice his changed appearance.

"Henry, what are you wearing?" Eli pulled at his own collar. "Miriam's *dat* might have something to say about your hair, too. Tell him hello for me. He and I had a nice talk after church today."

He winked at Miriam before walking away.

"Eli Brenneman." Miriam spoke between her teeth. He didn't acknowledge her.

"Don't let him bother you." Henry waved a hand. "It's only Eli."

He winked at her before joining a conversation with several friends. She took care not to appear angry as she went to put Henry's things away.

"Hmm, doesn't really look like the same Henry, does he?" Eli must have followed her into the dark bedroom, where she put Henry's hat and coat down next to her things. "That camp sure is changing him."

Miriam looked around. The oil lamp was dimly lit but she didn't see anyone else in the room. "Hair grows, and he's been working so hard his shirts were worn through."

She wanted to tell Eli that it was none of his business, but she knew better. Everyone knew everyone's business in the community. That was just how it was. Sometimes it was through the expected chatter that help arrived when you needed it; other times it

caused hurt feelings and misinformation being relayed from home to home.

Eli didn't respond, which infuriated Miriam. In defending Henry, she was reminded
of how she'd done the same thing before
Kathryn finally left. Though this situation
was completely different, she reminded
herself. Henry had had no choice in joining
the Civilian Public Service.

Eli followed Miriam back into the kitchen.

"I had fun with you tonight," Eli said.
"Until Henry came."

Miriam's head whipped to see if anyone
else had heard him before she glared at him.
Surely he was joking. But his wild blue eyes
showed no hint of humor. Her heart thudded in her chest. She loved Henry. Eli knew
that.

"Are you ready to go home?" Henry
walked up to Miriam and Eli, seeming not
to notice the tension between them.

"I'm ready." Miriam ignored Eli as she
walked back into the dim room to gather
their things. Ida May was also ready to
leave, and even though she was angry with
Eli, she and her cousin giggled about Henry
for a few moments as they put on their
capes and bonnets.

"Eli's as mad as a bull," Ida May whispered.

Ida May had never brought up Eli's interest in Miriam to her before. Heat instantly rushed through her. If Ida May noticed Eli's attentiveness to her, who else did? She'd shrugged it off for so many months, and it angered her to have to deal with it now when all she wanted to do was focus on Henry.

"He'll just have to stop." She waved a hand, hoping her best friend wouldn't notice how infuriated she actually was. "I'm with Henry."

For the rest of the evening, she and Henry talked and ate pie in the dimly lit empty kitchen of the *daudy haus* where Miriam lived. Her parents had gone to bed before even realizing Henry was there. It took her a short while to relax after the anxieties of the evening. She had to force herself to stop thinking about Eli's advances and Henry's changes. She let herself laugh and enjoy herself more than at any other time since Henry's draft notice. All she could think about was that she'd get the chance to see him again the following evening. A thrill jumped through her.

In her sleep that night, a haunting scene played over and again in her dreams: Henry and Eli pulling at her heart like taffy, forcing it to toughen. They weren't working together like the couples at the Singing, but against each other. She felt Eli's grip tighten. She couldn't move. It squeezed, weakening her breath. Henry's hold was soft and gentle. It moved her instead of holding her solidly in one place. Didn't he want to hold her tighter? Didn't he want to win?

CHAPTER 2

November 1943

It was early the next morning when a ticking on her window woke her. She pulled her head up from her pillow and noticed it was still dark outside. She heard the ticking again, and suddenly she remembered that Henry was home. She sat up in bed and rubbed her face with her hands. The icy air in her room sharpened her senses quickly, and she climbed out of bed. The floorboards chilled her feet as she walked to the window at the side of the house and opened it, instantly overwhelmed by the cold wind.

"Good morning." Henry held a flashlight.

"What are you doing?" She laughed quietly and looked around. Darkness lined with the coming morning's sun was everywhere but the circle of light around Henry. He tossed a few remaining pebbles from his hand.

"Come down, I want to show you something." He waved at her.

"Give me a few minutes," she whispered down at him.

She closed the window. Her body felt so light she floated and bounced around the room, trying to ready herself. She took off her long nightdress and sleep bonnet. She pulled out her brown dress, then shoved it back into the closet. She didn't want to wear brown; it seemed so sad. She had only a navy-blue and dark-brown dress for church and an older blue dress for weekdays besides her brown dress. For a moment she imagined wearing her royal-blue wedding dress. How much prettier would she feel? She pushed the prideful thought away. Of course she couldn't do that. She brought out the brown dress again and decided it was the best option.

After getting dressed, she tried to see herself in the small handheld mirror using her flashlight. Her strawberry-blonde hair was in disarray. She pulled it out of the bun and brushed it. Her locks reached her lower back. She twisted it around in a bun with a few pins. Though displeased with its messiness, she left her room. As quietly as possible, she grabbed her coat and her headscarf, tying it around her chin, and left the house.

As she stepped outside she inhaled the cool air, and as she exhaled watched as her white breath faded around her. Fannie's house was asleep, and her parents could probably sleep through a tornado. She wrapped her arms around herself as the cold began to chill her.

"Henry? *Voh bish?*" she whispered loudly, asking him where he was. She peeked around looking for him.

Suddenly, strong arms came around her from behind and he kissed her cheek before letting her go.

"What are you doing here? The sun isn't even up."

"I wanted to show you something." His eyes looked at her so intently, almost as if he saw through her.

"I'm glad you came," Miriam said, blowing warm breath into her hands.

He took her hands between his own and kept his eyes on hers.

"We should get married."

"Married?" Miriam repeated with laughter lacing her tone. "I thought you wanted to wait until your service was finished."

"But what if we could get married sooner?"

She searched his molasses-colored eyes and a surge of energy and passion enflamed her heart. He'd asked her to marry him already; she'd said yes without hesitation. Then his draft came, and everything changed. She'd marry him that Thursday along with Ida May and Jesse if she thought it would work, but she knew it wouldn't. He would still be leaving soon after.

"You know I'll marry you as soon as you come home to stay. Just like we planned."

A cloud passed over his eyes, stopping Miriam's heart for a brief moment. He bent down and kissed her and when she looked into his eyes again, they twinkled at her and he smiled.

"Follow me." He pulled her hand.

"Where are we going?" She giggled as she trotted behind him, trying to keep up.

He didn't answer her as they made their way through the small pasture behind the barn. She held his hand tightly as they followed the small beam of light. She was almost out of breath once they got to the fence on the other side.

"Henry, the farm is going to be awake soon."

"What are they going to say? That Melvin Coblentz's girl was seen running around before sunrise with that Mast boy?"

Miriam giggled as she continued to try to keep up with him.

Her family could wake up. If they noticed she was not in her room, they would wonder where she was. She knew it was sinful not to care, but she didn't. All she could think of was spending as much time with Henry as she could. He could take her anywhere he wanted to go. Henry was the most sure-footed and dependable person she knew, but he also was always ready for something out of the ordinary. The mystery behind his dark eyes was what drew her in every time.

Sometimes he did small things that would surprise her and their friends, like building his own buggy instead of buying one. Once he hitched rides and walked all the way to Lancaster, because he couldn't afford a train ticket, to help with a barn raising. His uncle's barn had burned down. When asked why he went when there were plenty of people in Lancaster able to help — and after all, how could one seventeen-year-old boy make a difference? — he'd said he needed to follow where he felt God leading him. While he was there, he spotted a three-year-old boy who'd snuck up a ladder. When the boy fell, Henry was there to catch him. This was his answer; this was why he was supposed to be there. That was what he believed. Miriam had always loved that about him — that sense of certainty.

Even though she hated the fact that he was at the CPS, she saw it as just another one of Henry's adventures. He was experiencing something no one in the community could understand. As much as he didn't want to go, he'd embraced it as a way for him to learn more about God's plan for him. She had a difficult time understanding this. Didn't all of them have the same plan — to live a good and separate life? Wasn't that the plan for all of them?

"Here we are!" Henry pulled her through the last of the brush and into a clearing.

The glint of morning edged the sky and the moon was shyly fading away. Miriam looked around, taking in the view. It was flat in the small area around them with dry, dead weeds; nothing was in bloom at this time of year. She'd seen it in the summer often enough, when it was grassy and beautiful.

"Why did you bring me here?" The cool air invigorated Miriam as she stood close to Henry, looking up into his face.

"Trust me." He pulled her toward a large tree at the edge of the clearing.

"I can't go up there." She pointed at the homemade ladder leading up to a tree house her nephews had made several years ago.

"Please?"

Miriam never could resist the wooing of a simple *please* from Henry. She sighed and followed him up the ladder, being careful not to snag her dress. They sat with their backs against the trunk of the tree, facing the large clearing. The light was spreading and the clearing was more visible.

"Big white house, windows everywhere, a porch for us to sit." He pulled her closer and kissed her cheek. "Can't you see it?"

"Henry?"

"Maybe we could build here. You know, someday, when we can finally get married."

Miriam leaned into him as his arm tightened around her and she imagined it in the silence of the morning. She could already hear the laughter of future children and see the heaps of snow in the winter and the huge flower garden in the summer.

"Can you imagine it?"

"Yes." She breathed the word more than spoke it. "Do you mean it, that we could buy this land and build here?"

She watched as he looked out into the new light that was blooming and up into the moon that was getting lighter. The breeze jostled the limbs above, dead branches cracking against each other. He looked up for a long time, as if he were reading a message in the sky. Then his gaze landed ahead of them for a long moment. His eyes were glistening. She wasn't sure if it was from unshed tears or the light of the morning shining in them, but he had never looked more handsome to her than he did in that moment. Dreaming their dream together meant everything to her.

"Ja." He nodded his head before he looked at her. "I know we'll have a big house someday. We'll have a family and we'll grow old together."

"I want that to happen more than I can say. It's been so hard waiting while everyone else moves on." She had to look away from him for a moment. She didn't want the disappointment that she was sure was in her eyes to make him feel bad for circumstances that were out of his control.

"Look." He pointed at the land beyond them.

They watched in silence as the sun rose. First it was a quiet orange and yellow, and then it blossomed into a warm reddish purple. Their town was called Sunrise. Just a small community outside of Dover. Until that morning she'd never given the name of her town much thought, but now as she watched the sun rise over the beautiful countryside where someday she might have a house and live and raise a family, it felt like the most important moment in her life.

As Delaware's level landscape appeared in the growing light, neighboring houses and farms became visible. She sat up straighter to get a better view. Small specks of light glowed far into the distance. It warmed her as she pictured her fellow church members waking in their own warm houses, preparing for another day with their families. Working alongside sons on a farm or baking with daughters, and sending the younger children to school. That was what their lives were all about. It was what she longed for.

"Beautiful." His voice was so breathless it almost blew away on the wind before reaching her ears.

"It is." She nodded.

He turned her chin toward him. "No, I mean this moment — you."

She felt her face grow warm. He traced it with his finger. He untied her headscarf and for a moment her body stiffened. She shouldn't let him uncover her head, but she didn't stop him. He pushed the strand of hair that had come out of her bun behind her ears, and all she could think of was how she never wanted to be with anyone else.

"Your hair in this light looks just like the sunrise." He didn't say it poetically, like in school when they would read out loud. But he said it in his Henry way, strong and sure, yet in a whisper, as if the trees or wildlife would meddle into their business if they heard. "Will you take it down for me?"

Without thinking, she pulled out the few pins and let it fall. She knew she should feel self-conscious. Wasn't this sinful? Prideful? Henry gathered a handful of hair and combed his fingers through it, letting it fall between them instead down her back.

"I want to capture this image of you in my mind and never forget it," he said, handing back her headscarf.

They didn't talk as Miriam put her hair back up and retied her headscarf under her chin. They didn't even talk while they climbed down to the ground, Henry stopping on their descent to carve their initials into the tree just below the tree house as the sun continued to rise. In silence, Henry led them back to the farm. Miriam's brother-in-law Truman and her nephews were out in the barn doing their chores, and they saw Fannie throw potato peels out the side door. No one saw them from where they stood. Henry turned toward her.

"Just when I think I understand you, you surprise me," she said to him.

"What do you mean?"

"I love these little adventures. It's like you

see things in a way no one else does."

"The way I see it is that God usually has us on this narrow path where we can only see the step right in front of us. Then sometimes," he paused and looked away again, "sometimes I feel like He opens a huge door or a field or, I don't know, opens something that shows me how big His plans are, and suddenly I have all this room to move around. Sometimes it's way off the path I expect. Do you know what I mean?"

Miriam wasn't sure. She nodded anyway. "All I really know is that whether it's a path or a field, I just want to be with you. No matter what."

When he kissed her goodbye there was a desperation in his touch. She didn't know why, but she was sure he had something hidden behind his dark eyes.

Miriam put her pointer finger in her mouth. The taste of her own blood was bitter as she stifled the pinprick. These little wounds eventually created a callus, but it had been months since she had done much sewing and her fingertips weren't prepared. Her hands endured an enormous amount with all the housework and laundry, so the delicate work with a fine needle had become awkward.

Since she lived with only her parents, she wasn't constantly sewing patches on pants for young boys or making dress after dress for the long line of girls. All of her older Amish siblings, three sisters and four brothers, were married with families. Miriam didn't know if her sister Kathryn, the one sister who wasn't Amish, had a family.

Kathryn could have made this dress in half the time. Miriam groaned quietly, her impatience growing. Sewing was the last thing she wanted to do on a day like today, when Henry was only a few miles away. It was all she could do to continue on with her Monday laundry and the seemingly constant cooking and cleaning. Her fingers went up and down, weaving the needle and thread through the pieces of fabric. As she did her best to make the pieces fit together perfectly, she wished the pieces of her life would fit as seamlessly. With the unexpected events of Henry's draft, their postponed wedding, and his surprise return, all the pieces of her life were mismatched.

"Vie kompts nae'es?" Her mother, Rosemary, asked Miriam how her sewing was coming along. Miriam turned as her mother entered the small sewing room off the kitchen. Her gaze roamed, as if trying to catch Miriam's eyes.

"Pretty well." She held up the maroon dress she'd wear as a wedding attendant to show her mother, just as she would have if her mother actually had normal sight. This was something Miriam made a point of doing even though she knew that the details were lost to the older woman.

Her mother held a bowl in her arms and spun a wooden spoon through the batter with a delicate air. She still moved spryly for a woman in her sixties, and given her poor eyesight, was still able to do a good amount of housework and even some sewing. But her eyes were not the only way she was aging. Her once full, expressive lips were becoming thin and pinched, and her formerly golden-red hair had gone pure white more than a decade ago.

"Ida May will look nice in royal blue. Has she finished sewing it?" her mother said.

"*Ja,* she finished it months ago." Miriam's voice was flat. "You always say everyone looks nice in royal blue."

"Royal blue's a good color," her mother admonished.

"Did everyone wear royal blue when you and *Dat* were married?"

"It was expensive fabric to buy, so not always."

There was a short silence as Miriam

considered this.

"As much as I like royal blue, it would be nice to have a choice."

"Nah, it's good that everyone does the same thing. Makes it so no one's better than the other."

Miriam didn't respond. That had been the answer for so many of the church's dress standards, and while she was fine with the response, she really didn't need to hear it over and over. The swish-swish of her mother's spoon in steady rhythm through the mixture in the bowl filled the room as Miriam studied the hemline she'd just sewn on the dress. Even considering the pinprick, she'd sewn it all quite well so far. She'd often imagined herself wearing the beautiful royal-blue wedding dress that she'd sewn more than a year ago, with a perfect white cape. The image pushed against her mind like a stamp. Her heart shuddered.

It was difficult for her to think of anything but Henry as she sewed, especially after their early-morning jaunt. How different things would be if he'd never been drafted. On the day the notice came for Henry, Miriam had perfectly folded her own royal-blue dress to avoid wrinkles and placed it in brown paper tied with string to protect it. She stacked it deep on her closet shelf, behind her other few belongings. She didn't want to be reminded constantly of what should have been. She knew Henry wouldn't marry her just to leave her behind to take care of herself. It wasn't his way. Another option was for them to marry and for her to go with him to Hagerstown. She would find a place to live in town and some work, maybe cleaning homes. Henry would never agree to this, believing it wouldn't be safe for a young Amish woman. They'd accepted that the best option was to wait. The thought made her sigh.

"I know you must feel left behind." Her mother's intuition surprised Miriam. "Henry will be back for good before you know it, and it'll be your turn."

She nodded, swallowing hard, refusing to cry. She turned her attention back to the hem, not wanting even her mostly blind mother to see her emotion. Besides, the last thing she wanted to do was be sad while he was home. She was going to make sure that the next few days were perfect. Perhaps her father would allow her to go to Henry's family for supper one night, and maybe he could come over after supper the other nights and spend the evenings with her. She'd decided that while it would make his awful haircut visible to her father, it would be worth it to spend as much time with him as possible.

Her mother broke the silence. "Don't mope about it, though."

"I know, but it's frustrating to think that by the time I pull out my wedding dress, Ida May will probably already be a mother."

Her finger began to bleed again and the droplets of blood tasted venomous to her. The dark mood had attacked when she least expected it. Shaking it away, she turned back to the new dress. Miriam was one of the honored *navah hockas,* one of two bridal attendants, for Ida May. She'd been paired up with Eli Brenneman, since no one knew that Henry would be home for the wedding. Now that Henry didn't have to catch a bus until later on Thursday, she wondered if Jesse and Ida May would ask Eli to step down, allowing Henry to be partnered with her. She feared that being paired with Eli at a highly anticipated wedding would instigate more rumors among the community.

"God's will is best." The spoon's motion paused for a moment as Rosemary patted Miriam's shoulder, then began again as she walked out.

God's will is best. The words rang in her ears and she let them soak into her throat, hoping it would push the lump of tears down into her chest. But she didn't let the phrase penetrate her heart. She couldn't. She wasn't sure she believed it anymore. Her heart was weary of those words.

CHAPTER 3

November 1943

Miriam woke to a drenching rain. She groaned, knowing that this meant she would be stuck inside all day and wouldn't have the chance to take even a cold walk with Henry. She was hungry for more of him, like the morning before. For so long she had been starved for his touch and attention.

Her intuition also told her that there was something he wasn't telling her. He'd already put her questions off the first night and she wasn't about to let it happen again. She couldn't imagine what was so terrible that he couldn't tell her right away. If his time was extended at the camp, she would be terribly upset, but they would manage. They would have to.

"Henry asked me to go to his house for supper tonight. Then after we'll probably play some games with his family." She kept her head down as she ate her breakfast. She had chosen her words carefully, not exactly making it a request though not announcing her plans without her father's blessing, either. She desired his approval and coveted his peace with the family.

Since her sister Kathryn had left, her father had been known to go into fits of temper at the spur of the moment. He had never done that before, and they had all learned to try to keep him happy.

Out of the corner of her eye she saw her father raise his head. His mouth was tight, declaring that he was troubled. She decided not to say anything further but wait for him to respond in his own time. It might have been five minutes or ten before he finally spoke.

"Tell your young man that it would be best for his hair to be cut properly next time or he should skip a visit," he stated, sipping honeyed hot peppermint tea. "It's disgraceful how he looks. Just because he's at that camp doesn't give him free rein to go against the *Ordnung*."

At the mention of the church's rules, Miriam's heart constricted. Everything they did was according to the *Ordnung*, and while her father was right, she couldn't help but wish that he would try to see Henry's situation for what it was. But then she realized that she'd scrutinized him as well, only she'd done it with a kiss on his lips and a tight hold of his hand. She was no better.

"You just be careful." Her father's voice suddenly grew louder.

"Be careful of what?" Her words snapped like a whip across the table. She cringed as they rang in her ears.

"He's not the same. Being in a camp like where he is for several years will change him — *has* changed him." Her father appeared dispassionate as he continued eating. As several moments passed, his breathing quickened and he became more agitated. "I wouldn't be surprised if he leaves the church. He's going to have freedoms that can twist the world into something better than it is. Don't be blinded, Miriam."

"*Dat,* how can you say that?" Miriam tried her best to keep her voice calm. She didn't want to be disrespectful. "He's always going to be the same Henry. Hair grows. I'm sure his next visit will be different. All of this is just temporary. It's not going to be much longer. It's not like it was his choice to go to the camp, and it hasn't been a good reflection of the world anyway. He has to work very hard without any satisfaction of working his own property or at least helping his community. He doesn't want to complain, but I know he can't wait to leave. He even has to pay the government to work at the camp. If it weren't for those Peace churches —"

"I know all about those Peace churches. They have all sorts of riffraff in those camps, even people who don't believe in God at all. They're called atheists or something of the sort. What kind of church would allow that? The longer he doesn't live by our standards, the harder it'll be when he's through."

"You know he's always been one of the most upstanding boys my age. He's never been in trouble and is admired by the community. He's a good man, *Dat.* He even wants to be a preacher."

"No one chooses to be a preacher. The church selects you, and it would do you and him good if you kept those kinds of visions quiet. Just you watch keenly and keep your eyes open and don't let your infatuation with a boy get between you and the church." His manner of speaking had always been sharp, his words clipped, but this morning he was fairly barking.

Miriam fell mute, feeling aptly scolded, but for what, she did not know. Had she actually done anything wrong?

The breakfast table remained silent for the rest of the meal, and she felt on edge even after her father left the table to attempt to fix the large sliding door of the barn. It had grown stubborn, as he put it.

Later, she washed the dishes using the hottest water she could stand, letting the water heat her skin as if her anger wanted to be sated. It didn't help. The rhythmic drumming of the rain on the roof, however, eventually settled her heart, though it did not wash away the deeper fear that gripped her.

Was Henry really changing too much? What if her father was right?

The farmhouse across the drive was a flurry of activity, as always. Her eldest sister, Fannie, and her husband, Truman, already had eight children and had another on the way. They were the picture of what she wanted. She pushed away her fears and her father's opinions for the moment and focused on her adventure with Henry the previous morning.

Miriam was glad that Henry arrived to pick her up a few minutes early. The rain kept her inside for most of the day and the bitter exchange that morning made the close quarters unbearable. Her father hadn't been able to fix the barn door, saying he was shaky on the ladder. He read his Bible and napped the entire afternoon. Her mother didn't say she was concerned over him giving up on the chore, so Miriam tried not to be either, though she couldn't help but calculate the amount of times he had left a job undone. The count came to zero.

"I'll be back later," she said over her shoulder to her parents, who were sitting at the table over reheated stew and bread. She imagined them sharing a mute meal together. She hoped that wouldn't be her and Henry someday. They'd shared such companionship when they were together; surely theirs was a love that could sustain affectionate talks and touches. Had there been a day long ago that her parents felt about each other as she and Henry did today?

As she hopped in the buggy next to Henry, she willed herself to forget the image of an unseeing mother and an unhearing father sitting stoically at a rickety table. Apart from Henry, they were the two people she loved most in the world. Her loyalty to her family had willed her to live after the grief of Kathryn's shunning.

She and Henry kissed before leaving the drive. Nestled in his arm, with a blanket wrapped around their laps and legs, they set off for the drive to his home. Though it was only about five miles away, it was just long enough for them to take comfort in their blessed aloneness. This was something young Amish couples coveted above all else. Living amidst large families and the ever-seeing eyes of the church compelled them toward times of pure, lighthearted enjoyment of each other — apart from so many prying eyes. No matter that she and Henry had long been baptized in the church, they still longed for a piece of their lives to be on their own terms, a secret from the rest of the world, for only them to savor. Nothing imprudent happened — nothing she should be ashamed of if she had to admit it to her elders, but they indulged in private conversations, personal dreams, and intimate talks of their undying love for each other that were definitely meant only for their ears.

"*Mem* and *Dat* said we would have the front living room to ourselves tonight," he said, as both their bodies swayed in rhythm with the canter of the horse-drawn buggy. It was a comfortable feeling, and Miriam relished it. "Of course, Sylvia and Rachel said it was unfair because they always have to share the room after Singings."

"Well, the next time their boyfriends are

away for months and months on end, then they can have some privacy," Miriam said righteously. She bit her tongue from saying more. His sister Sylvia had never been friendly with Miriam, likely because Miriam received all of Eli Brenneman's attention. She pushed the thought aside, refusing to let it ruin her evening with Henry. It was not an easy thing getting leave from the camp.

Only two other boys had been drafted from their community, and both were in Hagerstown, Maryland, working alongside other conscientious objectors, or C.O.'s as they often were called. Miriam didn't want any other girls to have to deal with the burden of having their boyfriends far away, but she was annoyed with his sisters for complaining about letting them enjoy the short time they had together.

The dinner was a typical affair; the subdued conversation revolving around the regular work of his father's carpentry business. Henry's mother, Linda, was a jolly woman. She was the type to bring the conversation back to her returning son and his time in the camp. Linda was as conversational as she was, Miriam had always concluded. She liked Linda and was glad that she would be her mother-in-law some-day.

Miriam looked around the table as they all ate. Ten children, none married, crowded around a sturdy oak table. Two long benches flanked both sides, with chairs at either end. Amos sat at the head and Linda next to him on a smaller chair on the corner, since there was no room with four girls on one bench and five boys on the other. She was an ample-sized woman, and sitting on a bench with four other children would be uncomfortable at best. Miriam's long and thin frame fit perfectly on the bench of four and Henry sat opposite his father, as the eldest son and child.

Miriam noticed that all the girls, even the ones who were in their *rumschpringa* years, were dressed in the same dark green, a color rarely worn in their community. She adored it, wishing her father would let her wear any shade of green, but he and her mother would say it was too progressive, and unless the preacher's family wore it, she was not allowed. A sunny canary yellow flashed across her mind as she remembered watching her sister leave the house for the last time. The beauty of how the color glowed in the dimly lit house was cured in her memory. How would it feel to wear such a shade, and in a style that wasn't Amish?

Henry nudged her from her right side, bringing her back to reality.

"What?" she said dumbly.

"*Mem* just asked you how Fannie's doing." Henry winked at her.

"Oh, you know Fannie. She'll call the midwife after cleaning up lunch, have the baby, and prepare dinner an hour later."

The girls choked over their food, and the amused looks Miriam got from Amos and Linda told her she'd said something out of line.

"I'd heard that she was getting cataracts like your mother," Linda said, delicately. "I hope that she is up for a new baby."

Heat rose from Miriam's toes to the top of her head. How could she have misunderstood that question? Of course, Fannie had been anxious for weeks as she felt her eyesight failing. And here she was, blabbing about her sister's labor and delivery in front of her future father-in-law. No one ever asked about something as personal as a pregnancy. Why had she assumed that was the information they were seeking?

"*Ja,* of course." She kept her eyes on her plate and pushed the potatoes around. "She has a doctor appointment later this week to have them checked."

No one else spoke until they all bowed for the silent prayer at the end of the meal. Miriam nervously clutched her hands under the table, still embarrassed about what she'd said about Fannie. When she heard the shuffling of feet and clanging of silverware, she raised her head and began clearing the table herself.

"Now, you and Henry go have some time together," Linda said, smiling as she reached out to touch Miriam's hand. "The girls can clean up just fine."

Sylvia and Rachel glanced at her out of the corners of their eyes. Miriam had won no friends that night.

"I would gladly help," she said.

"We can take care of it." Sylvia abruptly took the plates from Miriam's hands without meeting her eyes. Cold air seemed to wrap around Miriam, and she let go of the plates and gave up trying to help.

The house was mostly quiet except for the on-and-off footsteps they could hear upstairs. Everyone retreated to their bedrooms except for Miriam and Henry. The younger children were likely asleep, but Miriam suspected the older girls at least were gossiping over her and Henry. She was glad that they would have the living room to themselves on the first floor of the house while everyone else was on the second.

It had been quite a while since she'd been at the Mast home. She took in the living room around her. There were two large couches, a wooden floor, and two hickory rockers. The colorful rag rugs were perfectly in order, despite the young children in the family. What struck her in this moment was that it was the image of most of the living rooms of the large families in their community. A measure of comfort settled over her.

She'd waited all evening, wanting as much privacy as possible, before asking Henry again to tell her what was bothering him. Before she could say anything, however, Henry brought up her indiscreet comment about Fannie. They stifled the sound of their laughter with the couch cushions. The evening had reminded her so much of their early dating years and she remembered how sweetly they'd enjoyed each other. The teasing, joking, and innocent flirtatious touches stirred Miriam's heart. However, every time she brought up their future together and how she was so jealous of Fannie's large, perfect Amish family, his demeanor altered.

When the footfalls from the second floor finally ceased, Miriam felt ready to talk seriously with Henry.

"Now, I deserve to know what's bothering you. There's been something on your mind ever since you've come home."

She turned toward him, pulling a leg up onto the couch, ensuring her skirt was covering it. Her goal was to be able to look at him straight in his warm, brown eyes, knowing she would be able to detect any hesitation or burden in them.

He pursed his lips, sighing. His head hung, and Miriam decided to give him the space he needed. She needed his stubbornness to fall away.

"A month or so ago, Norman Hershberger went into town to get some new shoes. He was jumped by a few locals and left lying on the sidewalk."

Miriam gasped. "Why didn't you write to tell me? Do his parents know? Is he okay now?"

He took her hands, nonverbally asking her to be quiet. They didn't need any attention from the rest of the household, and apparently whatever he had to say was going to be difficult. Miriam was relieved, however, that it was about Norman and not personal. He had learned to care for Norman while at the camp. That made sense. Norman was young and shy, and Henry had taken him under his wing.

Henry grew increasingly tense as he continued talking.

"When he didn't come back for supper, a few of us went out to see if we could find him. I don't know how long he was lying there, but we got him in the car. He wasn't waking up very well and was beat up pretty badly, so we decided to take him to a nearby doctor's clinic. He woke up just as the orderlies were trying to get him to walk on his own to a room. He refused to talk to any of them about how he was feeling; he said he'd only talk to me." He paused as if regaining the strength to continue. He was almost hurting Miriam's hands in his tight hold. "He told us several men started harassing him, then started punching and kicking him until he stopped moving."

"What? Why would they do that?"

"There are a lot of people out there who don't understand our position and some who are really hostile about it. He only needed a few stitches but was weak for a few days. He's fine now, but it was scary." He shook his head.

"They should've sent him home."

"Oh, no. The camp would never do that. They can't." Henry's hard and bitter tone rang unfamiliar. She longed for warm words from his soft lips to fall upon her ears instead.

"Did someone let Norman's parents know?" Mervin and Rosella Hershberger would want to know what had happened to their son.

"No, and don't tell them." He clipped his words. "Norman made me promise not to tell them. He didn't want to worry them. You know how his *mem* is really sick already. He was afraid this kind of news would make her worse. Besides, none of us are allowed to go into town alone anymore."

"Well, if Norman's going to be fine, why are you so worried about him?" Miriam prodded. "You've been agitated with something ever since you arrived. Did you get more bad news? Is your service being extended? Are you not going to be able to come home for Christmas again? I know this isn't about Norman, Henry."

Miriam's walls shifted and her heart lost its foundation when the gap of silence became strained and uncomfortable. His eyes grew darker, like storm clouds ready to burst. Hot tears pushed against her own eyelids as she watched him and waited.

"When we came into the clinic there were other people there waiting to be seen," Henry said, sniffing and clearly fighting tears. "They sneered at us. They called us Hitler's Helpers because we don't fight."

"Hitler's Helpers?" Miriam repeated the English words.

"Even the doctor made a few jabs at us. The orderlies were cruel and unfeeling toward Norman. You should've seen how roughly his stitches were done. They didn't care, because he's a C.O." His voice faded. Miriam hated the label. It sounded so military and governmental.

Her hand was nearly numb in his grasp, and his burden burrowed deeply inside her heart, her pulse growing unsteady. She felt fury herself over the angry accusations. How could someone, anyone, say such things about Henry? He was a good man. A sob rose in her throat. She fought the urge to release it.

"Do you know what is happening over there? Jewish families aren't safe anymore. Hitler is targeting them."

He whispered as he let go of her and clenched his hands into fists.

"And, what if another Pearl Harbor happens? I just can't sit back anymore. I don't want to be called Hitler's Helper. I just know God has a real purpose for me. I believe it in my heart."

Her back became rigid as she sat up

straighter. She felt her façade breaking as a flood of fear pushed at her nerves.

"You know we need to have faith that God's will is best," Miriam said, hating her words as she spat them out, mimicking his raspy whisper. Words she'd been told her whole life when anything bad happened, though she hadn't repeated them often. She'd always longed for more explanation herself.

"But what if God's will is for us to protect them? They are His chosen people according to the Bible. What if something like that happened to us? We already look different from the English. What if suddenly our freedoms were taken away?" He paused. "And with people yelling those things at us, it just made it worse. I just don't want to be stuck at that camp to uproot trees and dig ditches. I'm not helping anyone there. I want to help."

"What are you saying, Henry?" She knew he had grown discouraged and longed for his service to be completed. But now, with all this talk about the war, heat began to penetrate her from inside, and she closed her eyes to the spinning room. "What are you saying?" she asked emphatically.

"I enlisted." His voice didn't carry the urgency that it had only moments earlier; it was resigned. He said it with such a calm that Miriam almost mistook it for peace, but how could that be?

Her pulse quickened and her breathing hastened. The room they sat in suddenly grew smaller. It seemed the air had escaped somehow, and she wanted to follow it.

"But what about the church? What about us?" she whispered, afraid to use a louder voice because of the sleeping house. Her tears surfaced without protest. She pulled a handkerchief from her apron, dampening it with fresh tears. "You'll be shunned. And then what?"

His silence made it final. His decision had been made. Miriam felt a burst of emotion, one she had never experienced with such force. She ran from the room and the house, not even taking the time to grab her cape and bonnet. She'd been so caught up with the conversation that she hadn't realized it was raining again.

Lightning burst ahead of her, lighting the soaking earth. The clouds sobbed with her. She ran toward home. She couldn't stay there, not with his news sitting between them.

She wasn't sure how far she'd gotten before she heard a horse and buggy behind her. Quickening her pace, she refused to look back. If it was Henry, she wanted nothing to do with him. If it wasn't, she didn't want to embarrass herself.

The sound of the horse's hooves stopped and a few moments later she was grabbed and pulled toward the buggy. She fought Henry every inch of the way; she heard his voice in her ear, talking over the thundering rain and wind.

"I'm so sorry," he kept saying. "I'm so sorry, Miriam."

She finally gave in to his strength and collapsed in his arms. He wept with her, squeezing the life out of her with both his arms and his words. She was dying a slow death and she couldn't fight back.

Her legs felt weak when he finally led her to the buggy. He picked her up, cradle style, and set her on the bench seat inside. She sat like a cut of stone, and even when the buggy shifted as he sat on the bench beside her, she was unmoved. He tried to close the space next to her, but she did not warm to his touch. He wrapped her cape around her and carefully put her bonnet on her head. His thick hands shook as he did his best to tie it. Miriam forced a fog to cross over her eyes, not wanting to see his face, even though it was so close to her own.

They drove in silence, both of them having stopped crying. The thunder and lightning around them was nothing compared to the storm inside her. Sheets of water branded the dirt road, and Miriam's life washed away along with the mud. Nothing could make this right.

In front of her home, she sat still, not wanting to stay and not wanting to leave. Leaving felt too final, but staying made the gap that grew between them more solid with every passing moment. Since their first date they had seldom fought, not wanting anger to rule the day. They'd prided themselves on how reasonable they were with each other.

"I will come home. I will marry you, if you'll still have me. Then we will have everything I've promised you. I just know I have to do this."

The conviction and strength behind every word was not lost on her ears. She knew a shunning didn't happen overnight. Sometimes it took a year or more. If he returned during the course of his shunning or after it was final, would he be able to find his way back after such defiance? Even if he confessed his enlistment as sin and was accepted back into the safety of the fold, life would never be the same, would it? His life was corrupted now, and hers along with it.

Miriam had no more energy to speak. Henry was quiet, allowing her to grieve the news before he spoke again.

"I love you, Miriam."

With that, Miriam stoically got out of the buggy. When he jumped out after her, trying to hold her, she pushed him away and walked through her front door without a word. She stood there in the dark for several long minutes before finally watching his buggy drive away. She had the very vivid sense that she had just watched her life fall away into the blackness of the storm.

Lightning lit her view and she was careful to notice that her English neighbors, Ralph and Nancy Poole, still had a light on. Maybe Nancy would understand. Her boys were soldiers. Maybe she could make some sense of how Miriam felt. She'd helped so many in the district with this or that, and now Miriam needed help. Before she knew it, she was at their front door, knocking.

CHAPTER 4

November 1943

"Miriam?" Nancy opened the door. "What are you doing out in this thunderstorm?"

The wind picked up and the rain pounded louder than ever on the porch roof above Miriam. She looked up for a brief moment before looking back at her neighbor. Now that she was there, she didn't know what to say.

"Can I talk to you?" The words fell from her mouth unconsciously.

"Of course, come in, come in." Nancy pulled Miriam into the house and closed the door. "Dear me, you're soaked through."

The older woman walked into the living room and grabbed a knitted blanket from the couch. The radio clanged loudly in the living room. The announcer's abrasive voice barked in her ears, stretching Miriam's nerves tighter. Why would anyone want to constantly follow such dreadful news? She

70

was sure his voice would follow her into her sleep.

"Ralph, turn down that radio." Nancy's voice mimicked a screech owl.

Turning back to Miriam, she led her to a kitchen chair. Miriam took off the bonnet and *kapp* and wrapped the warm blanket around her. She began shaking uncontrollably, even though she sensed a tender warmth from both the blanket and Nancy. After setting tea down for them both, Nancy pulled a chair up to face Miriam.

She asked in a raspy whisper, "What's the matter, dearie?"

Miriam bit her lip and looked past Nancy. Her eyes landed on the pictures of the neighbor boys in uniform. Their jaws were firm. They both looked older than she'd remembered ever seeing them. Was that what Henry would look like? Would the tender expression he usually wore become hardened? Would his smiling lips become rigid and straight?

"Henry enlisted." The words merely fell from her mouth. It relieved her to confess Henry's decision to someone, though it surprised her that the first person to know was Nancy.

"Oh, Good Lord!" Nancy said. "Sorry, I don't mean that in vain. I am just so shocked. I didn't — I didn't know that was allowed."

"It's not allowed." Her voice was lifeless. "We would already be married if not for this war. He received his draft notice the same week we met with our preachers to set our wedding date. We were so close."

"I'm so sorry." Nancy's eyes drooped at the corners and Miriam accepted her sympathy. There was a short pause before she spoke again. "You know, your Henry, he's an awful good man. He reminds me of my boys, always has." Nancy glanced over at the photographs of her two sons.

The older woman shook her head and sniffed. She took up her knitting from the basket at her feet. It was filled with dark green yarn and overflowing with socks and mittens, and she began knitting at a furious pace. "It's a downright unholy thing, this war. And, quite honestly, I'm glad I'm a woman and wouldn't be expected to go fight. But these boys — they step right up. They do their duty. Henry has your church to shield him from this terrible war, yet he risks it all to do what his heart tells him is the right thing. You should be mighty proud of him. Mighty proud."

"But it's against our beliefs. We don't believe it's right to kill anyone for any reason. War is murder."

This conversation made Miriam uncomfortable. She'd never argued the church's position — her position. The Ten Commandments said *thou shalt not kill,* and that was enough for her. Why wasn't that enough for everyone else? Nancy sat there considering her response. "My father said that since we are supposed to love everyone, we can't do that by killing them." Miriam's words were spoken hesitantly and in pieces.

"I understand, really I do. But David himself, a man after God's own heart, the Bible says, he fought to save himself from a king who despised him. And what about all the battles God brought the Israelites through?"

Miriam couldn't think of anything more to say. Their beliefs on the matter were just different, and it wasn't the Amish way to argue with a neighbor.

"You remind me of Kathryn, the way you've come here tonight." Nancy smiled.

Miriam's heart jumped at the mention of her sister. She sat up a little straighter. This was her chance to learn a little more about Kathryn.

"Couldn't you tell her not to leave?" Miriam asked, feeling like a child. "Our family has never been the same, but no one talks about it. I don't even know what happened."

"Oh, I couldn't have told her not to leave. It wasn't my place. But I did tell her that she should do whatever it takes to make things right between her and your parents, even if she chose not to stay with the church. Kathryn didn't feel that she had any other choice, dear."

Miriam didn't understand. She didn't know how to respond. Of course, Kathryn could have chosen to stay.

"You should write her," Nancy suggested. "Better yet, visit her. She doesn't live far."

"I don't have her address." It was an excuse. She wouldn't even know what to say and didn't know how to approach this topic with her parents. From the day Kathryn left, Miriam was told to not pursue contact with her sister, that it would only bring heartache.

"Talk to you mother. She loves *all* of her children. Don't lose faith in her." Nancy leaned forward and put her hand on Miriam's knee. She looked her straight in the eyes. "And, as far as your Henry, even if you don't understand him you can still pray for him. Pray for all of our boys over there."

"The church will shun him. His family will be disgraced. And my parents . . ." She hung her head. "My parents . . ." She couldn't finish her thought. "How do you cope or make sense of it all?"

Nancy didn't say anything but went to a small stand where she picked up a large Bible, laid it in front of Miriam, and tapped it. "Faith," Nancy said. "We believe in the same God you do."

The next morning the fog was heavy on the ground. Miriam felt the same murkiness wrap around her, unable to break free from it, unwilling to try. She couldn't concentrate on cooking, cleaning, or any real conversations. She'd nearly burned the bread, and she'd stared off into nothingness too many times to count.

"Mail's on the table." Her mother pointed at a few letters as they prepared their lunch. "I think you have one from Henry, but I couldn't read it well enough to say for sure. Must be a letter he sent before he came for his visit."

She took it carefully. It was indeed from Henry, but it hadn't been sent through the mail. Her mother hadn't noticed that there was no stamp on it. He must have dropped it in the mailbox himself earlier that morning.

Usually she'd rip open his letters before

she could even get anywhere private to soak in his words. How often had she read and reread his promises, each one reminding her that his only thought was toward coming home to her, toward marrying her, toward their love and future life together? How she longed for more honeyed words. Even the feeling of the letter in her hand made her long for the moments back before his declaration of enlistment. Had it been only the night before? She'd aged a decade since his confession. She wanted to erase the words from her memory and engrave the joy of his love on her heart. If he truly loved her, he would not go.

She slipped from the house as Fannie arrived, leaving the two women to chat while peeling potatoes, something her mother could still do despite her vision problems. Usually Miriam would ready her ears to hear all the gossip herself, but not today. She didn't have the stomach for it. She headed toward the swing near the rear of the house, away from the front windows where anyone could see her. She opened the letter as she walked slowly, inhaling the crisp November air. A winter storm was looming.

My dearest Miriam,

I am so sorry for causing such pain. I love you more than you can even understand. How I wish things were different from what they are.

I have questioned my work at the camp for months. We dig ditches and build fences. It's honest work, but for what purpose? Who am I helping? Several of the Mennonite boys brought radios and we listen to the news on the war in the evenings after supper. Sometimes we play cards, but often we can't do anything but listen. A lot of the boys pretend it doesn't bother them, but there are a few of us, me and two of the Mennonite boys, who can barely sleep anymore because of what we know is the right thing to do. I think more of the boys back home would understand if they heard the radio announcer like I have.

Miriam's eyes went blurry, and her small white house and outbuildings began to spin around her. Like a baby learning to walk, she put her arms out to steady herself and tottered the rest of the way to the swing. Her heart screamed and her mouth was silent. The wind sobbed in her ear, mourning with her. A long, rattled caw came from the tree nearby, where a crow was perched.

Was the large black bird weeping or laughing?

The front door opened and whipped shut, clanging against the wooden door frame. Fannie always let the door slam. Miriam couldn't let her see her like this. After stuffing the letter into her apron pocket, she wiped her face with her hankie. As she stood, she took several long breaths and willed the icy wind to freeze her face so maybe the sadness wouldn't break through.

"Does *Mem* need my help?" she asked as her sister rounded the corner of the house with a bowl of potato peelings. She expected Fannie to ask for details of Henry's letters, the way she usually did. The CPS camps were new establishments for the war and everyone in their community was intrigued.

"Go ahead and finish your letter." Fannie winked. "Uh-oh, tears today? Even with Henry only a few miles down the road?" Miriam's sister clicked her tongue at her.

"Ich bin en bope." She called herself a baby and forced a laugh.

"I heard Sarah Brenneman asked you to be a maid instead of Marty Miller when the baby comes?" Fannie said. Miriam could not deny the inquisitiveness in her voice.

"Ja." Miriam often worked as a maid after a baby was born. Why was this time any dif-

78

ferent to Fannie?

"You don't think it has anything to do with Eli?"

"What?"

Fannie shrugged. *"Mach dei augen auf."*

Miriam had her eyes open enough. She didn't need her sister questioning her being hired as a maid when this had been her job for several years. She was glad when Fannie walked back into the house, but she couldn't return to Henry's letter. She took a few long pulls of the cold air, then went inside.

At lunch, she could taste nothing. Her father insisted on reading from Proverbs before they left the table, but the holy words couldn't find her ears. Even her eyes didn't have the strength to close for the silent prayer. It wasn't until the house was still, as it often was in the afternoon, when her parents usually wrote letters or rested in their chairs, that she dared to read the rest of the Henry's letter. Her room was darker than usual, as if the grayness of the day had grown through her windows like vines. She lit her oil lamp and placed it on the wooden floor. Somehow sitting at her desk made her feel too vulnerable.

Bending down, close to the small flicker, she found her place in the letter.

I have missed you so much, Miriam. I couldn't sleep last night, burdened with all of this, hating that you are now in the middle of my own personal war.

I wish I could explain how much I hate the way I feel. I hate that if I follow my heart, I will be shunned from the church — from you. I also hate that if I don't enlist, I won't be able to live with myself, knowing what I am supposed to do. I have never been so torn in my life. Don't stop loving me. I'm going to need your love now more than ever.

His heart was leading him to war? He had always told her that her name was written on his heart. Now the space next to her name was branded with his thoughts of war. She added the letter to the stacks she'd buried beneath a floorboard. She would be humiliated if anyone ever read her personal letters, and she had nieces nearing their running-around years who were known to snoop.

She fingered the strip of royal-blue material she used to hold her letters together. It was like an English garter that brides wore under their long white wedding dresses. Many of the young Amish girls secretly wore them under their wedding dresses too. Now all it was good for was to be tightly wound around her stack of letters. She replaced them carefully, along with her diaries, under the floorboard.

Resoluteness and steadfastness were sought-after traits in the Amish church, but Henry's strength was leading him outside the church. He was choosing war when he could work out his draft in the safety of the camp, then hurry home to marry her. By defying his beliefs, he would be shunned from the church and her, and maybe die in a country fighting for and with strangers. The realization that he could be killed sent her into a fit of silent tears. She had only enough energy to extinguish the small flame and lay her head on the floor, her body shuddering against the cold wooden slats.

Her life would never be the same. The war had just moved into the safety of her home, piercing her heart. Evil had arrived, and a shadow in the shape of fear was silhouetted against her heart.

CHAPTER 5

November 1943

Miriam let herself grieve only a short time before washing her face with icy well water to startle away remaining tears. Then she quickly packed her over night bag for Ida May's wedding. The evening began turning away from the dismal rain, and a pretty sunset framed the buggy that was coming down the road for Miriam. She said a quick goodbye to her parents and left the house in a hurry. Neither of them had asked anything about her time with Henry the night before and whether or not she would see him that night at Ida May's. There was a benefit to having older and inattentive parents. They hadn't noticed the blackness in her mood or the storm in her eyes.

It was customary for all the attendants and the groom to spend the evening before the wedding at the bride's home, but the thrill was lost for Miriam. She joined Eli Brenneman in the buggy, however, with a bounce in her step. She was determined that they would not know anything about the river of pain that flowed in her veins. She couldn't bear to have everyone know her soul's burden. Besides, she didn't want anyone to know Henry's secret, which was now also her own.

"Thanks for picking me up," she said. It was not ordinary for a young man to drive a girl anywhere unless they were seriously dating, but it made sense for Eli to pick up Miriam since he went right by her house to go to Ida May's, so her father had made an exception for the occasion.

He leaned over to her, winking, and she wondered what it would be like if she had continued dating Eli and Henry had never asked her out. The two boys were about five years older than Miriam, both were handsome, and both were coveted among many of the girls in the community. Eli, however, was taller and brawny, with a personality to match his imposing build. Eli's blue eyes danced around his words, charming even the mothers. Miriam appreciated his friendship, but she did not have the heart-stopping, lightweight floating feeling with him that she had with Henry.

For the rest of the night Miriam focused

83

her attention on her cousin, and no one knew that her heart broke a little more with every fake laugh. They spent their time in the living room. Ida May and Jesse sat on the love seat, while Lucinda, Ida May's sister, and Samuel sat on the long couch along with Eli and Miriam. The three couples had time to relax before the long, busy day to come. Since Eli had been paired with her, he wouldn't leave her side. While this was a rather traditional situation between attendants, usually they were a dating couple. Since she and Eli weren't, this was unsettling to Miriam, but she hid her mood for Ida May's sake. When Eli made it clear he would enjoy more alone time with her, she knew she had to keep him at arm's length. She was confused enough about her future with Henry and fully unprepared to add Eli into the mix.

The next morning, Ida May wore her black covering for the last time as she stood next to Jesse. Their eyes were cast down onto the wooden slat floor, arms at their sides. Ida May's hands were pink from all the hard work she'd put into preparation for her special day. Her waist was tiny, smaller than Miriam's. Ida May was thin, but wiry, not waiflike. Watching them now, Miriam couldn't help but think of the years she'd watched Ida May's dark brown eyes fairly dance when she talked about Jesse, and now she was to be his wife.

Instinctually, she pictured herself standing next to Henry. With her strawberry-blonde hair and freckled face, she always felt she resembled more a barefoot child in summer than a grown woman of twenty. She was lucky that the rest of her didn't look like a child. And when Henry held her, she certainly didn't feel like one. For several beautiful moments she felt lost in her love for Henry, and her heart melted into her soul. Then her stomach turned over, almost forcing her body to double over itself. Would she ever again curl her hand in his and feel the warm tingle that would follow?

While she tried to decide whether she needed to leave to vomit, she heard a strong male voice lead the congregation in the wedding song.

Miriam's voice followed the tune thoughtlessly, but her eyes began to wander. They followed the line of men sitting on the other side of the room, landing on a deep and familiar set of eyes. Even at this distance, they carried the burden of sadness she'd seen earlier in the week. Only a portion of his face was visible, but as her eyes soaked into his, everything went black except for Henry. Like a magnet, his eyes soon found hers. A lump settled in her throat. Tears formed in her eyes, and she forced herself to breathe evenly in order to keep her emotions from flooding.

Their eyes remained locked until it was time for the prayer. Ida May had returned to the backless bench and it was time for everyone to kneel. She followed suit. Her knee landed on a jagged slat on the floor and it made her wince, but she didn't wiggle it away. Feeling physical pain somehow measured the ache of her heart. It was like the hammer of reality pounding her mind. It was warning her not to expect the same future that she had expected before, and maybe not even to plan one at all. With everyone's heads bowed, she lowered hers and allowed several large, hot tears to fall, careful to catch them in her hands so they wouldn't blemish her apron with evidence of her grief.

Weddings were such a blessed happening in an Amish community; everyone looked forward to them. Since the church didn't announce weddings until three weeks before the date, during the months before the fall and spring wedding seasons people would make their guesses at who would be marrying whom and when.

The reception was filled with numerous rows of tables and benches and happy chatter. Miriam noted that there was the usual amount of food at the reception. Weddings were large events for the Amish and with the current rationing, the host family would never have been able to feed everyone, so she, along with several others, gave as many of their rations as possible to help, especially with sugar, coffee, and butter. She and her parents cut their consumption of these items in order to help.

Now, sitting at the head table next to Ida May, with Eli at her side, she felt drained of her energy but was determined to keep the smile on her face. The only people who asked about Henry were a few girls who wondered if he was jealous that she'd been coupled up with Eli.

"It was too late to make changes," she'd said. "Besides, Eli and Henry are best friends."

She didn't believe her own words. The strain between Eli and Henry was unmistakable the first night Henry had been home, and today, they circled one another like rivals. Henry sat at the table right in front of the head table, watching Miriam and Eli.

It was against custom for Miriam to break away from Ida May or Eli at the reception, so it would be up to Henry to approach her if he wanted to talk. When their eyes met across tables, her knees went weak in an instant and her resolve to be angry with him faded. She wished for him, longed for him, ached for him. The vision of his handsome face, gentle eyes, and sad smile moved her heart to begin beating again. She sat at the table, returning his gaze and wishing to fall into his arms.

But what had changed in the day and a half since his admission? Though her rage had lessened, the burden felt heavy on her heart. She wanted to talk with him, feeling certain she could sway his decision. All she wanted was to be his wife, give him children, and make him happy for the rest of his life. She didn't want to give that up, but how could that happen if he was fighting in a country across the ocean, defying the church they answered to? If he returned, if the war didn't kill him, the church would shun him. To return from a shunning was difficult and uncommon. She didn't know how the church would react to his actions. Would he even be allowed to confess and return from a shunning after such an act? Nothing quite like this had ever happened in their district, or anywhere that she'd heard of. There were so many questions to which she didn't have answers. The only thing she knew was that she loved him.

Her thoughts were interrupted when Eli's firm forearm moved tightly against her. His touch reminded her where she was sitting. The eyes of their entire community sat before her. It was important that she keep her composure.

Eli's mouth was close, only a twitch away from her ear. His words were moist on her skin.

"Why didn't you ask Ida May to swap Henry in my place?" Eli asked. He retracted his arm and met her eyes. Miriam noticed a thread of seriousness against the dance in his eyes, gathering that his question was more serious than not.

"I didn't think it would be fair." Her eyes diverted. Sure, fairness played a role in her mind, but she really didn't know where she and Henry stood with each other. "Besides, he's leaving today. Maybe he wouldn't be able to help as long."

"Oh, no." Eli shook his head and leaned back in his chair, crossing his huge arms in front of his barrel chest. "He's staying until tomorrow."

Miriam fought against the heat that began

to rise into her face. He was staying until tomorrow? She couldn't help but be hopeful that this meant he'd changed his plans and was returning to the CPS camp instead of to wherever he was supposed to go for the army. Her head whirled with the possibility, and their eyes met. It didn't appear that he'd heard what Eli said, but Miriam could hardly wait until she could step aside from her responsibilities so they could talk.

They wouldn't get the chance to talk until the middle of the Singing at the end of the reception. In the meantime, Eli made sure Henry saw every wink and whisper. He spoke loudly, drawing attention to his comfortableness and closeness with Miriam. She noticed that Henry saw every interaction, and she'd never seen his eyes darken with such anger.

Hours later, when most of the guests had gone and the Singing was about to start for the youth, Miriam realized that Eli had left her side. Relief flooded her.

Without a word, Henry motioned for her to come to him. She did. Miriam noticed a group of girls at the Singing whispering, likely about them, as they walked together away from the gathering toward the darkness of the lined-up buggies. She knew that she should stay at the Singing, but this might be her last chance before he left.

As they walked, his touch grazed her elbow. It felt not only like the softest cotton, but also like the needles that sewed it. He took her behind one of the smaller barns where they could be alone without the eyes of the rest of the youth on them. Miriam looked at her surroundings. The full moon revealed rows and rows of buggies lining the yard. She loved the order of it, loved the symmetry and predictability. She leaned against the old shed, noting how far away Henry stood. While he was only a few strides away, it felt as though an impenetrable fog had risen to block them from each other.

"How are you?" he asked so simply, Miriam wasn't sure whether to scoff at him or answer him honestly.

She decided against answering.

"I heard you're staying till tomorrow morning."

They both stared at the large white moon. It hung cold and uninviting in the night sky, making her feel even more alone.

"Yes, I am."

"Does that mean —"

"It doesn't change anything." His voice broke, and then he cleared his throat.

"Oh."

The silence sneered, reminding them that they'd never been uncomfortable in each other's presence.

"Then why are you staying longer?" Miriam began, needling at the seam of her white apron.

"The bus that leaves tomorrow morning will still get me to Camp Lee for basic training on time. I haven't told *Mem* and *Dat* yet. I, uh, I don't know how I'm going to do that." He paused, pursing his lips. "And I wanted to make sure we had some more time to talk."

Miriam felt his burden with him, not envying him his duty. At the same moment, however, indignation arose in her. He had created the obstacle.

"I told Eli. But I wish I hadn't."

Miriam let out an exasperated breath. Henry was too trusting. Now that Eli knew, everyone would know soon. What bothered her most was that Eli had pretended not to know all day. Why didn't he just say that he knew?

"Have you told anyone?" he asked.

"No. I mean, yes. I told Nancy Poole."

"Nancy Poole? Your neighbor?"

"I went to her the other night." Her tongue went dry, making it difficult to speak. "She's always told us to go to her for anything. I thought maybe she could help me."

He only nodded.

"She told me to pray for you. She also told me a little about Kathryn and how it was for her."

"What do you mean, how it was for her? What did she tell you?"

"She wouldn't give me any of the details, of course, but we talked about her leaving and getting shunned." She reminded him as if he should have understood what she meant.

"She wasn't shunned until more than a year later. It doesn't happen overnight."

"You know what I mean, Henry." She sighed, frustrated. "I don't want us to be like this. I hate this."

Her comment stifled the conversation for several long minutes. The wind picked up, pulling at the decaying field in front of them. It would not live again until spring, when the ground could be tilled and prepared. The life cycle of farming always brought Miriam hope. What was dead would live again.

She thought about all the moments that had led up to this. She would bake for him. He would eat an entire pie in one sitting. He carved small wooden trinkets to sit on her nightstand. She sewed a shirt for his birthday. He wrote her poetry. She giggled loudly when his smile was bright with laughter. He always tried to find a better way of doing something, expecting a better outcome, while she was the picture of consistency, following a well-thought-out recipe for everything in her life. They agreed on the church's standards, almost always staying within the rules. When they occasionally strayed, it was with only minor infractions. This was their relationship. Now everything was different because of one decision he'd made.

"I love you, Miriam." Henry broke the silence and closed the gap between them. He took her hand.

Her throat caught with emotion. She clenched her jaw, not wanting to cry. It wasn't like the people in the church to wear their emotions on their sleeves, and they definitely did not let tears line their faces. It was far too embarrassing to show such intimate emotions in front of the community. Surely everyone would know immediately that she and Henry were having problems and rumors would circle, tightening around her.

"Do you still love me?"

"Henry, yes, I love you. There's nothing

you could do that would make me not love you. But I still don't understand. Why are you doing this?"

In the dim light of the moon, Miriam could see the corners of Henry's eyes move downward. His head hung and his brow furrowed. His voice was more sober than ever before, his eyes too labored, his touch too final.

"Miriam, I know I can't expect you to understand. It's not fair to you."

He ran a hand through his cropped hair. The muscles in his face tensed and he looked into the distance as if he saw something there that mattered. When he looked back at her, the twinkle in his eyes had been replaced with something she could not describe. It was not a hardness, nor was it rebellion. Was it compassion? A compassion that went too far, that would go far enough to kill him.

"All I want to do is stay. Build a home. Have my own wood shop. And most of all have you as my wife. A quiet little life away from — everything. I wouldn't let anything, any of the awfulness of the world, touch you. All I want to do is protect you."

The wind caressed her face and jostled the ties of her covering. Henry cupped Miriam's face.

"The only way I can protect you and be the kind of man you deserve is if I do this. If I'd never gone to the camp, maybe I would feel differently. Maybe then my conscience wouldn't be pricked because I would have no cause to hear what was happening. But I was picked to go. I think God wanted me to go and hear about what's happening so that I could make this decision. It's one thing to be deaf and do nothing. It is another thing to hear and still do nothing."

Why did what he was saying resonate with her? Yet, she wouldn't — couldn't — let him go.

"God didn't send you to the camp, Henry, the government did."

"A Baptist preacher who came to the camp said that God has everything planned out in our lives and that He doesn't let mistakes happen. I'm not planning to leave the church. This decision was completely separate from my loyalty to the church. I know that's probably impossible to understand. And I know I'll be at risk of being shunned while I'm away. But I will be back. I promise you."

Miriam paused, trying to swallow down her argument. He had always been one to talk of spiritual matters. At first she'd been taken aback at his seriousness, not always understanding what he spoke of, but she loved his enthusiasm to learn.

"The Bible says thou shalt not murder." She tore her hand away from his. She could spout out biblical lines also. "Did the Baptist preacher not remind you of the Ten Commandments? Have you forgotten those as well as your baptism?"

He sighed, and a tense ball of muscle held fast in his jaw.

"I can't argue with you, Miriam. I love you way too much," he said with a tenderness Miriam knew she didn't deserve. "But I can't give you the answers you are searching for. The Baptist preacher said that ultimately I was only accountable to God for my actions. He also encouraged me to get a Bible, an English one, and read it every day, especially now. He prayed with me — out loud. He prayed that God would tell me what I should do."

"So God is talking to you now? Seems awfully vain."

"Miriam, the anger I see in you is frightening me." He turned her face to his. "Please tell me that you'll try to support me — even in your fear and anger. I have loved you since our first date. Remember how you sat and watched me eat that entire lemon meringue pie? I was afraid to stop until it was done because I didn't want you to think I didn't like it. You were afraid I was only eating it to be nice. It was delicious, except I did have an awful stomachache by the time I got home."

Miriam lunged at him, wanting him to hold her, needing him to. He held her close, and she could feel in his touch that he didn't begrudge anything she said to him. She was sure of his love for her and her own love for him. It was her strength that she doubted, not Henry's. She'd always loved the certainty of his convictions.

How could she do this with him? How could she break her family's heart and support him going to war? Her family's name was already besmirched by Kathryn's shunning. Could they handle another blemish? It was far from the same thing, as Miriam was not leaving the church. But what would she do if Henry was never accepted back into the church, even after returning from the terrors of war?

Miriam was caught off guard when Eli's commanding presence entered the space around them, breaking the magic, or the curse — both existed between her and Henry. What was he doing there? Had he been listening?

"Just thought I'd check on my partner," he said with a smirk in his voice. "I was getting worried."

"Eli, we need a few more minutes. Can you give us a little more time?" Henry said the words more as a statement than a question. "Besides, I think Miriam's duties are done for the night."

"I think you've had plenty enough time with her," Eli said, weaseling his way between Miriam and Henry.

"What do you think you're doing?" Henry wasn't as big as Eli, but he had a tall, strong stature, just the same.

"You don't deserve her, Henry." Eli put a finger to Henry's chest. "You're going to war to kill some Germans. Miriam isn't going to want to marry a killer."

"Stop it, Eli." Miriam was unsuccessful at trying to push him away.

"Miriam, come with me." Eli turned to her, putting a heavy hand on her arm. "Come on."

"Not so tight." Miriam pulled at her arm. "You're hurting me."

Henry forced himself between Eli and Miriam. His jaw was clenched and his brow furrowed.

Eli's grip on her arm tightened.

"You heard her," Henry said through

bared teeth. "Let her go."

"Henry's the one really hurting you!" Eli yelled, spraying saliva into Miriam's face. "He's going to war. He's going against the church and everything we know."

"Let her go." Henry's voice was as black as the sky.

Eli released his grip, but she was still backed tightly against the barn and was afraid to say anything. She'd never imagined the anger she saw between Henry and Eli. Her heart raced.

"Please, stop it, both of you." Her whispered words were spoken through clenched teeth. She caught the attention of both of them. Henry's face softened. Eli's entire body flexed tighter. The two of them gave her an inch of space, only moving slightly. The three squared off for several long moments before Henry spoke.

"Eli, please, just give Miriam and me a few more minutes." His voice was quiet yet stern.

Miriam was surprised to see Eli's expression lose some intensity. He moved back a small step. He seemed agitated as he tried to speak.

"Miriam, I'm going to be right over there." He pointed around the corner of the small barn. "I cannot let him take you home."

"She can make —" Henry began to say, before Miriam gently touched his arm. He stopped instantly.

"I appreciate your offer, Eli." Miriam's voice shook from the weariness of the night. "But this is my last night with Henry. I want him to take me home."

The muscles in Eli's neck and the veins in his forehead began to push against his skin. His gaze darted between Miriam and Henry several times. He was still breathing like a bull when he finally turned and left.

"Take me home," Miriam said quietly, and without waiting for a word in return, she walked toward Henry's buggy.

As Miriam waited for Henry to hitch up the horse to the buggy, Eli ran his horse out of the drive and down the road. A chorus of voices from the Singing poured through cracked windows. Had anyone else heard the altercation? She hoped not. How would she explain the angry words and happenings? And what would happen now?

They sat close, but not in the way that their shoulders melded together. Even the rock of the buggy barely moved Miriam's stiff posture.

"I need to tell my parents tonight," he said, solemnly. "Will you come —"

"I can't," she said too quickly. She knew

she couldn't handle any more sadness, debating, or hurt. She was afraid for Linda and the range of emotions she would experience and the anger his father, Amos, might express. Surely this would be a night of utter grieving in the Mast home. She knew she could not travel that road again. "I just can't."

"I understand."

Henry reached over and took the hand that lay in her lap. A warmth coursed through the rest of her body, starting with her hand. Hot tears ran down her cheeks, dripping from her jawline. When one marked the top of Henry's hand she felt him sigh next to her. After several more minutes they were settled in her drive in front of her home. He carefully wiped the tears from her face, his brow bent in sadness. She could read his love for her in every touch and between the lines of his face. Her love mirrored his. She would not leave him when he needed her most.

"I love you," he said, his voice faltering.

She could see that his eyes met hers with a humble desire to hear the words in return. She hadn't been able to return those words in the time since he admitted his enlistment. It was not because she didn't love him. She loved him more than ever, but saying it out loud made the hurt of his decision sink deeper into her soul.

"I love you." Her words broke him as he dropped his head into her hands and lap. Her heart melted and broke at the same time. She kissed the top of his head, his hair feathering against her skin.

He raised his head and kissed her generously. She matched his passion, not knowing when she would feel his lips on hers again. She memorized the heat in his hands as they went from her face down to her shoulders and arms to her back as he pulled her close. His touch was always gentle, but this time, there was an undeniable intensity like never before.

Watching him drive away proved a test of self-control. She wanted to run after him and call for him to stop and never let her go.

With a sobered mood, she walked into her house. She took her cape and bonnet off and walked into the living room to say good night to her parents.

"Miriam, sit down." Her father didn't even look up from the letter he was writing when he spoke.

Miriam obeyed, noting her father's tense jaw. He sat at his desk, where he sat every night, clenching his hands. Her mother sat looking out the window, her unseeing eyes glistening in the lantern light.

"I heard today that one of our young boys is planning to join up with the army." He almost seemed to lose his breath, and she watched his chest rise and fall at a faster pace. This news affected him in a way that she had not anticipated. "Miriam, you've been deceitful."

Before Miriam said a word, she imagined who might have told her father about Henry. News traveled quickly in their small community. Once Eli knew, there could be any number of people who had learned of Henry's enlistment.

"Please, let me explain," she began, hoping he would hear her out.

"There is no need." Her father's large lower jaw pushed out. "Your young man has changed you."

"*Dat,* no, it's not true. Henry isn't leaving for good. He wants to return. He wants to give me the life I want — here with the church and —"

Her father put a hand out to her. "You are to have no contact with him, do you understand?"

All Miriam could do was shake her head no.

"Do you understand?" he repeated, unwavering.

Miriam looked at her mother, who was weeping into her hands. Memories of the same sort of sobbing flooded her memory. She could not do this to her parents.

"I understand." She stood, composed, and smoothed down her apron.

Miriam's father had sad eyes as he turned back to the letter he was writing. His hands shook as he tried to continue. She closed her eyes tightly against the disappointment in her father's face. It was enough to abate the panic she felt about agreeing to have no contact with Henry. The night had been too much. She pushed against the thick air and walked out of the living room.

Her legs were tired as she climbed the narrow closed staircase. Relieved to be in her bedroom, she went to the small desk in front of the window and pulled out a pen and paper. How could she tell Henry, after everything they'd shared with each other, that she would not be able to write him?

She sat unmoving for minutes or hours, she wasn't sure which. She watched the stars rise. Her sister's house went from a golden light to black, and her own parents' slow footfalls ceased. Then a light flickered on across the road.

Like a beacon, it poured out of Nancy Poole's front door. Her soft, motherly shape was silhouetted against the glow as she waved someone inside. Then, she saw him. Henry. He had a small bag in one hand and wore his hat hard on his head. His shoulders were hunched. He stood by the door in front of Nancy, and Miriam wished to hear what was being said. She couldn't see Nancy past the tall, broad image of Henry. Her heart swelled at the sight of him. The lump in her throat began to beat like her heart.

Then she saw thick white arms pull him downward into a hug. He returned the affectionate gesture. The older woman released him and then took his arm and led him into her home. Was he going to stay there? His parents must have forced him to leave the only home he'd ever known.

Though he was not yet officially shunned, the excommunication had begun.

CHAPTER 6

January 1944

The days passed away into nights, which poured into weeks. Snow had arrived and covered the ground with the color of Christmas, though it had already come and gone. It had not been the joyous holiday of years past without Henry. If he'd been home, she would have sewn him a new shirt for Christmas and maybe given him some new whittling tools. He needed them. He would have surprised her then by whittling some creation that would remind her of his love. But all that was gone now. Miriam would hear snatches of conversation in which his name was mentioned, but people would stop speaking about him once they saw Miriam. Suddenly conversations would shift to the weather in Sunrise. The consensus was that it hadn't been overly cold this winter. Then a veil of silence, as heavy as a workhorse, would linger for several long moments until someone found something else to talk about.

Attending church had grown uncomfortable for her. She was constantly waiting for his enlistment to be brought up to the members by the bishop. It was part of the practice of church discipline. Since this was what happened when someone strayed from the fold of the church, the anticipation of it grew heavy.

Miriam made efforts at being attentive at church this week, but lately it was a challenge. She looked around. The men sat in the large living room, and she and the other ladies were in an adjoining addition that used to be a porch. Miriam watched as the master-bedroom door behind the men opened. Inside, she could see the crowd of nursing mothers and women who would be mothers very soon. She could hear the squalling of infants coming from the room for a moment, and then it was shut. All that could be heard was the rhythm of the bishop's tenor voice and the on-and-off-again little voices of toddlers.

Miriam had often worked as a maid, helping a new mother after a baby was born. She was used to babies crying, but today, their cries seemed to remind her that her life was moving on, and that she was farther and farther away from having her own family. The nearby window diverted her attention and she watched several squirrels running around on the skeleton of a tree. Their humorous scampering saved her mood. They chirped and clicked at each other, almost as if they were arguing. Part of her wished she could nudge her mother. *Mem* had always enjoyed nature, but the entertainment would now be lost on her mother, whose sight was worsening.

Miriam didn't pay attention again until she heard the ancient bishop speak up, asking all the members to stay and everyone else to leave. The unbaptized boys amidst the men retreated quickly from their ranks and left the house. Likely they were gathering in the barn to talk about their week. Sundays often provided the social gathering that the youth enjoyed, as they had little opportunity to visit each other during the week.

The older daughters who weren't baptized shuffled around the rooms to gather up the younger brothers and sisters, her older nieces among them. A few of the toddlers cried for their mothers as they walked outside but were easily quieted. As the young women left and a few others rearranged their seating, there were a growing number of whispers and glances. Her eyes met Henry's sister Sylvia's, but she turned away as soon as Miriam's questioning expression caught her. The girl's lips twitched and when she passed by her mother, Linda, she placed a well-trained hand on her shoulder for a brief moment. Linda patted Sylvia's hand in return. Her other hand held a hankie. Miriam's body grew warmer and her heart beat more rapidly.

As the rooms regained their sense of calm, a sense of curiosity hovered above them. All eyes were on the bishop, who sat on the front bench facing the men. Though Miriam was surprised to see how stooped his posture had become over the winter, all she could think of in the moment was what he would say. Church preachers didn't ask nonmembers to exit unless there was a proclamation of great importance.

Due to the shifting in the room, she could now see Eli through the wide archway that led into the living room. Their eyes lingered when they met. His eyes narrowed. When he looked at her that way, she was sure he could read her thoughts. She looked away.

A few minutes later she could hear shuffling. The slow-moving bishop came to the center of the open area. His face was turned toward the men, but on occasion he would turn to look at the women as well. Though his voice was always sobering, today it felt strained and old, as though his throat had been thinned and stretched.

"I asked you to stay because we have a matter to discuss. In November, Amos and Linda Mast's eldest son, Henry, came home from his duty at the camp in Hagerstown, Maryland. And, oh, what a burden he brought home to his parents. What a disappointment! Henry has turned his back on the church."

Miriam's breath quickened and tears formed in her eyes. Her mouth went dry, and her palms dampened with sweat. Her mother shifted uncomfortably next to her before clearing her throat. Miriam's three sisters were nearby as well. Bertha and Martha both pursed their lips. Bertha started turning her head toward Miriam but returned her gaze forward a moment later. Miriam inhaled, then exhaled deeply and quietly. She needed to keep her composure, and she forced herself to keep her eyes on the bishop. She'd tried to prepare herself for this ever since Henry's departure. It was something everyone knew would happen. Now that it was here, it was almost as if she were standing in the corner of the room watching everything happen. Was this real?

"He told his parents that he was leaving the good work he was doing at the camp and enlisting in the army. He knows this is not the way of the Amish and is not right in the eyes of the Lord. One of the preachers, Ira Mast, his uncle, talked with him and told him he needed to turn back from his sinful ways. Henry's heart was unchanged. He said he believed God was telling him to do this. We all know that it is blasphemy to say such things. In the sixth commandment, God says thou shalt not murder. He was told unless he changes his mind, he was to leave his home."

Miriam could no longer hold her gaze on the bishop and her eyes snapped to Linda, who sat in a nearby bench. What torture this would be for her. A flurry of anger arose in her for Henry's mother. Tears rushed to Miriam's eyes as she saw her hunched back shudder in silent sobs. Linda's sisters sat next to and behind her. They patted her, shushing her gently.

Tears clogged Miriam's throat. She thought the bishop to be heartless, but then she noticed that he, too, was crying. His brow furrowed deeply and his mouth quivered as he spoke. Miriam suspected it hurt him just to mutter these words, let alone announce them to the congregation. He was in a delicate position. Such merciless words brought out the heart in everyone. Many were weeping. Norman Hershberger's mother was crying. Norman was the only other boy from the district at the camp. Was she afraid that he would be next? Several others kept their gazes down and dabbed their eyes with a handkerchief. So many, in their own ways, were feeling the pinch of pain from Henry's decision.

Miriam's defenses were breaking. She'd never bared her soul for the church to see. Where were her sisters? Was there no one willing to support her? Did everyone just expect her to forget her commitment to Henry or bear the burden alone?

The bishop went on to say that he would not be formally shunned yet and that out of courtesy for his mortal soul, they would wait until he returned from the war, *if* he returned. If he was shunned from the church without being given a chance of confession, his soul would surely have no place in heaven. *What if he died while fighting in the war?* Miriam questioned rapidly. *Where would that leave him?*

Her head fell forward onto her chest and she covered her face with her hands. Her body quaked at the power of her sobs. Since the night he left, her emotions seemed to have been hiding, deep down inside her, in some unfamiliar place. And now that they had surfaced, she had no strength to quell them.

"Henry left town the morning following his admission of his enlistment to his parents, like he was escaping the Lord's wrath. We have since written to him only to receive the same response as before, that he considers this to be following the will of God." The old man hung his head. His warbling voice declaring his burden. "Oh, how I will pray for his soul."

At this point the bishop's voice was lost in her pain. She could only sense the growing ache in her heart and among the members around her. Henry's mother would now grieve him as if he were dead. That was how it was in the eyes of the church, even if his shunning wasn't official yet. His name was written in the furrows on the brow of every person that filed out of church. Just as she was taught to push away the burdens in order to fulfill duties, she sensed this on everyone's shoulders as they moved on to the next order of business: serving and eating lunch. As she dished out food on plate after plate, concern about Henry was reflected in everyone's eyes.

When her own eyes looked up to meet the most familiar in the group of hungry men, she choked back a sob. Eli. He alone wore an expression she couldn't read completely. There was something else mingling with the sympathy in his gaze; was it that he had won the battle, or that he was just beginning to fight for her? She couldn't tell, and as much as she didn't want to care, she did. She cared whether or not she mattered to anyone. At the moment it seemed as if she meant something to Eli and no one else. His sharp stare weakened her; then he broke the tension with a playful wink and moved on.

When her kettle of potatoes was empty, she picked it up and took it to the kitchen. Henry's mother, Linda, was the only one there for the moment. Miriam hadn't talked to her since the terrible night she ate supper with the Mast family and Henry told her his plans for enlistment. They'd seen one another at church, but neither had initiated any conversation. Miriam had no idea what to say to her and she suspected Linda felt the same. They'd always gotten along, but Miriam found herself on uneven ground.

"I'm empty," Miriam said, trying to sound casual.

"Here you go," Linda said without looking up. She stirred the potatoes in the new pot a few more times, and as she handed off the large stainless-steel pot their eyes met.

Miriam's eyes met Linda's older brown ones. There seemed to be a knowing, a sympathy even, that traveled between them, until Linda looked away. It reminded Miriam of the days that passed so slowly after Henry's draft notice arrived in the mail. Linda and Miriam never spoke of it, but silently they shared the same burden and sorrow. He was the first of the community to go. Everyone expected him to honor their district with loyalty and good behavior despite the temptations of the new life he would be living. No one expected this. The weight of the heavy pot was transferred to Miriam, and her hands sank as her heart did. If she could have found some companionship with another person among her Amish community, she was sure her heart would feel lighter. She sighed and turned around to go back to the assembly line of ladies.

"Have you heard from Henry?" Linda quietly asked.

Miriam turned, meeting her eyes again. The lump in her throat grew at the sight of tears in the older woman's eyes that were so much like Henry's. In them she saw the reflection of her own pain and felt guilty for finding comfort in it.

"No. *Dat* has forbidden me to write him. Eli wrote to tell him." She let her gaze fall to the floor, unwilling to share the grief in them. "I'm sure he'll write to you soon."

The older woman nodded her head and pursed her lips. She turned away so her back faced the open door, telling Miriam the conversation was through.

Miriam walked quietly through the thin night air. She didn't mind coming home alone from the Singing. It gave her time to think, wrapped in the blanket of darkness. This would be the only time she would allow tears, knowing no one would see them before she arrived home. Muted light fell through the windows of the houses, just enough to see the haze of what was ahead of her, but like a dull memory, it gave no details.

As she followed the dim beacons home, she heard the canter of hooves behind her. She stepped a little farther to the side of the road, waiting for the buggy to pass. She smiled and waved at her friend Becky, who it seemed had finally gotten a date with David Bontrager, a boy she had been eyeing for some time. Her friend's voice chattered away as she waved back. A sharp ache dug into Miriam's chest, and her hand instinctually went up to her heart. She swallowed hard and forced herself to keep walking. She was almost home.

Several more buggies passed and Miriam kept waving and smiling. She couldn't help the joy that she felt in seeing newly paired couples, knowing the excitement of falling in love. Yet it was agonizing to watch as everyone around her continued to move ahead while she stood still, stagnated by Henry's leaving. It was as though he'd died. That was how the community reacted to the news. Even before the announcement was made in church a few weeks back, his mother had begun wearing black to church. His father constantly wore a mask of placidity, which was unlike him; he was usually much more jovial. It was as if he wanted to be void of all emotion.

"Miriam," a familiar voice mounted over the clip-clop of the horse hooves behind her.

Her head spun, pulling her out of her agitated thoughts. It was Eli. He was the only one out of all her friends who talked with her about Henry. Everyone else, including Henry's mother and her parents, pretended as if he'd never existed. His name was never spoken, and no one talked of the CPS camp. When Norman visited for a few days, he was welcomed with open arms, but the grief that blemished the community remained unspoken and nameless.

"Hello," Miriam commented quietly, still walking.

"It's freezing and wet. Why didn't you let me take you home?"

"You didn't ask." She flipped her head back around to watch where she walked. She wasn't vexed with him, but she was nervous about giving him too much attention. She didn't want to give him, or any other young man, any handy ideas. Though she couldn't write Henry, it didn't mean her heart wasn't with him.

He kept his buggy moving, pacing his horse at the speed of Miriam's walking.

"Why don't you get in now?"

She shrugged. "My house isn't that far away."

"Come on, Miriam, get in. You left before I could ask you." He stopped the buggy in the middle of the road.

Another buggy was waiting patiently behind them. Sylvia, Henry's sister, and a young man were inside. Miriam waved and smiled, but Sylvia responded only with noticeably cold eyes. Miriam shivered at the chill of the look and pocketed the worry for another time.

Miriam sighed. Then, reluctantly, she got into the buggy. She was surprised about the distance he gave her when she climbed up into the buggy. Maybe he didn't want this to be a date. He hadn't been forcing himself into her life since Henry left in November. Maybe it was because of the argument that they had at the wedding, or that he just understood that she wasn't going to be swayed away from Henry.

They chatted over the community happenings, touching on nothing important. Before she knew it, they were in her driveway and she realized that Eli's warm body was close enough that she could feel the pulse of blood in his veins. When had that happened? When they talked about him making a trip out to his cousin's wedding in Pennsylvania, or when he mentioned he might buy land between his parents' home and hers to build a house? Or was it in the midst of all the jokes? She hated herself for not moving away, enjoying the warmth of a real body, and the safety and comfort it had always brought her.

"My *mem* mentioned that she asked you to come over to help after the baby's born?" Eli raised his eyebrow at her.

"Well, with all you boys in the house, she can't expect much help there," she teased. "It's been a slow winter for babies; I haven't really helped as a maid for anyone since early fall. Fannie barely needed me, so I am excited to help your mother. New babies are always so much fun. It keeps me busier than at home with *Mem* and *Dat.*"

She sat silent for a spell. She didn't say what she was thinking, that the break from her home would be a good change. It might get her mind away from her burdens for even the few days that she would help Sarah Brenneman. Sometimes she would stay a week or more, depending on where the mother and new baby lived, but since it was just in the community, a few days was all Sarah would need. After that, she'd have sisters or cousins arriving from out of town, or nieces even, who would be able to give more long-term help. This was okay with Miriam also. Spending more than a few days at the Brenneman home could cause some problems, since Eli lived there.

The wind died down around the buggy, but only warmth grew within. She felt guilty as she sat so close to Eli that her head was almost resting on his shoulder.

She loved Henry with everything she could feel, but the last thing she wanted to

121

do right now was feel.

"Better be careful, Miriam — if you fall asleep leaning on me I'll pull you out of the buggy and throw you in the snow." He laughed.

"You would." She laughed with him and slapped his arm.

"Maybe next time I can drive you home from the Singing, instead of halfway down the road." He winked at her.

"We'll see." She paused for a moment. "Well, thanks for the ride."

Miriam began leaving the buggy and he grabbed her hand.

"What, no invitation for pie?" His eyes were twinkling.

"This isn't a date, Eli."

"But I did ask to drive you home and you did say yes. Isn't that a date?"

Miriam rolled her eyes and actually laughed. Eli was good for that. She supposed it was harmless to offer him a piece of pie. He wasn't Henry, but she was aching for real company and conversation.

"I suppose you can come in. But it's still not a date."

He winked at her and then took his horse and buggy to the barn to get them out of the cold weather. Miriam walked into the dimly lit house, taking off her cape and bonnet first, then going to see her parents in the living room.

"Eli's coming in for pie," she said.

Her mother's eyebrow twitched as she crocheted and rocked on the hickory rocker, and her father stopped writing for several long moments. She was sure they would be happy, maybe even overjoyed, at the prospect of Miriam actually moving on. While this didn't change Miriam's love for Henry, she couldn't help the urge to please her parents, either. Her loyalties were divided in the worst way. Inviting Eli for pie was simple enough as long as he understood that there was only friendship between them.

She and Eli spent the next hour together with tea and a pecan pie. For the first time since Henry's confession about his enlistment, she was at ease. Eli enjoyed teasing and showing off, both things that made her laugh. Anything other than crying was a comfort. It was easy to be around him.

CHAPTER 7

April 1944

Miriam had received word after breakfast that morning that Eli's mother, Sarah, had given birth to her first daughter. After six robust boys, this was more than a blessing to the aging woman. Eli was already twenty-five, and she'd had him when she was newly married at only eighteen. Then five boys followed, with numerous miscarriages and even two stillbirths throughout the years. The two stillborn babies had both been girls, but this girl was born with a healthy scream. Everyone would be rejoicing with them.

Miriam saw her father bring the buggy up the drive. She grabbed her handbag with a few of the items she would need for the next several days and nights. She waved at her mother, who was sitting at the window at Fannie's house helping her with mealtime preparations. Fannie would look in on their parents while Miriam was away from home. She was glad they lived so close.

"I'm ready," she said to her father. He clicked his mouth and the horse started out.

Miriam really wanted to walk to the Brenneman house. It was a beautiful early-spring day, even though there was a chill in the air. The buds were on notice and any day now the breeze would carry the sound of the eggs hatching, opening up a choir of new songs. The sky was a perfect blue, and puffy white clouds hung lazily above her. Unfortunately, the Brennemans lived more than five miles away from the Coblentz home. While she'd walked a lot greater distances over the years, her father offered to drive her since he had business in that direction anyway. They needed a new horse, and Simon Pieterscheim, the Brennemans' closest neighbor, was the man to buy from.

They mostly rode in silence, only briefly chatting about when she would need to be picked up again. Her father suggested asking Eli to drive her home if it was after dark. He didn't like to drive the buggy after dark much anymore. He said he felt the automobiles were driving too wildly on the old dirt roads lately, and the horse was too easily spooked. Miriam knew her father would never tell a falsehood, but she wondered if he secretly wanted Eli to drive her merely to get them alone together.

Miriam hopped out of the buggy, and without as much as a goodbye, her father left, and Miriam turned toward the house. She had always admired the Brenneman home. It was a very large farmhouse and had the greatest number of milking cows in the community. Eli's father, Mark David, was known to be a good businessman. No one wanted to use the word "shrewd," but Miriam suspected that it fit the bill. Eli was always hard at work as the oldest son and would likely take over the farm someday, including the extraordinary farmhouse.

"Miriam," Eli waved from a distance. He trotted up to her with a crooked smile and a twinkle in his eyes.

In the few moments it took him to reach her, she couldn't help but recognize how handsome he was. No one would disagree with her or even make her feel guilty for noticing him, despite her insistence that she loved Henry. He wore an old, faded blue shirt with the sleeves cut off just around his large forearms. His suspenders were strapped tightly against his barrel chest, and rubber work boots reached his knees.

"Eli," she said, cheerfully. "A little girl!"

"Not just one, but two," he said, nodding.

"*Mem* cried more than the babies."

"I can't believe it. I'd better get in there." Miriam beamed with joy.

Sarah was sitting up in bed and fairly glowing when she walked in. Miriam couldn't believe the beauty of the two nearly identical girls. Sarah had named them well, Emmy and Betty. Sarah cradled them both with an expression of disbelief, looking back and forth from one to the other. Dark hair, blue eyes, and fair skin. Breathtaking.

"That's Betty." Sarah nodded her head at the baby on her right. "She was born second. This is Emmy. They are named after my two favorite aunts."

The woman blushed and looked at Miriam, then down at the babies in her arms.

"They are both so pretty." Miriam grazed little Betty's cheek with the back of a finger.

The silence in the room was comfortable as they admired the babies. Betty made a small grunt and twisted, and Miriam could feel she was a strong baby even though she was less than twelve hours old. The women giggled when they heard the rumble in the baby's diaper.

Miriam went ahead and changed her diaper, then put both babies down together in a small cradle. They seemed to sense the other was close and curled inward. Miriam convinced Sarah to stay in bed and sleep as well.

Miriam went about finding her way around the home. She decided to do laundry even though it wasn't a Monday, since the girls would start going through diapers way too fast. But first, she began preparing lunch.

All the boys who weren't in school anymore came in for lunch, and Miriam felt a little awkward as she sat with Mark David, Eli, Mark, David, and Moses. Abe and Enos were still in school. She witnessed the fastest eating she'd ever seen. She could hardly keep herself from laughing. Eli ate slower than the others, and sat across from Miriam. His eyes passed over her continually. Self-conscious, Miriam ate half the amount she usually would.

The men and boys went back outside as soon as they finished lunch. After helping Sarah get the girls ready for another nursing, Miriam returned to the kitchen to wash dishes. Music played in her mind and heart as she scrubbed the pots in the hot water. It was just something she did when working chores. Several songs she'd learned during her years of running around before she was baptized lingered with her, and she wasn't sure she'd ever forget the words to them.

The words to "Cheek to Cheek" ran through her mind. The heavenly lines, the happiness the singer expressed — she couldn't help but relate a bit after taking in the scent of the two sweet babes and the joy radiating from Sarah. How could she let her own selfish burden muddy up the almost angelic mood in the home? Her eyes closed for a moment as her body remembered a familiar rhythm to move to, though she had heard it so seldom.

Suddenly, strong arms flanked her and a heavy chest leaned against her. She jumped and threw soapsuds on the window in front of her. In her startled confusion, she turned around. She was only inches from Eli's face, their bodies touching. His breath warmed her face, and he winked playfully, seeming to enjoy her discomfort.

"Eli." She pushed against his chest, not hard but with enough force to make her desires known. "Someone will see."

"*Mem*'s in her room and everyone else is outside," Eli said, unmoved. "No one is around."

Miriam stopped leaning back and relaxed slightly. Her heart beat faster than normal. She could smell the April breeze around him. His arms closed around her more tightly, and he brought his face a bit closer and his hands to her waist. Every move seemed so easy for him, as though he had planned it perfectly and acted it out a million times. The smile he wore only spoke to his confidence, and it unnerved her.

He leaned toward her slowly, and Miriam inhaled and countered the move. What should she do? She wasn't frightened of him, but she was afraid of what she would feel if he did kiss her. She didn't want to fall for anyone, including the very handsome Eli Brenneman, the most coveted unmarried man in the community. Her feelings toward him always wavered between easy companionship and almost despising him because of his forcefulness.

"I would never leave you," he whispered in her ear.

Miriam, still holding her breath, wished he wouldn't compare his staying to Henry's leaving. No one could compare his circumstance to Henry's.

"I think one of the babies is crying. I need to go."

His hands tightened the moment before he let her go.

She moved quickly through the kitchen and was cradling Emmy to sleep in her arms in a matter of moments. Neither baby settled well throughout the evening, but finally, both were quiet. This gave Miriam just a sliver of time to get back in the kitchen to make a simple dinner as the men finished their day of work. Just before she was finished, all the Brenneman boys came inside with their father. Miriam watched with a smile on her lips as they teased and bantered with one another. Her family had never been quite that funny with each other. She enjoyed the Brennemans' informal ways.

After they cleaned up, several of them took turns looking in on their new sisters. None of them could leave the room without a great smile on his face, and they all commented on how perfect they seemed. All Miriam could see was how well Sarah had reared her boys; her girls were born into a delightful family.

Mark David's presence commanded attention as he called for quiet when he was ready to lead the silent prayer. Everyone obeyed in a moment, even Eli. The respect he showed his father appealed to her. Of course, this reverence was expected, but Miriam had never watched him in his home setting and had never seen him interact much with his father and brothers.

Throughout the meal the boys spoke and chatted. This wasn't common. She'd eaten with many families in the community, but none were as verbal and entertaining as the Brennemans. It wasn't as if they were laughing boisterously, as perhaps happened more often during the Singing games; there was just the comfortable and happy chatter of sharing a meal. Even though it wasn't her family, the warm sense of belonging wrapped around Miriam's heart.

Miriam had a difficult time as she tried to fall asleep late that night. She was put in Eli's room, since he was the only one who wasn't sharing a room anymore. Usually a son of twenty-five was married and out of the house. His room was as simple as the rooms in the home she'd grown up in. Even though in her mind she knew it was just another iron bed frame and a coverlet just like one of many quilts she'd slept under, the bed bothered her. Only the night before, Eli had slept in that bed.

She suddenly felt like God Himself was orchestrating either a new love or her demise. Her heart loved Henry, but her loyalty was to her family, her church, and the only life she'd ever known. Eli was part of that world. Was her loyalty stronger than her love? Did it even matter? She hadn't heard a word from Henry since November.

It was almost as if the burden of his probable shunning was more like a grieving over his death. She hadn't spoken to Linda since their brief conversation in church and wondered if he'd written to her yet.

As the thoughts coursed through her mind, she eventually gave in to a tempestuous sleep. Before she realized it, the morning sun fell upon her through the east-facing window, showering her with light and warmth. The yellow shaft soaked deeply into her, bringing the only relief she knew she would receive. She felt no more revived than when she'd lain down.

She took a few deep breaths before leaving Eli's bedroom for the day. She felt her heart wish, long, and hope that Eli would be occupied today. She didn't want to be alone with him. Even though she cared for him, until she knew something about Henry — anything — she wouldn't be able to move on. She had to know if he still loved her and if she should wait for him to return. And she had to figure out in her own time whether she wanted to do so.

The day was like the day before. She continued to force Sarah to stay in bed at least until Suzie Kline, the midwife, came to check in with the twins. Then the midwife gave Sarah strict orders to stay off her feet for at least another two days. As glad as Miriam was to help Sarah, she wondered when Sarah's niece would be arriving to take her place. The walls were closing in on her with Eli being nearby all the time. She didn't want to lead him on when she had no intentions with him. Or was it because she was actually tempted to fall for him?

She ignored every wink and smile and pretended not to notice when his foot nudged hers under the table. By supper, his brow was furrowed, and his frustration satisfied her. She knew that Henry's training was going to take months, and she was sure he wouldn't go overseas to war without writing or maybe even coming home. She had to wait.

Hours later, she combed out her long strawberry-blonde hair with the warm water in a small bucket. A larger bucket was cooling next to her, as she'd just finished giving herself a sponge bath. The house had been asleep for well over an hour when she started, but in the last few minutes she'd heard the babies. One of them cried with a gusto she hadn't heard from either of them in their short little lives. It was the type of cry that was painful for a baby as well as anyone hearing it.

She grabbed her sleep bonnet and rolled

her hair up quickly, hoping the tightness of the strings would keep her long strands up. She pulled on her robe as she walked toward Sarah's room, feeling her way down the hall. She'd been told earlier that Mark David slept like a dead man, and it was okay for her to go into the room to help Sarah, though she did so with hesitation. Sarah's face was drawn and beyond exhausted.

"Betty's kicking her legs like she has a stomachache," she whispered. "Colic?"

Her question sounded so sad, and even though she was an experienced mother, she appeared anxious. Was she afraid that another blessing would be taken away from her?

"She's fed," she said, handing the screaming baby to her. "Emmy's hungry, so I'll feed her while you have Betty."

"I'll take her out," Miriam whispered loudly. "Most of Fannie's babies were colicky; I know just what to do."

Miriam gathered the small squirming bundle into her arms. Even in the dim lantern light she could see that the baby's face was bright red from crying. Her legs went from straight to drawn up to her stomach and then back down again. She shushed the baby in her ear as she walked through the hall. It did not help Betty's frustration, and her cry became louder.

Once she'd returned to Eli's bedroom, she lay the baby on the bed and unwrapped the blanket. She changed her diaper, then gently took the baby's legs and began circling them up against her stomach and back down in slow movements. As she sang the sweet song her mother always sang to her grand-children, Betty slowly began to calm. The more her bloated belly was relieved, the more her eyes drooped. Before she fell completely to sleep, Miriam laid out the blanket and began swaddling the tiny infant snugly inside. As she'd learned to do over the years, she kept her arms down and gave her little chance to squirm out of the blanket. This was a comfort to a newborn who had just been tightly held beneath her mother's heart, with little space to move.

"You sure are good with her." Eli's tenor voice strummed like a guitar in the small bedroom.

Miriam's hand went to her chest, startled. Eli leaned against the door frame of his bedroom. In the small light of the oil lamp on the nightstand, she could see that he wore only long johns. She'd never seen anyone except her brothers in anything other than regular day clothes. She quickly moved her eyes back on the baby.

"Eli, what are you doing in here?" She finished the final tuck of the swaddle before picking up the baby, curving her gently into her arms.

"I heard her." He nodded toward his baby sister. "I couldn't sleep."

"Well, she's okay now," Miriam said almost in a song as she gently swayed back and forth. "Just some colic."

Eli's light golden hair lay in disarray around his forehead. How was it possible that even in the dark room, his light eyes still illuminated flirtatiously? He stood upright, filling the door frame, then slowly made his way into the bedroom.

"You shouldn't be in here," she said, but his presence instantly brought some comfort to her after the energy it had taken to avoid him all day. In the quiet of this room, she found herself repeating her words. "You shouldn't be in here."

"Do I make you nervous?" He winked at her.

"No," she giggled. Eli was always a tease. "I don't like the way this looks."

Eli looked around, as if searching for something.

"I don't see anyone looking." He smiled. "Don't be so tense. Don't tell me that you and Henry never —"

"Don't you dare," she spat out in a loud whisper, catching a spark in his eyes. She realized he was teasing her. "Eli Brenneman."

She threw one of the clean diapers at him. He always knew how to lighten her mood.

"Okay, okay." He lifted his hands in defense, smiling. "I'm sorry."

When their quiet laughter subsided, the silence of the muted room filled Miriam's ears. She moved her eyes back onto the sleeping baby. For the space of several minutes, neither of them spoke. Miriam wouldn't have known what to say anyway, but she secretly wished Eli would either talk or just leave. Both of those things would be an improvement to standing together wordlessly.

Eli came closer and put a heavy hand on her back and even through her robe and nightgown, its warmth seeped through. A tingling sensation ran along her scalp, then suddenly she realized her hair had fallen out of her sleep bonnet. It hung loosely down her back. He was combing through her locks much more gently than she thought possible given his thick, callused farm hands, and her face grew warm with embarrassment. The memory of that early November morning when Henry sweetly requested to see her hair in the sunrise came to mind. That innocent moment was so different from now. Here she was with Eli, in the middle of the night, alone in his room, with a silent house wrapped around them.

"Can't you see it?"

Eli waited, but Miriam didn't respond.

"This could be us in a year."

Miriam's heart thudded as his hands continued to comb through the length of her hair. Her eyes shut him out as she angled herself away from him.

"We could get married this spring and in a year, maybe less, you'd be rocking our little baby." His voice wasn't dreamy and inspiring, like when she and Henry would dream of their future, but it was more exacting, like walking in narrow paths instead of roaming fields.

She wanted to tell him to stop, but there was something in the companionship that hushed her ability to resist imagining the scene he described.

"Isn't that all you've ever wanted, Miriam?" He moved to face her, his hands on her forearms. "To get married and have a family? Why question this? Don't you think that maybe Henry left for a reason?"

She looked into his bright blue eyes. For one of the first times in all of her memories

139

of Eli, she could see he was serious. The twinkle of his childish nature wasn't in his eyes.

"I'm sorry, Eli." The words came out sincerely, but they took great effort. "I love Henry."

"Even though he chose war, Miriam, over you?"

Miriam had no response.

He closed the gap between them, and his hold on her arms grew tighter, forcing her to stop swaying with the baby. The pleasant soft breathing of the baby she held between them was the only thing that could be heard. Their eyes locked. He bent toward her and she began debating how to handle this. She liked Eli, but she loved Henry. Miriam held her breath and was surprised when he tapped her nose with his finger, smiling.

"Good night." He winked and left the room before she could say anything.

Miriam was glad to leave the next afternoon when Sarah's niece, Barbara, arrived. Barbara was full of energy, and Miriam knew she would feel at home in the Brenneman household. They never stopped talking, joking, and laughing. She couldn't help but wonder how the two tiny girls would do with this boisterous family.

Her father was able to pick her up, and

she was glad that he wasn't the type to ask questions. They rode the entire way home in silence.

Monday, several days after Miriam returned from Eli's home, she worked against the weather to get the laundry on the line. The sun shone, but it was bitter cold. Though spring was only a whisper away, it didn't feel like it, and Miriam couldn't sense the hope that the new season usually brought her. Just as she wished the sun would wash away the cold around her and she lifted her face to the golden light, a gray cloud hovered over the rays and a heavy shadow moved slowly over her.

She hadn't seen Eli since the night he'd questioned her love and loyalty. His words had been swimming in her mind for days, and she couldn't answer his questions. Thoughts about Henry choosing war over her and their plans haunted her.

She was just about to release a heavy sigh when she turned to notice her father carrying a heavy ladder out of the barn. His teeth bared and his face red, he struggled with every step. She moved past the clothesline and jogged down the long drive.

"*Dat,* where are Truman and Fannie's boys? They should be doing this for you."

She picked up the front of the ladder, helping him position it against the barn door that was still not sliding properly. "Please, don't climb the ladder. Let me find Junior or Levi."

"They're not here," he said, not meeting her eyes. He never had seemed to warm up to her since the situation with Henry.

"This door can wait until they come back." She felt like a pacing animal in a cage. She did not want her elderly father climbing the ladder.

"I've been climbing ladders since before I was schoolboy." His voice was stern and harsh. This change alone concerned Miriam. He usually softened his gruff exterior toward her when they were alone. "I'm fine. Now go, your laundry isn't going to put itself away." He tried to chuckle at the end of his last word, but it came out more like a cough.

"Just be careful," she reminded him.

She watched as he climbed the first few rungs. His body strained with each step, but he seemed unwilling to heed her warnings, so she said nothing more. Perhaps she was being overly cautious.

"Miriam!" a voice called.

She turned around as Nancy Poole trotted across the road. She held her coat tightly around her large frame. Her face, always cheerful, carried news, Miriam sensed. What was it? She looked back at her father to see that he was still making his way up the long ladder, then she jogged out to Nancy.

"Miriam, I have a letter." Nancy puffed between words, her face flushed. She tried to talk quietly behind her hand, but her raspy whisper was loud. Miriam was glad that Fannie's household wasn't outside at the moment. "Wait, let me catch my breath."

Miriam pulled back at her desire to force her older neighbor to talk so she could get to the bottom of this. Was the letter from Henry, or maybe from Kathryn? Eli had assured her that he'd written to Henry to let him know that she was forbidden to communicate with him. She had grown desperate to hear from him and was secretly disappointed that he hadn't broken the rules and written to her anyway. She wished she had the courage to do just that.

"Sorry," Nancy said, finally. "I was just so excited to give you this."

Nancy looked around before slowly pulling out a folded letter from her coat pocket. "It's from Henry."

Miriam gasped as her hand went to her mouth. She watched seemingly from a distance as her hand went toward the letter.

This could be the pot of gold at the end of the rainbow or the bumble of a beehive. The tingle she felt upon touching the envelope made her take a deep breath. Joy, rebellion, elation, and hesitation surged in her heart.

A loud slap and a dull thump jerked her back to reality. She spun around only to find her father on the wet ground, with the ladder beside him. She was at his side before she realized what she was doing.

"Dat, Dat." Her voice rang frantically, moving none of the cold air that towered around her. "Don't move." She palpated his arms and legs, not knowing what she was doing, only wondering if he had a break.

He grasped his chest and coughed. "I'm okay, Miriam," he rasped. "I just lost my breath." He rolled to his side and despite Miriam's urgings, sat up.

"Should I get my car and take you to your doctor?" Nancy stood behind Miriam.

"No. No." Her father waved his hand at Nancy, grimacing and scowling all at once. "Help me up."

Miriam knew there was no use going against her father. He was as firm as the sun was bright. He hadn't always been so gruff, but in his latter years it seemed to be his way. His laughter grew less frequent, and the smile that sat above his long white beard was unfamiliar. Miriam reached for his straw hat and placed it atop her father's full head of white hair. After standing, she helped him up, holding him steady for several long moments to ensure he wouldn't fall over.

"I was on my way down already," he said, jutting his jaw out. "I didn't fall from very far. I'm fine."

"I hope you let one of the boys take care of the door, *Dat,*" she said, emphatically.

"I will do as I choose." He looked past her as he began slowly walking toward the house. "I'll go in now. Come along, Miriam, I'm sure *Mem* needs your help with lunch. Goodbye, Nancy."

Miriam looked at Nancy, surprised at how abruptly she was dismissed. She began following her father in when she realized her hands were empty. After spinning around she found Henry's letter in the mud, wearing her father's boot print. She picked it up and brushed off what she could before rolling it up so she could tuck it in her folded fist. With a sigh, she wished for pockets like the English.

She mouthed a thank you to Nancy, who winked back, but she couldn't help but feel the heavy thud of guilt weigh her down. She had told her father not to attempt the climb up the ladder, yes, but had she been there as he made his way back down, she could have kept him from falling. Her attention to Henry's letter and hiding it had kept her from her first responsibility. She hated the taste of the guilt but chewed it anyway, refusing to swallow.

March 25, 1944

Dearest Miriam,
I'll be home in July for about a week. I don't want to cause problems for you, especially since I know your situation has changed, but my feelings haven't changed. I love you, Miriam. All I want is to have a chance to talk to you, just once more, alone.

I love you,
Henry

What did he mean about her situation changing? Did he mean that he understood that her father did not want her to have contact with him? What else could he mean? She traced the lines of his handwriting with her finger.

She glanced over at the calendar on the wall of her closet door. July seemed like an eternity away. Would she really have to wait so long before she could trace her finger along his face instead of just a letter? She reread the letter.

All I want is to have a chance to talk to you, just once more, alone.

What was he planning to accomplish with that one last talk? And did it have to be the last talk? The thought scared her. Did he expect to never come home or did he assume she didn't want to see him again? Unanswered questions flooded her thoughts.

I wish I had someone to talk to. Someone who would understand. She almost said the words out loud in the small square-walled room. The thought reminded her of what Henry said about praying out loud with that Baptist preacher. A swell pushed through her heart. It seemed too bold, too self-important. Who was she to speak to God with her voice even a whisper? Her heart contradicted her mind. *Who else do you have?*

CHAPTER 8

May 1944

Miriam awoke to a late spring shower. Every raindrop appeared like the miniature prisms that she held in front of the window as a child. Her brooding mood taunted the pretty sight.

She usually saw Eli only at church and Singings, and since they were held only every other week in a church member's home, it made avoiding him easier. She averted her eyes from him at church and made excuses to anyone who would ask why she didn't attend the Singings on church Sundays. Her parents weren't the type to ask, which made her change of routine even easier. For more than a month she had begun to see a life as an old maid formulate. She would ruin her family's reputation and her relationship with her parents if she followed her heart and stayed with Henry. Could she care enough for Eli to marry him? Maybe. Though caring for someone could never be confused for love. While Eli hadn't asked her to marry him outright, his conversation that night with his little sister cradled in her arms made his intentions quite clear. He was handsome and funny. He would be an excellent provider to anyone who married him. But his arrogance infuriated her.

She sighed aloud as she lay in bed wishing the day away, and in the midst of her exhale her voice breathed, "Henry."

She said it so softly it almost didn't reach her own ears. His name on her lips brought warmth. She closed her eyes and remembered the feeling of his arms around her. The security of his embrace and the unashamed desire they shared for each other rested heavily beside her.

She didn't just miss Henry, but missed writing to him, their telling one another everything. Her promise to her father spoke loudly against her ears. She wanted to respond to him after his final plea for her love in the last letter, but she couldn't write him back. All she could think about was July and seeing him, but until then, she needed to follow her father's rules. Her heart did not bend to the strict guideline, however, and with each beat she could hear Henry's name. She filled her journal with all the things she wished she could tell him.

She rolled over, carelessly slid onto the wooden floor, and pushed against the slat almost beneath the bed. It raised the other half, reminding her of the old teeter-totter she used to love. As the youngest child, how often was she left to sit far up and away from the ground, her feet dangling? Her brothers sometimes enjoyed teasing her and sitting squarely on the bottom. How she would cry and plea to be let down! She was still afraid of heights.

She pulled out the stack of letters bound with the garter. The other girls had probably long forgotten the sweetness of the untraditional garment, while Miriam had yet to wear it. Fiddling with the once important piece, she returned it to the stack of letters. It would do better to wrap around her letters than fit around her leg. Though it had begun as a silly promise, now it became her symbol of reuniting with Henry.

Miriam was putting the wooden slat back in its spot when she heard the slap of something falling outside and a familiar thump. She sped to the window and saw her father lying in the muddy drive, unmoving.

She grabbed her house robe and wrapped

it around herself as she ran down the stairs. She began yelling for her mother and then for Fannie once she was outside. The large, pretty drops of rain had lost their glimmer as her nightclothes became dotted and wet. Her feet felt cold and sensitive against the abrasive ground, but her eyes were locked on the still figure of her father. She reached him and knelt down at his side, her night-gown soaking through from the mud puddles that had formed.

"Dat, Dat," she yelled, feeling the breath rasp in and out of her throat. "Can you hear me?"

Fannie was out there only a few moments later, and Miriam rolled back and sat on the dirty drive, crying. She watched as Fannie yelled orders and instructions to her husband and older sons and daughters. Miriam didn't hear much of what she said, but she saw a few of the boys run down the driveway to the Pooles' house across the street. A few ran into the house, and before she knew it, she saw her father was rousing and arguing that he could stand by himself. Fannie's girls wrapped some blankets around him to keep him warm and helped him walk toward Nancy's car. They opened the back door of the car and moved her father into the narrow backseat. She'd never been in the Pooles' car. It had been only a few months since they'd purchased it after selling their truck to a neighbor. All Miriam knew about their new car was that it was a beautiful shade of a blue, almost teal, and Mr. Poole cleaned it almost daily. The word *Chevrolet* sparkled near the back driver-side wheel.

She saw her mother's blank eyes as she found her way into the car. Nancy helped Miriam up and she felt her shoulders being shaken. She came back to reality with a jarring clarity and rushed to get to the car. As she climbed into the front seat, she realized she was wet and muddy, from the hem of her robe and nightgown to the bottom of her thighs, and she cringed at the dark mud smeared around her feet and legs.

"What will Mr. Poole say?" she said, gesturing to her feet. "And my father's dirty also."

"Dearie, don't you worry about him. His car is his baby — he'll clean it up just fine."

Nancy knew right where to go. Most of the Amish went to the same doctor, who had a small clinic at his home. The drive was a blur, yet it felt never-ending.

"I'm trying to hurry, but the speed limit is only thirty-five right now. I haven't been able to get used to that."

Miriam didn't know much about the government's rules on vehicles because of the war. She knew that driving faster apparently wasted fuel and rubber. They all had their own ration cards for food, but that was the extent of her understanding of national standards.

Her father complained of chest pain. His voice was strained and weak.

"We'll be there soon," Nancy said, and she made the car go a little faster. They were in front of the clinic only five minutes later.

Miriam squeezed her eyes shut against the reality. She fought her instinct to run, but instead forced herself to get out of the car and walk toward the front door. She rehearsed the words in her mind. Her father had collapsed, he needed help, he was pale and in pain. Was he going to die? She pushed open the door to a room with a small desk and a few chairs. No one besides a nurse was in the room yet, which relieved her.

The nurse spoke to her but Miriam heard nothing. She took in her small white hat with her hair smoothly pulled back beneath it. The nurse's tiny waist was cinched tightly by her mid-calf dress. She'd seen nurses before; why did these details suddenly seem so important to her?

"Miss, can I help you?" She finally heard the nurse's voice. It was kind, and her brow furrowed as she took in Miriam's appearance.

"My father is in the car. He fell. I don't know if he can walk."

The nurse instantly called for a man named Wayne. When he came through the door, Miriam first noted how white his starched uniform was. Then she inhaled as she caught sight of his mutilated face. He had an ear missing, and his skin was stretched and scarred over his jawbone. He smiled at her but looked away and walked past her before she could smile back. She followed them out and watched as they helped her mother out first and then convinced her father that he needed help walking.

As Miriam watched, all she could see was that suddenly her father looked decades older and her mother's skin sagged on her face as she tried to follow what was happening. Her eyes swept from side to side, trying to follow the nurse and the attendant's voices.

Her father began stuttering that he wanted Fannie and her mother to go with him. Miriam winced that he didn't want her, but rather her older sister. Perhaps she should have stayed behind.

"*Dat,* go with them — we will be right behind you," Miriam encouraged him gently.

His right hand held onto the left side of his chest as he let the young man help him out of the car. His eyes fell on her mother, but she made no indication that she recognized his gaze, and his eyes moved to Miriam. His mouth was slightly agape as he breathed heavily, and his brow was lined with fear. He was as frightened as she had ever seen him.

They walked up to the clinic, which was really only a small house next to the large house where the doctor lived. Miriam looked up when she heard the bell sound at the top of the door. She hadn't even noticed it when she ran in before.

Her father was standing there hunched over, and next to the tall doctor who had come into the room, he appeared especially small. Miriam didn't know Dr. Sherman well. Fannie did, however, and usually liked him. There had been times where she insisted he was wrong and she was right, but that was Fannie. He was in his forties, with gray hair and bright, kind eyes. He wore a white coat and a smile as he patted her father on the shoulder.

"I'm going to examine him and then you can come back," he nodded as he spoke.

Miriam nodded back as she watched Wayne take her father back. The nurse followed them as well.

She led her mother to a chair and helped her sit. She watched as her mother pulled out a hankie. She didn't use it, but only began wringing it in her hands. Miriam sat next to her mother, hoping to feel less fidgety. Nancy continued to stand and jingled her keys. Miriam sat on her hands and wished for a muzzle so she wouldn't shout at both of them.

Her mother and Nancy interacted primarily with Nancy's initiation in the past few years since the situation with Kathryn. Miriam felt an uneasiness being with both of them at the same time, especially because Nancy had helped Henry.

"I think I'll check with Mrs. Sherman about some coffee or tea." Nancy's nasal voice sliced through the blaring silence.

Her mother's head snapped over, her eyes almost finding Nancy's face. Her smile twitched.

"Yes, please," Miriam said for both her and her mother.

A moment later the orderly returned, and Miriam stood.

"He's calm and okay right now. The doc will get you back there soon," the young man said.

Miriam nodded and sat back down. She tried not to be distracted by his scarred face, but she wanted to take it in and imagine what it would be like to be his girl or wife. What if that were Henry?

The bell chimed and everyone looked at the door. A beautiful woman walked in with a baby in blue in one arm and a young girl holding onto her other hand. Her hair was immaculately done with a flawlessly coiled roll on one side, and the other was puffed to perfection. The length of her brown hair was waved toward her face, falling over her shoulders.

She shushed the crying baby tenderly as she walked in. Miriam continued to watch the woman and was surprised when a man walked up behind her with an obvious limp and a long white sleeve that hung loosely at his side. His hair was shiny and well styled for an English man but he wore a frank expression of boredom, irritation, or even apathy. The family found a few seats, and the mother continued to hush the children and seemed to constantly be laying an open hand on the baby's forehead, checking for fever. The husband sat, unaffected by the tears, cries, and anxiety on the woman's face.

"Hey Sarge," Wayne said. "How's the, well, ya know." He motioned toward where the *Sarge's* arm used to be.

"How do you think?" the man said, rolling his eyes.

Miriam watched and listened with fascination, having had very little exposure to anyone involved with the war efforts. The two spoke briefly about a few other men and who they'd learned recently had died or returned wounded. The conversation made Miriam wince. Was this Henry's future? Would his gentle demeanor be lost to a hard edge? Would he return whole? Would he return?

Miriam suddenly became intensely self-conscious. Usually her plain appearance didn't bother her. She was among the English enough to ignore the stares and pointing that all the Amish still got. But she wasn't usually in nightclothes soaked in muddy water. The beautiful woman didn't seem to even notice Miriam, completely consumed with her two needy children.

Nancy came back without tea or coffee. She apologized too often and loudly that she couldn't find any. She seemed nervous and her hands shook.

The three of them found silence again, and Miriam put her head in her hands, trying to break free from the sight of the wounded men. She did her best to call to memory all the prayers she'd memorized over the years.

. . . bind us with a bond of peace . . .

. . . preserve and defend my family . . .

. . . give me a strong, firm faith . . .

Lines, phrases, sometimes only words poured through her thoughts, but they brought little peace. The vision of her father's panicked gray eyes was branded in her memory. She looked at the clock on the wall. They'd been there for less than twenty minutes. She sat back up and kept her eyes on the door her father had gone through, willing it to open. She vaguely heard the bell above the front door chime. Then a soft hand touched her arm.

"Miriam?" a voice said, gentle and lilting. It was familiar, yet, like the wrong puzzle piece, it didn't fit. It was as if the voice was from a different place and time.

Miriam turned to meet eyes that looked like a younger version of her mother's. They didn't have the unrelenting mask of sightlessness. Her eyes scanned the woman's face in the next instant; how had her mother grown young? Without warning, her unsee-

159

ing mother next to her stood, her eyes sparkling with unshed tears and her arms reaching to cup the woman's face.

Kathryn.

Miriam watched in stunned silence as her mother and sister embraced. She felt a pat on her shoulder, and Nancy's voice coming from somewhere far away telling her that she would return to check on them in a few hours. That they would be okay now, Kathryn was here.

Kathryn was here.

CHAPTER 9

May 1944

Miriam observed Kathryn for a few more moments as she gathered herself. She looked so different. Her dark auburn hair was still long, but it was styled like that of the woman with the uninterested husband. A roll and long waves cascaded over her shoulders. Her lips weren't as red, but everything looked rosy and glowing about her face. Her eyes and smile were mixed with sorrow and sadness. Their mother was crying.

Miriam stood as if in line for the next hug, but when would her mother release her grasp on her lost daughter? Kathryn had broken the heart of their family and changed everything for Miriam.

"Miriam," Kathryn said again when she was finally released. "It has been so long."

She pulled Miriam in for a warm, tight hug. Miriam surprised herself with tears of her own, not realizing how much she'd missed her older sister in the past five years. As she hugged her, she felt a roundness against her abdomen and pulled away to look. Her sister's belly was swollen to what looked like six or seven months.

She found Kathryn's eyes and they shared a smile and giggle. Kathryn's hands instinctively curved around her middle, looking affectionately at the place her baby grew.

"James is sure this one's a boy," she said, "but little Nan says it's a girl."

"James? Nan?" Miriam questioned.

Kathryn looked stunned, instantly making Miriam feel more uncomfortable than ever.

"Miriam, has no one ever told you? I married James Poole and we have a daughter, Nancy Rose."

Kathryn turned and gently pulled a little version of herself from behind her legs. The girl was biting her lower lip as she looked up at Miriam. Her curly auburn hair hung in pigtails.

"Nan, this is your Aunt Miriam," Kathryn said, still speaking in their Pennsylvania Dutch dialect. "You've never met her. And this is your Mammie, who hasn't seen you since the night you were born almost five years ago."

Miriam was almost choking over the new

162

information, especially that her mother was at Nan's birth. This was James Poole's family? James Poole, the neighbor boy, Nancy's eldest son? It all began making sense. How Kathryn rushed over to Nancy's house when she left, and how Nancy had told Miriam it would be good for her to write Kathryn. She knew there was a story to tell, but that it should come from Kathryn herself.

"Hi, Nan," Miriam said, then looked at Kathryn. "She understands Pennsylvania Dutch?"

Kathryn nodded.

"And I can speak it, too," the little girl said in perfect dialect.

The three women all chuckled. Then, Nan and her grandma sat to get reacquainted and Kathryn handed Miriam a bag.

"I brought you some clothes."

When Miriam looked confused, she continued with an explanation.

"Nancy called and told me about *Dat* and that you were still in your nightclothes. I still have one of my old dresses. It's old, but it should fit you." Kathryn opened the bag and pulled the sleeve of an older faded blue dress.

"I'm just so confused about all of this," Miriam said, shaking her head. "Why did you wait until now? Why couldn't you come

163

back earlier? I've needed you, Kathryn."

A surge of frustration surfaced. For years she'd been the primary person responsible for her parents, and now she was carrying Henry's burden without help. She rebounded from anger over Kathryn's abandonment to relief that maybe she was back for good, even if not Amish.

"*Mem* and I have written all these years," Kathryn explained. "When her eyes got bad enough that she couldn't write, *Dat* wrote for her."

Miriam recoiled. Her parents had been in touch with Kathryn all this time, but hadn't told her. The church resisted the continued communication of a shunned member, but it was not completely forbidden, either. Of course, her father wouldn't have wanted Kathryn's influence on Miriam, but it angered her that these years had been taken away from her.

"I know, I was surprised, also. Nancy and Ralph came to visit me at my house, but I don't visit at theirs unless I know I won't be seen. I felt like it was just throwing it in everyone's faces."

"And you and James Poole?"

"You make it sound so shocking. We fell in love. Plain and simple. I couldn't give him up."

Miriam only nodded. She understood more than her sister realized. But making such a rash decision to leave her family behind was something she couldn't fathom, regardless of whom she loved.

Half relieved and half confused, she changed into Kathryn's old dress. In a matter of an hour she had learned so much new information that she wasn't sure how to process everything. Her father probably had a heart attack. Nancy had called Kathryn, who was married to James Poole. Kathryn was here with her four-year-old daughter and was expecting another child. In this moment, something occurred to her. Nan was four, nearly five, and Kathryn had left about five years ago.

Kathryn had been expecting before she left the church.

Miriam looked across the drive as several of her nieces pounded on rugs. The wind pulled the billows of dust through the June air. Over and over, the grime and dirt was forced from the rug and quickly dissolved into the warm summer breeze. It was as if the dust had never even existed. What would it be like to be so free and invisible? This was where pain and pleasure interlocked.

Miriam had been far from invisible, not

having a moment to herself since taking her father to the doctor a week ago. Dr. Sherman said her father's heart was weak and he needed to be on bed rest for at least three weeks. This infuriated Melvin, who insisted he was fine.

"Keep his activity low for several months to be safe," the doctor told Miriam and Kathryn.

His words rang in her ears anytime she felt selfish of her time, her future, her life. It was her job to preserve the life her father had left. She would ensure that their family would not go without its patriarch. She worked around the clock to provide for his needs. Her mother was little help but remained as steady and consistent as always. After some debate, Melvin Coblentz finally agreed to step back from their portion of the farm and allow his grandsons to work where he couldn't. The frown on her father's face became permanent, and he grumbled about how he wasn't good for anything anymore.

The greatest benefit to all of this was that Miriam finally had a relationship with Kathryn again. After some discussion Miriam had overheard between her parents, they decided they would allow regular visits as long as the limitations that were set, according to the rules of the ban, were followed. Their father wanted to be very clear that they would follow the guidelines of her shunning to the letter of the *Ordnung.* This meant no meals together, no driving in Kathryn's car together, and they couldn't accept any gifts from her. Despite this, her visits provided both strength and encouragement to Miriam and their mother. Miriam wished they'd had the years since Kathryn's departure back, but didn't want to add more stress to her father. She knew he hadn't wanted Kathryn's English influence over her during those years when it could have made a difference in her future with the church. It continued to amaze her that their mother was able to keep Kathryn's letters a secret from her for so many years.

Miriam had known that James enlisted in the army early on in the war and understood that he had a wife and child. She hadn't, however, known that the wife he'd left behind when he'd gone to war was Kathryn.

After supper, Kathryn came over. She helped Miriam clean up while their parents sat in the living room. This gave coveted private time to the sisters, who had not been given much opportunity to talk one-on-one.

"So, you haven't written to Henry at all

since he left for training?" Kathryn asked, her voice declaring her surprise.

"No, *Dat* told me I couldn't," Miriam said, trying her best not to sound pious in her obedience. She knew Kathryn would never have agreed to that.

"Well, I don't want to tell you what to do, but if you love him, which I know you do, don't you think writing him is worth getting in trouble over? It just seems so harmless to at least write him and encourage him. It means so much to the soldiers."

"I'm not you, Kathryn," she told her. "I don't want to leave the church. I want to marry and have my life here. Besides, I am the only one left to take care of our parents."

"Is Henry asking you to leave?"

"He enlisted. I'm not sure there's any other way I can take that. He insists that he didn't do this to leave the church, but to follow God's will, but I have a hard time seeing how it's possible to make a decision like that without it forcing you out of the church."

"You're angry with him," Kathryn stated.

"Well, wouldn't you be?" As Miriam said those words she wanted to bite them back. In the short time that Kathryn had been back in their lives, she had never spoken ill of her husband's enlistment.

"No, I am not angry, and neither should you be," she said with gentle conviction. "James is fulfilling the duty he feels God gave him."

"That's easy for you to say. You're not Amish. You don't stand to lose everything because of a decision the man you're supposed to marry made."

Kathryn looked down and bit her lips. Her brow furrowed.

Miriam wanted to pull back her words. Of course her sister understood what it was like to lose everything. She'd done it. She did understand what it was like to be far away from the man she loved. Then why wasn't she wracked with anxiety over his departure? How could she calmly smile and warmly rub her protruding belly when she knew she would never truly be accepted back into the family, not like before she was shunned? Miriam couldn't imagine the feeling of isolation and despair she would have felt if she were in Kathryn's shoes. Of course, she would never be in her shoes. She would never get pregnant before marriage.

"Ever since I left the house, I haven't gone a day without some sadness over losing everything I've ever known. And, now, with James fighting over there, now I stand to lose it all again. But my days are filled with so much more joy with Nan, and soon this new babe. With rekindling this relationship with all of you — how can I be blue? James wouldn't want that anyway."

"But, before you were married, you were —" She couldn't say it.

"Are you trying to say that I was expecting before I was married and that's why I left?"

"It's true, isn't it?"

"Partially." She paused, wiping the last of the dishes. Her eyes wandered past the window, past even the house across the drive. Beyond. "I was expecting Nan. Yes. But I was given a choice. I could've stayed."

"Then why, Kathryn?" Miriam's passion had gotten the best of her, and her question came out urgently and on the verge of anger.

"I could've stayed if I had agreed to marry within the church. Someone I didn't love."

"Marry whom?"

"I could have married Henry."

"Henry? My Henry?"

Kathryn met Miriam's eyes and nodded her head. Miriam studied her sister as confusion set in. Her large eyes, soft and comfortable to look into. She was no longer the wild-eyed young woman she'd been years ago. She'd matured, grown up, and appeared so happy. Where had the loud, abrasive talking gone? Where had her manner of disrespect for authority and the church gone? Why did she seem so — what was the word — settled? It didn't seem right or fair. It stirred anger and resentment Miriam hadn't realized she'd been harboring toward her sister for years.

Miriam got up and pulled on her coat. She couldn't handle any more new information. Kathryn and Henry? Henry was going to marry her sister before Miriam was even in her running-around years, and no one had thought to tell her. Henry hadn't even been honest with her. Was that why he hadn't been married by the time Miriam was running around with the youth? Was it because he had been thwarted and heartbroken over Kathryn?

"Please, Miriam, let me explain."

Miriam stopped walking when she heard her sister's voice, but she didn't turn around. After a moment she continued to walk. Any chance of her rebelling against her father and writing to Henry was gone. She had nothing to say to him or to Kathryn.

CHAPTER 10

June 1944

Miriam sat on a backless bench in the heat of June, sweat glistening on the side of her face where her covering glanced over her skin. The first wedding of the season was over and another couple, several years younger than she, was making their thank yous and goodbyes and probably still enjoying cake and pie.

Again, she was amidst the youth, at the customary Singing held at the end of the wedding. The last time she was at a Singing after a wedding, Henry was with her. He and Eli had argued and she'd learned that she would not be allowed to write him. Now, even if she could write him, she wouldn't. Not after what she'd learned about Kathryn.

Less than an hour later she stood at the bottom of the closed staircase, waiting her turn to be numbered. A favorite Singing game after a wedding was called Love in the Dark. She and Henry used to love this game and would figure out how to be numbered together.

Since you were paired up by numbers and the boys usually were numbered first, Henry would stomp his feet at the top of the stairs in succession and then Miriam would make sure she was the same number in the girl's line. That way they'd be paired together. All the courting couples had their little tricks to be paired up, but there were always a few mistakes or people who didn't have a steady date and it was always a mystery whom they would get matched with. Even though the game was simply for a boy and girl to sit together in the dark for about fifteen minutes, it always gave her and Henry a chance to be almost alone.

As she stood, she heard someone cough three times, and another boy clapped seven times. The girls around her giggled and adjusted in their lines. She noticed Sylvia, Henry's sister, sneak ahead of her into the third position. She wondered which boy Sylvia wanted to be paired with. She'd dated Marvin Hostetler for several weeks in a row, and Mark Brenneman, Eli's younger brother, had made it clear he wanted to date her as well. Sylvia briefly looked in Miriam's direction, then after a small lift of Sylvia's chin, she moved into the place in line she wanted, causing several people to release exacerbated sighs and reshuffle.

Miriam went to the back of the line and was paired up with seventeen-year-old Enos Yoder. He was a nice boy, smaller than she and shy, but funny. She laughed for the whole fifteen minutes as they sat in a dark corner of one of the upstairs bedrooms. One other couple was in the opposite corner, doing less talking. Enos kept clicking his flashlight on and off in the black room, making ridiculous jokes that didn't make sense. The other couple grew irritated when he shined his light in their corner. He and Miriam were barely able to stifle their laughter.

Then one of the older boys, Rufus, who was leading the games that night, called everyone to the main two rooms to begin the next game. Miriam kissed Enos on the cheek in friendship as they concluded. Even in the dark room she could see him blush pink.

Everyone was chattering when they returned. The paired couples were the typical ones until Miriam saw Eli. She had to keep her mouth from falling open when she saw him taking slow steps through the door frame with Sylvia Mast behind him. They were together? Sylvia's eyes found hers. Miriam's heart was pounding. Was Sylvia gloating?

She decided to look away. She didn't want to give Sylvia the satisfaction of noticing her shock at seeing her and Eli together. It *was* a shock, though. While it wasn't that he shouldn't or wasn't allowed to date around, Miriam couldn't help but remember that in April he had all but proposed to her.

Rufus called out that next, they would play Please and Displease. Miriam had to fight from dropping her head in her hands. After taking some time away from the Singings, she'd forgotten how foolish some of the games were. As a young person just starting her running-around years, they had been exciting, often the only outlet from all the work and scheduled obligations throughout the week. Now, when she should already be married, they felt childish.

"Raymond, go give Lissy a kiss," Rufus called out.

The group collectively began giggling. The two had been dating for a few weeks and were shy with their affection for each other. No one wanted to disappoint the others, however. Lissy chuckled and pursed her mouth as she awaited Raymond's response.

It was clear she was pleased.

"Pleased," Raymond nearly yelled, and he leaned over and kissed Lissy squarely on the lips. The dreadful smacking sound at the end turned Miriam's stomach, but both looked far too overcome with pleasure to seem to care how their kiss was perceived by anyone else.

"Sylvia Mast, go with Marvin Hostetler to the next room and hug him for five minutes." Rufus winked at Marvin.

There were a few chuckles amidst the group, and Marvin, beaming with his trademark closed-mouth grin, awaited Sylvia's acceptance. Miriam couldn't help but analyze Sylvia's haughty expression. Her mouth twisted in a smirk as she glanced at Eli.

"Displeased," she said confidently.

"She can't handle five minutes alone with me," Marvin laughed loudly, his buddies following suit. No one wanted to be embarrassed by a displeased retort.

Rufus went on to dare several more couples to hold hands, kiss, and sit in the dark room across the hall for several minutes. One of the boys even had to serenade his girlfriend with a silly child's song about barnyard animals. They all had a good laugh about that one, even Miriam.

"Miriam Coblentz," Rufus called out, saying her name slowly and deliberately. He looked around the room, tapping his mouth, as if really wanting to make this a good one. "You take Eli Brenneman into the closet across the hall and hold hands in the dark for five minutes."

Miriam's face grew warm, and every eye bore down into her, especially Sylvia's. Miriam's head snapped in Eli's direction, but he wasn't even looking at her. He seemed indifferent. The room itself seemed to hold its breath waiting for Miriam to respond.

"Pleased," she said, undaunted. She didn't want the group to know how embarrassed and nervous this made her.

Eli's eyes met hers. After waiting one pregnant moment in the silent room, he stood. He walked across the wooden slats over to her. He held his hand out to Miriam, and when she took it, the room began to hoot and holler.

His hand was warm in hers and she followed him out of the room and across the hall. He opened the closet door with his free hand and stepped inside. After a moment of hesitation, Miriam followed Eli. She was instantly aware of how small the closet was when, as he closed the door, their bodies pressed against each other.

"Rufus wanted us to hold hands in here?" Eli whispered. "We can't do anything else but hold each other. There's no room for us not to."

They both chuckled quietly, not wanting to give the awaiting room any fodder upon their return. They were quiet for about a minute when Miriam broke the silence.

"So, you and Sylvia?" Miriam said quietly.

Eli's chest rose and fell against her, as their hands grew sweaty.

"You turned me down." Eli's voice still carried an air of humor in it, making Miriam wonder how serious he was about anything.

"But why Sylvia?" She looked up at him. "I thought your brother Mark was after her."

"She's awfully pretty to look at."

Her eyes adjusted the darkness and she could see him smile and wink at her.

She gave him a weak slap on the arm. The closet was too small to do much more.

"Is that all you think about? Pretty girls?"

"I'm only thinking about one pretty girl right now."

Miriam only shook her head; her heart began beating harder. Eli dropped her hand and put both arms around her waist. Miriam closed her eyes, hating that she felt pleasure in his closeness. She didn't want it to be like this, but Henry had betrayed her with her own sister. Maybe it really was time to move on. Eli was the only boy she could imagine moving on with, even though she didn't love him and sometimes didn't even like him. His rude and brash ways might be all she deserved.

"You know I'm with Henry." Her voice broke while she spoke. She hated that he likely sensed her nervousness. Even as she said the words, she felt anger rise in her about what she'd learned about him and Kathryn. She wondered if Eli had known, but she didn't want to bring it up.

"Can't we just forget about him?" He began stroking her back, pulling her tightly against him. His hands moved to her arms, rubbing them up and down, then back to her waist, pulling her tightly. "I just want to be alone with you. Our five minutes are almost up."

In the brief moments that Miriam considered this, she realized how good it felt to be held, even if it was by Eli instead of Henry. She'd missed the sweetness of Henry's touch so desperately. No one else touched her in any way, since her family had never been one that hugged or touched often. Eli broke the boundaries of her stoic and cold existence and it was like an icy pond crack-ing in the spring. Her body relaxed under his touch.

It was easier to force the anger and hurt away and enjoy the moment with muscled arms around her. And Eli had said he loved her. What if she married him and forgot about everything else? Just moved on. What would happen when Henry returned?

She looked up at Eli, opening her lips slightly. She wanted to say that this was wrong and that they shouldn't be doing this, but she couldn't find the words. They could see enough of each other that she knew he could see her welcoming him. The tightness of his hands held her so close that even if she wanted, she wouldn't be able to wiggle free. She moved her hands from his muscled forearms up to his thick neck. She could feel the tightness beneath her fingers, his pulse racing, triggering hers to follow.

She fingered the firmness of his jawline, and without thinking, she pulled his face down to meet hers, lifting her chin. She didn't just let him kiss her, but kissed him in return. The hunger she'd felt in his lips and touch the night at his house came back in droves. His passion was strong and unrelenting. His hands gripped her too tightly. His kisses grew hungrier instead of abating with satisfaction. She forced away her apprehension and continued.

His mouth found her neck and felt hot against her skin. If it weren't for the knock on the closet door, she wondered how much longer this would have continued. It had felt like an eternity, but it was really less than a minute.

"Time's up, lovebirds," Rufus said, laughing.

Miriam and Eli remained paralyzed in position. They didn't move until they heard Rufus's heavy footsteps walk out of the bedroom. Miriam leaned her forehead on Eli's chest for a few moments, then inched slightly back to replace her *fahoodled,* rumpled, covering. She took a hankie out of her tight apron waistband and wiped her sweaty face. The air in the closet suddenly felt thick and moist, and it was getting smaller by the moment. Her breath was quickened now, and not due to passion; her entire body was squeezing from the inside out. She needed to get out of there. She began to panic when she couldn't open the door.

"Hey," Eli said, taking her hands. "Slow down. It's okay."

"No, it's not," she snapped, "this is completely embarrassing. I shouldn't have done this. Everyone knows that I am engaged to Henry."

"No, you're not."

"What are you talking about?"

"You haven't written, talked to him, or even heard from him since November, unless there's something that you haven't told me. How can you be engaged to a man who doesn't even write you? If he really loved you, he would find a way."

"Well, then he really loves me, because I got a letter from him in April, telling me he'll be home for a few days in July before he goes overseas." Her voice came out raspy, as her throat was raw from intensified whispering. She stuffed the hankie back into her waistline.

She tried to open the door again, but Eli held her hands tightly. She struggled to no avail.

"I love you, Miriam," he said.

She believed him and held his eyes for several long moments. But, no, she didn't love him in return. She hated him for tempting her and for challenging her every time they were together. She hated herself, too. She had just been unfaithful to a man she supposedly loved. Maybe she and Eli deserved each other.

"We have to get back." She opened the

closet door, but instead of returning to the bedroom where the Singing games were being held, she grabbed her cape, bonnet, and purse from a downstairs bedroom and left the house before Eli could stop her. She couldn't face the other youth. The expression she knew she wore would give everything away.

She was almost home from the walk when there was a familiar whistle behind her. It wasn't a real melody, but a tune she recognized. She stopped in the dark and looked around. The moon was only a gold sliver, and she couldn't see much. The tune came again.

It couldn't be.

She puckered her lips and joined in the tune. Her heart began beating wildly and her chest rose and fell with the thought of what this meant. She turned around and looked toward the direction from which she'd just traveled. The whistle came and went, but a beam of light grew closer. All of the Amish boys and girls carried flashlights when walking home. She had a small one with her but clicked it on only every so often, not wanting to waste the battery.

She stayed still as the light came closer, the tune stronger. She again matched the song and wished her eyes could adjust to the beam of light now right in front of her. She still couldn't see who held the light.

"Miriam?" The tenor voice danced in the night air.

"Henry?" She raised her voice and tried to look past the light. It suddenly clicked off, and before her eyes even readjusted, she felt his arms around her. She reacted with her heart, and wrapped her arms around him in return. The thick material of what had to be his uniform was foreign beneath her fingers. Her hands moved up around his neck. She touched his hair, which was softer than she'd remembered. She was careful not to tip the hat off his head as she stroked his velvety shorn hair. He didn't feel like the Henry she remembered, though his voice and scent were the same. She returned his embrace, wishing he'd never gone.

"You're home."

He pulled back and cupped her face gently, his lips tenderly finding hers. He delivered a kiss that nourished her soul and reminded her of the unconditional love she had for him. Tears formed in her eyes and she smiled, satisfied with his touch, his love, his everything. Her heart swelled as she tightened her arms around him. She would never let go.

Then, in a moment, the intimacy forced her guilt to spill over. Even though she'd kissed Eli out of emptiness and hungry frustration, she'd still kissed him, and her unfaithfulness chided her.

She forced her lips away from him. She looked at him, letting her eyes adjust to the darkness, and though she barely recognized him in uniform, a lump caught in her throat. He looked so handsome. His neck looked thicker than she remembered, under the tight collar of his uniform instead of the looser Amish collar. His cleanly shaven face reminded her that he wasn't growing a beard anymore. Her heart pounded. Part of her wanted to take his hand and run away, go anywhere he wanted to go and never look back, but the other part of her grew. Her guilt over Eli and her anger over Kathryn burned in her.

"I'm sorry, Henry," she said, her voice weightless, "I can't. I can't."

CHAPTER 11

June 1944

"Miriam?" Henry questioned.

His voice rang so innocently in Miriam's ears that she swallowed up her words. Could she even tell him the truth? If he loved her half as much as he claimed, she knew her actions would be an enormous sting in his heart. She closed her eyes in the darkness and her mind instantly took her back to Eli, in the closet, his hands on her body and his lips on hers. Her purse slipped from her shaking arms and onto the gravel road.

She knelt down to grab the purse. Henry bent down beside her. They picked it up at the same time, and they stayed motionless with their hands both wrapped around the straps. The heat from his hands in the warm evening reminded her of being in the sweaty closet with Eli. She shook the memory from her head and stood abruptly, nearly toppling Henry over.

"I need to get home," she stated. "My parents will wonder where I am."

"Miriam." Henry touched her arm. He didn't grab. He didn't pull. "Please. Stay with me?"

The familiarity and gentleness of his voice caressed her ears, and her heart became dough. She kept her back to Henry but couldn't walk away. All she'd been dreaming of for months was to talk with Henry, be close to him, feel his touch, and marry him. But in the past weeks, there were two things that changed. One of them involved Kathryn and the other, Eli. She didn't trust either of them at the moment. Her path was filled with burdens and frustrations and pain. Would Henry's love lighten the load somehow?

"Did you get my letter?" he asked.

Miriam nodded, remaining turned away from him.

"I understand why you didn't write back," he paused for a moment, "but I sure wanted you to. I've missed you so much."

She willed her legs to move but they betrayed her. She was paralyzed. Part of her wanted to walk away now and finalize the separation, but the greater part of her wanted to never leave his side.

"I got your letter," she said breathlessly. "I

was going to write you back. I started a letter, even. But I couldn't."

Henry walked around and faced her. He grazed her cheek with the back of a finger once before dropping his hand back to his side. The crescent moon cast a mute glow on their path, and Miriam couldn't help but be glad that she could see his face. It fairly glowed in the warm air that curved around them, hugging them. His dark eyes brought her heart back to life. She released a long-held breath, took his hand, and moved his palm to her cheek. She leaned into it as his other hand wrapped around her, pulling her closer.

"I couldn't write you," she said.

He tilted his head, brow furrowed.

"Such a good girl you are, my Miriam," he said huskily, taking her face in his hands. "I know you take obedience to your *dat* very seriously."

She shook her head out of his touch. She could so easily let Henry believe that she was a good Amish girl and not defying her father's standards. The truth was that her resolve to stand firm in her father's rule had grown sour, and just when she was on the verge of writing Henry, Kathryn returned. Miriam was everything but good. She resented what Kathryn told her and was angry with Henry for his dishonesty about her own sister. She was disloyal and had kissed Henry's former best friend. Henry deserved much better.

The road beyond Henry was dimly lit, but it appeared long and lonely, without a bend in sight.

"It wasn't because of *Dat* that I didn't write," she said so quietly that she barely heard herself.

"Then why?"

She looked back into Henry's eyes, drawing a breath in to keep herself from drowning in them.

"Kathryn."

"Your sister, Kathryn?"

She took a few minutes to explain about her encounter with Kathryn and her father's health. Henry appeared as confused as ever, which frustrated Miriam. At some point in the conversation, he took her hand and began walking down the road. They weren't far from her house, and she assumed Henry was staying with Nancy again. Nancy, who once sheltered Kathryn from her disgrace, was now on the second time around with Henry. Miriam had often wondered why Nancy had put so much into helping Kathryn. She'd spoken with such intimacy months ago when Miriam ran to her home.

It made sense now, since James and Kathryn had gotten themselves in trouble. All of these thoughts rolled around in her mind as she spoke of the happenings of the past few months.

"Just a few weeks ago, Kathryn told me everything about when she left," she said, then was silent, waiting for Henry to explain his guilt away.

"If you mean that I should've told you about her and James Poole, I'm sorry — I just honestly thought you knew. We never really spoke about Kathryn," he reminded her. "It always seemed prohibited."

"Well, you should've told me, and you also should've told me that you were going to marry her."

"Marry Kathryn?"

"Yes!" she exclaimed, her voice beginning to climb toward yelling. "Now you know why I can't be with you. You lied to me. I wasn't your first choice, I was second behind my own sister."

"Now, wait a minute. Your *dat* approached my *dat* once, and he told him that Kathryn had gotten herself in trouble with the neighbor boy. He asked my *dat* if they would encourage me to marry her for the good of the family, the baby, and the church."

"And you never thought to tell me?"

"When *Dat* told me, I was shocked. I decided to clear it up with your *dat,* and I did right away. When I told him that I couldn't marry Kathryn, he told me that she'd already left home anyway and this time, it was for good." He paused for only a moment, and then with his voice softening, he continued. "You know my eyes were on you since you were fifteen. I was already nineteen and hadn't gone on more than a few dates here and there, mostly for *Mem*'s sake. I was waiting for you. As soon as you were of age, I asked you. I've never loved anyone else."

"Then why didn't you tell me?"

"My *dat* said that it wasn't something I should be talking about, that the family had been hurt very badly by Kathryn's leaving and that I should just forget that we'd ever had any conversations about Kathryn Coblentz. He also told me that he thought it would've been a bad decision for me to marry a woman who was already expecting a baby."

Miriam fell silent. He had explained himself, and everything he said was believable. First, she knew Henry was an upstanding young man. She'd heard rumors that he was waiting for her but when Eli had asked

191

her to date during those first few weeks, she'd wondered if the gossip had been true at all. She knew that Eli and Henry were friends, and surely they hadn't both wanted to date the same girl.

"Why did Eli ask me to date him when he knew you had plans to date me?" she asked him out of the blue.

"Eli has always done whatever he wants. He knew — almost everyone knew among the youth — that I wanted to date you." Henry looked off far away as they sat on the front steps of her home, then turned to her, capturing her eyes deeply. "You were and are the prettiest of all the girls. Your hair always reminded me of a sunset, and your eyes are always smiling. And I love every freckle."

He gently kissed the blush of her cheek beneath one eye. His kisses were so gentle, but they carried the weight of romance and undying love. Her heart was open to him like grass longing for the nourishment of dew. He was part of her. But she didn't deserve such a gift.

"I don't know how much more of this I can do, Henry."

The chirping of the nature around them stilled in reverence to her confession. The moon hid behind a mask of clouds, tossing

192

a cool breeze at them. Miriam felt the rawness of the moment in her throat as she pushed down tears. How much more of this could she handle? How could she balance loving Henry from afar while being tempted by an immediate life with rough-cut Eli?

"I have never loved anyone like I love you. For months I have chosen to set you aside to follow my father's wishes. I have laughed, sung, and played games with the youth. I have calmed babies in their early days of life when all I wanted to do was scream and cry myself. And, my parents need me."

"And, what about Eli?"

Her face snapped to look at Henry in the darkness, the moon betraying her and lighting their faces again. His brow was still lined with burdens and his lips pursed. He gently rubbed a thumb over the back of her hand, loving her as she broke his heart.

"I," she began hesitantly, "I don't love him."

"But you let him kiss you. Touch you." She could hear his breathing quicken.

Could he see in her eyes the burden of her guilt and regret? Henry's intuition had always been sharper than anyone else she knew. She sucked in a breath and expected to find anger in his face, only to be surprised to be caressed by the love in his gaze.

"I don't deserve you." She hung her head, weeping. "I have been so lonely, and he keeps offering me the life I have always wanted."

She couldn't look at him anymore. His thumb had stopped rubbing over her hand and his grip had tightened almost urgently. His other hand traced her back, up and down, lovingly. He heaved a long, sad sigh.

"I want you to be sure who it is you want to be with, Miriam."

He leaned in and kissed her warmly on her tear-streaked cheek. Then he stood, grabbed his bag, and left. She didn't stop him. She couldn't stop him. He was right: she needed to make a choice. She watched him as he stood on Nancy's porch and the light flickered on. Then he was ushered inside. Darkness swarmed Miriam and even if Henry had looked back to see if she still sat there, he probably couldn't have seen her.

She turned around to enter her home. As she walked, she was overwhelmed by the sense of her feet sinking deeper and deeper into the ground, making it harder for her to move, as if she were walking in quicksand. Her distance from Henry was greater now than it had ever been.

She moved to her father's desk and

opened up his prayer book. She had memorized so many prayers over the years but not one of them came to mind. She flipped through the pages, barely deciphering the old text and the High German words.

. . . cast the bright rays of Thy divine light into our sin-sick hearts.

. . . let us die to the world, that we may live.

. . . give us true repentance for anything we have done against Thy will.

What was the will of God? Her whole life she'd always been pacified with those words, *will of God,* though never provided an explanation. Was God's will the same for everyone? Was it the glass dome she lived in, or could it be beyond? Where did His will end and the world's or hers begin?

CHAPTER 12

June 1944

The next morning after breakfast, Miriam did everything she could to keep busy. After the breakfast dishes were washed and put away, she pulled the rag rugs out and hung them over the clothesline to be beaten. She grabbed the broom and thrashed it against the rugs. The dust was minuscule compared to the energy behind every blow. She needed to keep her mind off the fact that Henry was across the road. More than anything, she longed to be there with him. No matter how guilty she felt about her unfaithfulness, she wanted to help him see that she loved him. The thought alone brought the army-green color of his uniform to her mind and her stomach churned. He was going to war. He was going away. He could die.

She let out a grunt as she hit the last rug with such force that she nearly pulled it from its hold. Deep, uneven breaths forced her to drop the broom and prop herself on her knees. A sob reached her throat as she tried to steady her breathing. With her last bit of energy, she pushed the emotion down and closed her eyes.

What did the prayer book say? One of the prayers said something about God wanting there to be no division between God's children. Another said God would protect us. Did He protect the American soldiers who were killing people in a land that was as foreign as the moon itself? What she really wanted to know was what God said about what to do when the division was between her loyalty to her parents and love for her intended husband. Was it better to honor her parents' wishes and eventually marry someone she didn't love, or was it more important to marry a man she'd promised herself to and loved without exception? Did the Bible answer those questions? Did God speak to individuals, as Henry had told her months earlier?

"Miriam."

Henry stood a few feet away. He wore his Amish clothing. That brought a tenderness to Miriam, making her want to run to him and throw her arms about him. Instead she stood still and bit her lower lip. It was a habit she thought she'd overcome. She furtively glanced toward her sister's house. Had anyone seen him walk over here? Then she turned and looked at the windows of her own home. Were her parents inside watching them? Was her father ready to come out and banish Henry from their property? She didn't see anyone. She let out an even breath and turned back to him.

"Hi," she said. "That sounds so dumb, just saying hi. I don't really know what to say."

He smiled warmly and trained his eyes on her. She felt captivated by his gaze and couldn't look away.

"After last night. Our conversation. I'm just not sure where we're at and what to think." She stuttered through her words, unsure of herself.

"I know. This isn't like us, is it?"

She shook her head before speaking.

"I really thought about what you said last night," she started, "about you or —"

She couldn't say his name. She wouldn't. She looked at her feet, considering how to continue. She had never loved Eli and would never love him. Caring for someone was not the same thing. Even kissing someone didn't amount to much when it came to her feelings. Henry supplied affection she'd lacked from her life, and she'd grown to rely on him for it. When it was taken from her, the longing wore her down greatly.

"Do you love him?" His voice cracked and she could see his chest rise and fall, breathing deeply.

Miriam's soul fell and broke. The words of his heart were written along the lines of his brow. His jaw clenched and his eyes glassed. She dropped her broom and ran to him, throwing her arms around him. She didn't care who saw. His warmth as he held her tightly against his chest was matchless. How could she have taken any comfort in Eli's embrace?

"I love *you,* Henry. No one else. I am so sorry." She pulled way and looked into his dark eyes. "Please forgive me. I should never have —"

"Of course you're forgiven," he said. "I feel it's half my own fault for putting you through this. I never intended to hurt you."

The silence between them callused over the sorrow, burden, and failure they both felt. They were both guilty of hurting the other. But there seemed to be no answer outside of their mutual love. Every wrong and right in their lives always brought them back to the same place — each other's arms. That was the only place she wanted to be.

"I want to marry you," he said, embracing

her eyes with his own.

"And we will. I will wait for you. I promise, I will."

"I don't want any more waiting. I want to marry you now."

Miriam's insides wobbled. Marry now? She wanted nothing more than to marry him. The idea of being his wife so quickly thrilled her. It was wedding season, and it would take some planning for it to happen fast.

"Well, I guess we could do it. I know the preachers would require you to confess, but then we could marry. But what about your enlistment? How would this even work?" She tried to think through the particulars but there were too many uncertainties.

"Miriam, I am still shipping out. I can't go back on my commitment with the army. It's against the law. But we could marry before I shipped out and then no one could keep us apart. You'd be my wife."

Wife. Hearing that simple word from his lips washed her clean of anxiety. Though it only lasted for a few long moments; her mood deadened after hearing again that he couldn't leave the army. She knew that, of course, but hated hearing him say it. *Wife.* She spun the word around in her mind again, pushing the reality of the war far away from her. She hadn't allowed herself to completely imagine her life as a wife for such a long time, her very body was weak with delight. Could they do this?

"But, I don't understand. No matter how much you confess, if you are still committed to the army, then you'd still be on the other side of the *Ordnung*. How could we possibly get married with that against us?"

"I don't mean for us to get married in the Amish church."

The words, the statement, the idea — none of it made sense. Her face contorted in confusion.

"What do you mean?" She almost laughed at the oddity of what he said.

"A bunch of fellas are marrying their girls at the justice of the peace or with an army chaplain before they ship out. It can happen quickly without all the planning. Then, when I come home, we can have a real wedding."

Miriam's tongue went dry. Get married in a courthouse with a judge? Without family and friends? Not a church ceremony where they would commit their lives to each other in front of God? No cake? No secret garter? Her breath came quick and labored. She pushed away from him for a moment.

"I can't do that, Henry. I can't." Her head

spun and she closed her eyes for a moment. "You wouldn't marry me before you left for the CPS camp because you didn't want to leave a wife behind you couldn't take care of. Why is this any different?"

"I should've married you anyway before I left. But now's our chance, I want to know that I have a beautiful wife at home waiting for me and praying for me. We will have everything we always wanted. God is everywhere, which means He's there in the courthouse, too. And, when I get back we can see if the preachers will allow us to have a real wedding."

The disappointment she would cause her parents would be overwhelming. What would the community say? Her life as she lived it would never be the same. But — she would be married to Henry. She would be his wife. He would be her husband. Wasn't that what she wanted? Wasn't that what she dreamed of? Still, the possibility of being excommunicated and cut off from her family without even a husband nearby to comfort her was too much.

"I don't know, Henry. What would everyone say?"

"Just think about it, will you, please?" He kissed her, then trotted away before someone saw them and before Miriam gave him an answer.

The rest of the day moved slower than normal for Miriam. When Kathryn arrived after supper, she was glad for the break in the routine. She'd been visiting at least every week. Miriam had avoided her ever since Kathryn had admitted to her that Henry was the Amish boy whom their father wanted her to marry, but now that Henry had explained things, she took the first opportunity she could to talk with her alone.

She followed Kathryn as she walked out to her car. Nan was bouncing around in the car, even though it was well past her bedtime. Their parents were heading to bed, and Fannie's house steadily got quieter and dimmer by the minute. Fannie had not taken much to Kathryn showing up, so she rarely made it over when their sister visited.

"Kathryn, can I talk with you?"

"Sure. Is something the matter?"

"Henry's back."

"Sis ken fashtant?" Kathryn couldn't believe it.

"He got back into town last night and found me walking home from the Singing. I was so surprised I hardly knew how to act. Then he came over today."

"To the house?" Kathryn said a little

loudly, and both of them looked around to see if anyone heard. "I mean, didn't *Dat* forbid you to communicate with him?"

"*Ja,* but he didn't see him. I was working outside when he came over from Nancy's."

Kathryn instinctively looked over to her mother-in-law's house and sighed. Miriam's eyes followed. Was Henry there now? Had he gone over to his family's home? There was so much uncertainty. She sucked a breath in and held it.

"That's Nancy. She won't even let a stray cat go hungry. She really thinks so much of Henry, she's told me so. And in all these years, I've never heard her say an unkind word, even when I was so hateful about the church and *Mem* and *Dat.*" Her eyes roamed the houses around them with nostalgia, then turned back to Miriam with a glassy look. "I was so angry, Miriam. I said some horrible things to them."

"Well, I knew things weren't good, but I realize now that I didn't know much of what was happening. I was so in the dark."

"Be thankful. It was terrible. *Dat* insisted I do everything possible not to involve you. You were so young, and they were afraid I'd woo you away from the church." Kathryn shook her head back and forth, needling her shoe into the gravel drive. "I wouldn't have. I just wanted to have my baby." She slipped a finger under her eye and brushed away a small tear, somehow still managing to smile the entire time.

She confirmed something that settled a question in Miriam. Kathryn had made a decision because she loved her baby and James. They wanted to be a family. Even though they went about it a little backwards, Miriam believed in her sister's instincts.

"I wish I could've been of some help to you."

"I thought you were angry with me." Kathryn dug deeper.

"I was." Miriam laughed a little. "But then Henry explained everything."

She paused for a few moments. The evening's nature came to life around them and soothed Miriam. "I shouldn't have gotten so angry."

"You never let me explain it all. I would never have married Henry. I loved James. And I am sure he wouldn't have married me anyway."

"I know, I know." She waved a hand at her sister. "He told me it was *Dat* trying to fix things."

"Did he remind you that he had his eye on you all along?" Kathryn winked at her. "No one could get close to Henry, because he was waiting for you. That really frustrated a lot of girls."

Miriam and Kathryn laughed, reminding her of the long years together giggling when they were supposed to be sleeping. The chuckle died down a bit quickly and silence took over.

"He asked me to marry him."

"I thought he already had. Weren't you just about to be announced in church when he left for the camp?"

"We were about to be called out. We'd met with the preachers. I already had my dress made by then." Her voice faded away.

"So why is he asking you again?"

"He wants to marry now, before he leaves for the war. He wants to get married at the courthouse."

Kathryn's eyes rounded in surprise. "Really? I didn't take Henry for a rebel."

"Kathryn, he enlisted. What's more rebellious than that?"

"I guess I don't see that as rebellious, because I really admire him for his enlistment. James is there, too. I think it's heroic for our men and boys to go. The church has blinders on. You don't see the war for what it is."

"Now you really sound like an Englisher if I've ever heard one. They are killing people over there. It goes against the Ten Commandments. It's not right."

"I'm not going to argue with you. But if you were out there in the real world," she said, pointing away from the surrounding homes, "you would understand. But let's not talk about that. I want to know what you're going to do about Henry."

"Well, you need to tell me what to do."

"Me? You want *me* to tell you what to do?"

"You have to — I don't know what I should do."

"Then I say you do it." Kathryn smiled.

"That's easy for you to say. You've already done it." Miriam didn't know whether Kathryn's advice excited or frightened her.

"No, I didn't marry at a courthouse. I had a wedding. I even wore a white dress."

"What?"

"Nancy threw us a small, beautiful wedding at their pretty white church in town. His family came and welcomed me so graciously. I wasn't showing at all by then, but we were honest with everyone. We knew we'd made a mistake, but we also knew that God forgave us and we were as white as snow. It was a nearly perfect day."

"But you were expecting."

"And that doesn't happen within the church? Come on, we both know it happens occasionally. It's just that no one wants to talk about it. And, really, why *should* people be talking about it? It's personal business not meant for everyone to be gossiping over."

Miriam couldn't help but agree with her this time. It was true. Though she had to admit to herself that she participated in the typical gossip, she wasn't one to encourage it.

"I won't pretend to understand your new English ways." Miriam shook her head.

"You could wear my dress if you married Henry at the courthouse." Kathryn winked at her, as if baiting Miriam.

"Sis ken fashtant!" I can't believe it, Miriam exclaimed, and started laughing.

"I'm teasing about the dress, but I think you really need to consider for yourself what to do about Henry. Of course, marrying him would keep that wild Eli Brenneman out of your hair."

"What do you know about Eli?" Miriam grew warm with embarrassment.

"I still have some connections in the community. Friends who keep me updated. I know Eli really wants you."

"I kissed him," she admitted blank-faced, and stared past her sister into the sliver of moon rising in the half-lit sky.

"You were lonely."

"How do you know? Maybe I am falling for him."

"Are you?"

"No," she said flatly. "It would seem easier though, wouldn't it?"

"Easier isn't always better. I know that for a fact."

Kathryn bridged the gap between them and gave her an unexpected hug. Miriam soaked in the loving feeling of her sister's arms like a sponge to water. In the far reaches of her mind she told herself that she would want to be that type of mother, giving hugs generously to her children. Why withhold something so easy to do that speaks volumes of love?

Henry was already that way. He was always ready and willing to provide tenderness and love. Not just to her, either. He might not hug his friends, but he was always the one with the listening ear and encouraging words. She knew she would never find someone better. She had to admit, marrying him would provide a greater sense of independence from her parents, something she longed for. No one could forbid her from writing to him or marrying him once he returned. Was it worth risking the relationship with her parents? What if they wouldn't let her live at home anymore? What if the preachers put her in the ban? She would have to deal with that alone while Henry risked his life on the other side of the world.

Kathryn pulled away and looked into Miriam's eyes. "You know I can't actually tell you what to do. You need to come to the answer on your own." She patted Miriam's shoulder. "Try praying about it."

Before Miriam could say anything further, Kathryn was driving away.

Then a thought came to her. What if she said yes to Henry and they kept the marriage a secret?

CHAPTER 13

June 1944

Miriam's parents were both napping after lunch, giving her the perfect opportunity to visit Nancy and see if Henry was there. She hadn't seen him since the day before and wasn't sure how long he planned on being in town. The conversation with Kathryn the night before had triggered something in her and she desperately wanted to talk with him again. Would it be possible to keep the marriage a secret? Nancy would help her with getting letters off to him, something she wouldn't feel comfortable doing if she were truly under her father's authority. If she were under her husband's authority, she would do everything in her power to show him her love. Then when he returned, no one could tell them that they couldn't get married, because they'd already be married.

"Hi, Miriam," Nancy said. "Henry's not here. He left earlier this morning with some of his friends."

"His friends? Really? Was Eli Brenneman with him?" She secretly hoped that he wasn't. Surely they weren't really friends anymore anyway, right? His presence would offer nothing except suggestions that Miriam was unfaithful to Henry and was falling for Eli. That was the last thing she wanted communicated at this point. Not only was it a falsehood, but the more she was around Eli, the more she realized he couldn't be right for her. Love had to be more powerful than merely pleasing her parents.

"No, not those friends, dearie. His soldier buddies."

"Oh," she said, her voice dropping. She wasn't part of that world, and without anything to contribute, she felt worthless to him.

"Why don't you come in for a cup of iced tea and some cookies and keep me company for a few minutes? Ralph has been awful company these past weeks; he worries something fierce over our boys. Makes him a grump. Makes me eat."

Miriam stepped inside Nancy's immaculate kitchen and smelled the cookies. Nancy chattered on and on about how pleased she was with how things were going with Kathryn's visits. She even went as far as calling it a reconciliation. Miriam wasn't sure she would go that far, for she knew that Kathryn would always remain shunned. She did agree that having Kathryn around was a good thing, though she hadn't gotten to know Nan that well yet, since the little girl often enjoyed staying with Nancy during Kathryn's visits. Kathryn had admitted to Miriam early on that Nan had confessed to being afraid of their father's beard.

A car engine sounded loudly in the drive, and loud laughter followed. Miriam saw, to her amazement, Henry stepping out of a long blue automobile. He was in uniform again, striking a chord out of tune with her. Nancy stood and went to the door.

"You boys want some iced tea or cold milk?"

A holler of yeses came from the car full of young soldiers. Miriam bristled. These were Henry's friends? They poured out of the car, four in all, arriving on the porch with Henry leading the way.

"You boys take a seat out there. It's cooler than it is in here." Nancy asked each what he wanted, iced tea or milk, then bustled around the kitchen filling glasses and piling a plate full of cookies.

Miriam felt indignant. These boys were not Nancy's sons or just some young kids arriving home from school. They were soldiers, and she was serving them milk and cookies on her front porch like children. She kept her back to the door as she sat at the table. She didn't want to accept that this was Henry's life now.

"Miriam?" Henry asked. "Is that you?"

The front screen door creaked open and a warm hand slid onto her shoulder. She tentatively looked up, finding the handsome face of the man she considered her future husband. As he moved toward her, she realized she didn't miss the beard. His now defined jawline added to his muscular stature, which appealed to her. His uniform only added to this strong, sturdy appearance. Without thought she touched the uniform, as if inspecting the collar and stitching, but really she wanted to feel something that belonged to the new Henry. The man Henry, rather than the boy she'd fallen in love with years ago. In the light of day, she could see how perfectly the olive-green uniform fit him. The pockets were flat against his chest and the belt around his waist proved he'd gotten thicker during his time away. He held his hat, which reminded Miriam of a soda jerk's hat, only it wasn't white.

Henry gently took her hand in his and

smiled before he spoke again. She savored the feeling of her hand in his more than ever before.

"Miriam, I am so glad you're here. I want my friends to meet you." He pulled her up and her mouth gaped in horror. He curled her arm around his, something they'd never done before. Was he really going to make her go out and meet his friends?

He walked her out to the porch, and the door slapping behind her startled her. Her nerves jumped awake to the three unfamiliar faces ahead of her. She gripped his arm with her own. When she saw the four young men in the same uniform, the image branded her mind. There was something remarkable about it. Maybe it was the strength it proved, their common purpose and determination. Their faces were tanned against the olive green. She noticed all of them had the same stripes on their arms and tight tan ties around their thick necks. The gold buttons sparkled even in the shade, and she wondered if they shined them. Her everyday chore dress suddenly felt incredibly simple in front of such an intricate uniform.

Her eyes met Henry's. He wasn't mocking her, she knew, but his smile over the nerve-wracking situation still vexed her. Before she could tell if she was truly angry or not, Henry began speaking.

"This is Miriam. Miriam, these are my friends."

"Hi, Miriam. I'm Buck." A short, square-shaped soldier stood and extended his hand toward her. She shook it with her customary firmness. He met her eyes, and Miriam saw a genuine smile in them. Beads of sweat dripped down the sides of his red, pudgy face.

For the first time, she realized how different Henry's English sounded in comparison to his friend Buck's. Henry's exaggerated pronunciation sounded foreign in the English world, but he was as American as any of the boys on the porch. She tried to stop it, but her chin lifted, as if she was glad that he didn't fit in completely. No amount of pretending would make him exactly like them. In the moment after this thought, she wondered if this was how she sounded when she spoke English. The heat in her face rose.

"I'm Abe. Hank's a good fella, but I am sure I don't have to tell you that. I'm so happy to meet you," the next one said. He held her gaze longer. His mouth pursed, as if the words behind them should remain unspoken. His shake was firm but gentle, and he used two hands. She'd never known someone to do that before and it softened her to him.

"Come on, tell her we call you Thump. No one calls him Abe. He's our Bible thumper. Doesn't go anywhere without that book," the yet nameless soldier said, addressing Miriam before tipping Thump's hat off, then moving into his own introduction. "My name is John Stephen Rossum the third, the pride of Virginia." He shook her hand and did a shallow bow in front of her. "But you can call me Johnny Boy." The boy burst out in a fit of laughter.

A grimace reached her brow in a moment, and the next, she wiped it from her face. Miriam wasn't sure what was funny but the other three all laughed too, though not so hard as Johnny Boy.

"So you're Miriam?" Johnny Boy continued after he'd slugged back half of his drink. A white film of milk sat atop his upper lip. "You're all Hanky-Panky talks about. But I don't remember him telling us how pretty you are."

Miriam looked down at her feet. And why were they calling him Hank and Hanky-Panky? It was a terrible nickname.

"Johnny, put a lid on it." Henry's arm went protectively around her. He had to have known what a humiliation it was to her to be paraded in front of his supposed friends. "I didn't bring her out here for you to be rude."

"Hank has told us so much about you, Miriam," Thump said. His voice sounded like there was a song behind it, and he had the gentlest eyes of the three friends. Miriam couldn't help but like him even though she knew nothing about him. "You have a good man here, and I admire how much he loves you."

"Aw, Thump, you're such a softy." Johnny Boy's wide mouth grew into a flippant smile.

"Thump's right, though," Buck said. He had no neck. It was as if his square head were glued right onto his wide shoulders. "Hank's nuts about you."

"Now you're embarrassing me," Henry said before clearing his throat and peeking out of the side of his eyes at Miriam. His face transformed from pink to red.

"So, you gonna marry this Yankee Boy?" Johnny Boy stood and punched Henry in the shoulder.

Everyone looked at her, even Henry. She wanted to slap him. How could she answer that question, and why would Henry expect her to in front of his friends?

"I need to go. Mother and Father will be waking from their naps soon." She was so self-conscious of her accent, she was barely able to get the English words out. "I don't want them to wonder where I am."

She pulled away from Henry and began walking away.

"Can I see you tonight?" Henry grabbed her hand and tugged her slightly. She looked back at him, his face melting into her eyes.

"Just whistle after dark," she said in their dialect even though Henry had spoken to her in English. "I'll meet you outside."

She heard Johnny Boy hooting and laughing behind her even though there was no way he knew what she'd said. She hated him. She knew it was wrong, but she couldn't keep herself from just despising him. He was so loud and brash; there was nothing appealing about a friend like that. Nothing.

Though it was only dusk outside and Miriam couldn't see Henry from her window upstairs, his familiar tune still reached her ears. It had only been five or ten minutes since she'd heard her parents walk around downstairs, so sneaking out now could cause a problem. She would have to be more than quiet.

She padded silently downstairs, avoiding the step in the middle that creaked. When she got to the kitchen, she recognized the

219

orange glow from the kerosene lamp in the living room. Her parents were still awake, which wasn't common. She carefully opened the door that led into the mudroom and crept out, making sure the screen didn't blow back against the frame.

Before she moved farther, Henry's arms formed around her, pulling her close. She stiffened, remembering how demeaned she'd felt earlier that afternoon.

"I'm sorry, Miriam." He loosened his hold and caught her eyes for only a moment. She avoided eye contact with him; otherwise she would lose her nerve to be upset with his actions that afternoon.

"I was so humiliated. I have never felt so uncomfortable in my life." She pushed him away half-heartedly, because she really didn't want to be angry. The last thing she wanted to do was argue with him, not with what her answer was to his question from the previous day.

"I should've known better, I just wanted them to meet you so bad. But I still scolded Johnny. He told me to tell you he didn't mean to embarrass you." Henry leaned back, putting him at eye level with Miriam. She met his eyes this time. "Forgive me?"

A small smile tickled Miriam's lips, and she nodded her head. "Of course I forgive you. Just, please, I don't want to be around Johnny again. But I thought the other two seemed nice. Except that they called you Hank. How terrible!"

He chuckled.

"I knew you would hate it, but everyone has a nickname." He winked at her. "Just like when I call you my Cherry Pie." He ran a finger over her freckles.

"Nah, schtopes." She told him to stop it, playfully pushing him away. "Why were they here? Don't they have families?"

"Well, Abe's from around here. He married his sweetheart just before he left for training and is having a wedding reception later this week. Johnny's from Virginia and his family already lost one son. His mother told him she can't handle seeing him in uniform."

"And, *Buck*? Is that what you call him?"

"He doesn't have a family. His parents died when he was young and he just moved around between aunts and uncles all his life." Henry was silent for a moment. "He's really a great fella. You'd like him."

"I just don't understand any of you." She shook her head. "Why do any of you want to go to war? You could be killed!"

"We don't *want* to go. We feel it's our duty."

A silence hung over them for several long moments before he hopped forward and pulled her close again and kissed her deeply on the lips. Their conversation grew unimportant as Miriam allowed herself to thoroughly enjoy the lingering moments, imagining that on a day very soon she would be kissing him as Mrs. Miriam Mast.

"I'm glad you wanted me to come over." His voice was husky and deep in her ear as they swayed to the music of the nature around them.

She reveled in the fluttering in her stomach for several long minutes. His simple faded blue Amish shirt opened one button too far, his suspenders down around his legs instead of over his shoulders, and even the rough prickles of new growth on his jawline brought all of her senses to life. It was so different from the uniform he had worn earlier, which held his posture straight and made his shoulders look so broad.

They walked hand in hand to the wooden glider swing at the back of the house. She sat, and Henry instantly laid his head in her lap. They often sat this way. She enjoyed tousling his hair when they swung back and forth after a Singing. Though she missed the way her fingers could wind around his lengthy hair, tonight she stroked his short hair, giving her a new sensation of touching the church's forbidden velvet fabric. Velvet was far too fancy for the Amish. Now her almost-husband was naturally adorned in it.

She finally broke the silence. "I have been thinking about what you said yesterday."

He sat up, and she noted his eyes sparkling as they found hers. He took her hands and brought them to his lips. Miriam could hardly understand how it was that she had gained the attention of someone so sensitive and willing to offer love and affection. She'd heard from most of her friends that they longed for more tenderness and affection from their boyfriends.

"And, what have you decided?"

"I want to marry you," she stated simply.

"But?"

How did he know there would be a condition?

"But, I don't want to tell anyone. I want to keep it between the two of us, and maybe Nancy and Kathryn."

Miriam saw either confusion or a quarrel in his expression and instantly jumped in to try to explain herself.

"That way when you get back, no one can tell me that we can't be together. We can deal with the church together."

"But how would that solve anything in the

present?"

"You would know that I'm here, as your wife, waiting for you to return safely. Just like you want. We could send and receive letters through Nancy. My parents wouldn't get the shock of us marrying at the courthouse. When you get back, after we clear things up with the preachers, we could still get married in the eyes of the church, and no one would be the wiser. We wouldn't be hurting anyone."

"Except that you'd be lying to your parents and the entire community. And what about Eli? Do you think he will leave you alone without believing you're my wife?" His voice grew excitable. He stood and began pacing. "This isn't a good idea, Miriam. You know I have never been anything but straightforward with you, my parents, and the church. It has never been my intention to sneak around in any part of my life, especially when I want to commit my life and love to you, as my wife."

"But my parents will never forgive me." Miriam stood but didn't go to Henry, a few paces away.

"It's better for you to marry me in secret than it is for you to just write me in secret?"

Miriam didn't have an answer to that. He was right. Why was it okay for her to go against her parents and marry Henry at the courthouse and then keep it from them but not to just write him secretly against her parents' wishes? Weren't both options rebellious and dishonoring to her parents?

"I am so afraid you'll never come back and then I'll never have the chance to marry you. But this isn't how I wanted it."

"It's not how I wanted it, either. But shipping off and heading to war knowing that I have a beautiful wife waiting for me will bring me back."

"That's not fair. So if I don't marry you, you're not going to come back? You're going to die?"

"I don't mean for it to sound like that. I mean that there's just something about marrying you that would encourage me with every breath, almost like it would be my responsibility to come home and take care of you, because you're my wife. I can't really explain it."

The two of them stood in the remnants of the day as the final veil of evening left them and ushered in the night. Miriam wasn't sure where to go from there. Their differences were weighing down the bridge between them, chipping away at Miriam's resolve.

"Okay, let's just do it. All I really want is

to marry you."

Henry bounded to her in one large step, crushing her in a tight hug. They both giggled with joy, knowing this time the decision was final. There would be no more discussion.

"Now, one thing," she said, pulling away enough to look into his face. "You'll have to trust me to tell my parents alone. Okay?"

He winced a little, but agreed with a kiss.

Miriam sighed as she melted into his warm lips. Soon she would be Henry's wife.

CHAPTER 14

June 1944

Before Henry left that night, they arranged to pick up the marriage license on Tuesday and then return on Wednesday to get married. He would be in town only until Thursday, giving them very little time to act on their plans. Kathryn would be coming Tuesday afternoon and would keep her parents occupied while she slipped away, and on Wednesday, Miriam would just have to come up with a reasonable excuse. She had a number of things that would work, though her parents rarely asked where she was going. Miriam had to fight her guilt over this, because their trust in her in was why they didn't question her.

She didn't attend the Singing on Sunday, glad to use the excuse that she had a headache, which was partially true. Summer had hit Dover and the humidity seemed to be locked between her ears. It was the in-between Sunday, so the Singing was held in the other district in the area and was much farther, so she wouldn't have gone to it anyway. It would have been nearly impossible to keep Eli from insisting on driving her home. She hadn't heard from him since they found themselves in a dark closet less than a week earlier. She was sure he would be expecting her at the Singing.

By the time Monday's dawn broached the sky and she was bouncing out of bed, she wondered that no one seemed to know that Henry was home. How he had managed that was beyond her understanding. It even seemed impossible that Fannie or one of her girls hadn't noticed. Miriam decided it didn't matter.

She went about her chores that day with vigor and energy. Her laundry was done in half the usual time, and she began her Tuesday ironing. Her mother, unnoticing, was with Fannie for much of the afternoon, cradling and rocking their teething baby. No one seemed to do it better than Grandma. Her father had gotten the energy up to follow Truman around the farm for a while. He would tinker at small chores on these good days. Miriam was glad he would get some fresh air. Since his heart attack he had become more ornery than ever, often refusing to even go out and get the mail for a little exercise.

Miriam kept herself busy cleaning, though her mind was only on Henry and their impending marriage. She even scrubbed the woodstove till it shined inside and out. She refilled the small squirt containers they used for kerosene and gas and the salt and pepper shakers, and made a few pies. She snuck one pie over to Nancy's as a dessert for Henry and her after they returned from the justice of the peace the following day. Her feet barely touched the ground all day.

Tuesday came with a wild wind and rain. Though Miriam had hoped the sun would be shining, nothing could dampen her mood. Her parents were particularly slow-moving and in low moods that day, mirroring the weather. They ate so unhurriedly that Miriam imagined feeding them like a toddler to hasten the process. The dishes and plates were cleared before they were half finished with their cabbage soup, and Miriam stood vigil waiting to snatch up the bowls beneath their chins as the last spoonful was eaten.

"You seem to be in an awful hurry," her mother said.

Miriam hesitated to say anything too

quickly, not wanting to seem eager with an excuse.

"Well, I have to keep up with Fannie somehow," she tittered after a few moments. "She can sew, cook, and clean circles around me usually."

"She was always my biggest help," her mother agreed.

Her parents then took their customary nap in the living room on their chairs after Miriam reminded them that she would be running out for a little while and Kathryn would be stopping by soon. She took every other step up the stairs and took her purse out of the closet, making sure her birth certificate was inside.

Miriam's heart tumbled when she walked slowly over to Nancy's house, trying not to notice if anyone had seen her. All she and Henry needed to do was get their marriage license and get her back home. Nancy had been pleased to offer to drive her into town and to the courthouse. By the time she climbed into Nancy's vehicle, she hadn't seen anyone notice her. She could come up with plenty of excuses as to why she had hired Nancy to drive her, though she didn't do it very often. She would have to make sure to stop at a store to buy a few items in case she was asked.

Her skin tightened around her knuckles as she held onto the door in Nancy's car. The pressure from the entire situation was mounting against her nerves. The fact that she'd hired a driver for such a short trip, the secret she was keeping from everyone, the possibility of being found out, and how she would do this all over again the next day so they could get married was almost more than she could bear.

Nancy chattered on about hearing from her sons and said that even Ralph had smiled over the letters. Miriam could barely contribute to the conversation over the drumming of her heart. She wished Henry had decided to drive in with them but understood that it would have been more difficult to go unnoticed that way. He had gone into town with Ralph hours earlier. She wound the window down and took a few deep breaths of the warm June air passing them by, letting it wash over her face.

When Nancy pulled into a parking spot, the courthouse itself intimidated her. It was exciting, like something in a novel, but fearsome as well. Would she regret this in the future?

"Do you want me to go in with you?"

Miriam didn't answer right away. She could use the moral support, and what if she and Henry didn't know what they were doing? Before she could respond, she felt a hand on her shoulder through the open car door. It was Henry, dressed sharply in his uniform. He was a welcome imposing figure against their intimidating task.

She exhaled and put a shaky hand over Henry's.

"I think we will be fine, Nancy, but thank you."

Henry offered her the crook of his arm as they walked into the building. This was something he'd never done before, and for the first time in her life, she felt like a lady. Not just a young Amish woman, but a lady who had a man willing to take care of and love her. His footsteps were sure and strong and when he released her arm and opened the door, he placed his hand on the small of her back and led her inside.

Where had this gentleman come from?

He had never been crude or abrasive as young boys could be, but the way he measured his movements and his gestures was beyond her. These English ways intrigued her, and she lifted her chin a bit higher and walked with a little self-confidence. Though Miriam wanted to get through this quickly, she still enjoyed the wait as she watched the people around her.

There were several other men in uniform with rosy young women next to them. Were they as sure of themselves as they appeared to be? Were they forgoing their own wedding dreams to marry quickly at a courthouse? None of them seemed to have the fear in their eyes she would have expected. Could they see her fear?

Henry filled out the document to file for a marriage license and had Miriam look over it and sign it.

"Everyone is looking at us," she whispered to Henry, glad to speak in their dialect so no one else could understand.

"It's because you're so beautiful." He winked at her.

She squeezed his muscled arm, and he flexed under her touch. They both quietly giggled. She supposed that all the other couples sitting there waiting had their own giggles and fears. She was learning through this that maybe she and Henry weren't as different from everyone else as she had always thought. Sure, she looked a lot different with her plain dress and her hair pinned back under a covering, and didn't have shiny lipstick or rouge, but didn't all women have the same angst about their plans? She suspected that they did. It brought her a measure of comfort, until the woman at the desk spoke.

"Next," she said. She wore pointy glasses, and her hair was tightly rolled on top of her head and in the back. Her high collar enhanced the pinched look in her face. Miriam was afraid of her and held her breath as they stood.

Henry curled Miriam's arm through his and they walked to the desk. It was a tall desk. Miriam could see over it, but the woman was on a higher level behind the counter and made her feel small and insignificant.

"We're here to apply for a marriage license," Henry said and handed the woman the completed form.

Miriam instantly recognized the confidence in his voice and that there was only a twinge of his accent in his words.

"I need to see your forms of identification," the nasal voice said.

Henry handed her both his and Miriam's birth certificates, and the woman went about writing and stamping, not saying a word through the process. After a few minutes she returned their documents, including the marriage license.

"You have a twenty-four-hour waiting period, then you can get married," she said, never meeting their eyes. "Next."

Henry took Miriam's hand and led her to the hallway, where they put their birth certificates away and inspected the marriage license.

Was this real? Would she really be married to Henry the next day?

Once they got to the parking lot, he opened the car door for Miriam and leaned into the open window, pecking her lips quickly.

"Can I see you later?" she asked, hoping.

"I had hoped so, but tonight is Thump's wedding reception. I'll be staying over." He winked at her. "This is the first chance they've had, since they just had a small wedding before he left for basic training. I only wish you could come with me."

She smiled, unsure of what to say. His conversation felt so English, she didn't know how to contribute. Part of her wished to attend with him and part of her wanted him not to attend, for fear of the English part of him becoming greater than the Amish. Yet another part of her wanted to just curl up in her bed and pretend these past months weren't real. She was preparing for a secret elopement. There weren't many things more romantic or frightening than that reality.

Miriam memorized his face. It was free of

lines. He had a wide smile, his eyes were bright, and he appeared as if he didn't have a worry in the world. She had imagined her wedding day for so many years, and that was how she wanted Henry to look. He was ready to be her husband and have her for a wife. His bright smile and the joy in his eyes were suddenly all that mattered to her. She wanted to make him happy as his wife for as long as she lived. Now she would finally be given that chance.

CHAPTER 15

June 1944

When Miriam arrived home, she was instantly faced with chaos. Black smoke floated through the open front door of her house. Several of her nieces were running into the house holding small buckets with water splashing out the sides. She charged toward the scene and reached the house only a few paces behind the girls.

"What's going on?" she yelled, then coughed from the smoke that filled the small house. The floor was wet and a heavy dark cloud poured out of the oven.

Fannie was already inside helping her mother out of the house. Miriam's nieces flanked her father, bracing him at his elbows. Miriam followed them again as they headed outside. Her heart raced, and her mind could not keep up with what was happening. Her nephews nearly ran over her as they doused more water over the oven.

"Where were you?" Fannie spoke harshly to Miriam when they got outside.

Miriam couldn't answer her as she watched her mother sit on a small wooden bench in front of the house and wince as she held her badly burned hand and arm. Her face looked blistered as well. Their father sat next to her. He seemed frightened but otherwise fine.

Miriam's hands shook and her purse landed on her feet when she dropped it. Her tongue was dry in her mouth, and she couldn't utter a word. Fannie, on the other hand, acted quickly. After her cutting remark to Miriam, she returned to action. One of her daughters ran from their house and handed her a clean white cloth and water in a bowl. With her jaw clenched, she applied the cool cloth to their mother's hand, arm, and face. Miriam felt her own tears burn her face as she watched her mother grimace at the pain.

"Go see if Nancy can take us to Dr. Sherman's. We need to take her in and get her burns treated," Fannie said to one of her daughters, then looked back at Miriam, her eyes sharp and narrow. "Where were you?" she repeated through clenched teeth.

"I, I, I —" she stuttered, "Kathryn was going to come."

"Kathryn, of course, Kathryn." Fannie tried to clear away any debris and fabric from their mother's burn. "Well, neither of you were with them, and now look at what happened."

"Mem, vas hoat kapent?" Miriam knelt in front of her mother and asked her what happened.

Her mother's lips quivered as she tried to speak. Her eyes reminded Miriam of a child who had just been told a story about the bogeyman for the first time.

"I just wanted to make some tea. *Dat* wanted some, and when I went to heat the fire I squirted the kerosene into the oven. And all of a sudden a huge flame just poured out. I don't know what happened." She whimpered and touched her red cheek with her good hand, then recoiled.

"I'm so sorry, I should've stayed. Kathryn said she'd be over."

Just then, Miriam heard the sound of a car engine and turned, expecting to see Nancy's familiar vehicle, but was surprised to see Kathryn barreling out of the driver's seat. Her round belly looked larger than ever as she ran toward them.

"Now you show up," Fannie said, not hiding her disdain in the least. "Nancy's here."

"I can take her," Kathryn exclaimed, look-

239

ing wild-eyed.

"No, you can't. You're shunned, remember." Fannie pulled their mother up and ushered her past Kathryn's car and into Nancy's.

Miriam hopped up and followed.

"You're not coming. You stay with *Dat,* unless you have another errand to run." Fannie helped their mother into the vehicle and closed the door, and then turned back to Miriam. Her eyes drilled into Miriam's before she spoke. "And if you want me to keep your secret that Henry's in town, then you'd better learn to sneak around better. Do you see what your sneaking around has caused our family? Not to mention, you're setting a bad example for my young ones."

Miriam's mouth fell open and her heart squeezed tighter. Fannie marched around the car and sat in the backseat next to her mother, who more closely resembled a strange old woman than her mother. Nancy looked at Miriam. The corners of her eyes were turned down, and her forehead was lined with concern. Miriam turned away in shame.

Is this what my sneaking around has caused my family? she repeated to herself over and over. She had caused this. It was her doing. If she had been home, she would have made their tea and would have realized that she'd unknowingly replaced the kerosene with gas. She had been too distracted yesterday because of Henry and made a horrible mistake. Kathryn wasn't to blame. She wasn't the one who lived at home with her parents as her sole responsibility. Her mother was on her way to the clinic, and her father sat, frightened, looking more like a child than a grown man.

What had she done?

"This isn't your fault," Kathryn said, as if she could read Miriam's mind.

"Yes it is." Miriam spat the words. "I was the one who was too distracted yesterday and didn't put the kerosene and gas bottles in the right order. We need them in the right order because *Mem* can't see well enough anymore. And I wasn't here. They are my responsibility, and I wasn't here."

"What do you mean?"

"Have you forgotten your Amish life so quickly?" She felt bad about snapping at Kathryn and tried to calm down. She took a deep breath. "I put the kerosene on the shelf of the woodstove so it's there when we want to start a fire. But I put the naphtha gas for the lights in the closet shelf. I must have accidentally switched them. You remember what happens if you squirt gas into the woodstove instead of kerosene. This! The fire! *Mem*'s burns."

"It's not your fault. You just said it yourself — it was an accident. You're allowed to make mistakes."

"Not the kind that nearly kill your parents and burn your house down. Especially when —" She bit her tongue. The last thing she wanted to talk about right now was that she'd just gone with Henry to get a marriage license.

Miriam piled the soot-covered rags in an old bucket. The last thing she wanted to do was laundry in the middle of the week, but her mother prided herself on always having clean rags. They might be a sleeve from an old shirt or even a sock that had been darned too much to wear, but they were spotless. Her back ached as she picked up the bucket. The wire handle indented her red, chapped hands.

"I think this is the last of them," Kathryn said, tossing another rag into the bucket. "Everything on *Dat*'s desk is clean."

Kathryn wore a crude ponytail under an old kerchief. Her face was streaked with black. Instinctively, Miriam touched her own face. It was moist from sweat. Her fingertips were smudged gray, as she'd expected. She sighed. Why hadn't she remembered to remove her white covering? She was sure it was ruined. Why hadn't she put a kerchief over her head? Knowing that wearing a covering at all was a sign of their devotion to constant prayer made her well up with anger.

Sure, she had prayed as they cleaned, feeling like it was the hardest and longest scrubbing she'd ever done. Prayed that she would be forgiven for her misjudgment in going to town. She asked forgiveness for choosing to marry Henry against her father's wishes. Or was she pleading forgiveness for the repercussions of her actions that played against the future she longed for? Was this God's will again? Had His plan allowed for her mother to suffer terrible burns as punishment for Miriam's disobedience?

"Where's Nan?" Miriam suddenly realized she hadn't seen her young niece in hours.

"Fannie's girls have her. She's happy as a lark."

There was a long pause, but Miriam could almost hear the words Kathryn was about to say.

Finally, Kathryn broke the silence. "So, where were you? Were you with Henry?" She squinted and looked at Miriam inquisitively.

Moisture layered over the dried sweat under Miriam's arms. She looked at her sister, then pivoted on her heels and walked out of the house. Kathryn's quick steps padded behind her, and Miriam battled with herself whether to tell the truth or a believable lie. The guilt of her sin already weighed heavily on her heart. The idea of adding another atop of disobeying her father brought her an instant headache.

Walking out into the dark, balmy evening gave her no more breathing space than the heat of the house. The humidity cloaked her, embracing her. Her hand wiped away dampness from her forehead only to further smear the smoky residue onto her hands. She set the bucket down in the soft dirt around the side patio area where she always did her washing. She began pulling out rag after rag and pinning them onto a small line nearby, one not visible from the road. Kathryn moved with the same deftness, and in a matter of a few minutes, the rags were hung to air dry, awaiting the scrubbing they would receive the following day.

They sat on the glider swing together, using their toes to keep it rocking. In the restful silence, Miriam noticed how lovingly Kathryn cradled and touched her growing belly. She had seen so many expecting women in her life, but none who seemed so aware of the life that was inside. Pregnancies were avoided in conversation, practically ignored, so as not to draw attention to how they happened. She wanted to reach out her hand and feel on the outside what Kathryn was experiencing on the inside, but she didn't.

"Henry and I filed for a marriage license today." Her eyes remained diverted into the small glowing orbs of light in Fannie's windows.

"I was hoping you would say that."

"Really?" Her eyes quickly found her sister's in the light of the moon.

"Come on, Miriam. I want you to be happy, and Henry makes you happy," she said with a chuckle. "I am shocked that no one else has figured out that he's here."

"Fannie has. She knows Henry's here. He probably shouldn't have gone to the Pooles' house with those soldier buddies of his in the middle of the day. Besides that, he's been careful. He doesn't want to ruin our chances to elope. His uniform does make him look so different, though. I'm surprised Fannie would even have recognized him. He doesn't want to ruin our chances to elope." She surprised herself with how easy it was to talk about. If there were tears to be shed, they were hiding behind her guilt. "But Fannie gave me a very clear warning before she and *Mem* left."

"Oh, forget Fannie. She's full of smoke," Kathryn said, waving a hand at Miriam's concern.

"Full of smoke?" Miriam said, smiling playfully. "Really, you couldn't think to describe her better?"

The sisters shared a laugh for a few moments. Miriam wondered how she could laugh at a time like this. There really was nothing funny.

"Well, Nan is already asleep, so I think I'll just stay the night. That way I can be here all day tomorrow, and you can leave and return before anyone has a chance to become suspicious. I won't lie, but I'll keep your secret as honestly as I can."

"There is no secret to keep, Kathryn." Miriam said, sighing as she spoke.

"Aren't you meeting Henry?"

"I am not going to marry Henry tomorrow. You know I can't. I can't believe you think this doesn't change everything." Her harsh whisper cut through the dampness in the air, drying up the lingering laugh that still floated around them.

"Why should it? This was an accident. I understand you feel responsible, but —"

"Why are you making this harder for me? *Mem* was punished because of my rebellion. If I had just followed the rules, she wouldn't have been burned. It *is* my fault, and now I need to suffer the consequences."

"But what about Henry?"

"What about him? He should never have put me in this position."

"He loves you. How can you not see how much he loves you? Most girls in your own community would take your place right now if they could, no matter what the rules. They know that Henry's a good man."

Miriam pursed her lips together. Just the thought of any other woman marrying Henry was enough to pull the tears out from their hiding place. Her eyes burned. She loved him more than she could explain to Kathryn, but how could she play games with her family's lives? If she married him, what more would happen? What wrath would be poured out to satisfy God, to punish them all for her rebellion?

"I wish things were different. If it weren't for this war and Henry's stupid enlistment, we wouldn't be going through this, this — pain." Sobs left her throat, and she haphazardly passed the back of her hand over her wet cheek. "I just can't risk it."

Miriam left Kathryn standing there just in

time to see Nancy's car enter the drive. She rubbed both her hands over her face, drying her tears. She could sense exhaustion settle on her face, and when she saw Fannie's still firm and stern features, she tucked her emotions safely away.

Her mother's burns were neatly wrapped with white gauze and medical tape. The three sisters helped her into her room, where their father was already snoring. Kathryn helped her undress and pull on her nightgown and bonnet. Fannie gave Miriam instructions on the pain medication and dressing for the burns. Her words were curt. She left the house without another word.

CHAPTER 16

June 1944

A beam of sunshine, birds singing, and a sweetly scented breeze should have helped Miriam's mood. Instead, her hands moving up and down, scrubbing the rags in the hot, steamy water, measured her bitterness and anger. The process brought just enough physical pain for her to consider herself fairly punished. Her knuckles scraped against the washboard, and the lye sunk deeper, stinging. She clenched her jaw.

She was glad Kathryn was helping inside so she could be outside and away from the reminder of what had happened the day before. The sunlight struck her eyes as she hung the pristine white rags on the regular line out front. The sun was high. It was noon. Her stomach reminded her that she'd skipped supper the previous night and breakfast that morning.

"Granny!" Nan squealed, running to the

round woman whose arms were always open. "I got to milk a cow with Cousin Mandy this morning."

"You did? Well, I can't wait to hear all about it. But first I need to talk with your Aunt Miriam, okay?"

The little girl ran back to Fannie's daughter, Mandy, who was near her age. Miriam had heard them all morning communicating perfectly in Pennsylvania Dutch. One little girl looked like she'd walked out of one of those Sears, Roebuck catalogs; the other little girl looked as Amish as Miriam. Yet there was no gap between them and no question that they were cousins. Miriam also noticed that when Nan spoke English to Nancy, she did so without the trademark Amish accent, having learned and used both languages equally. Miriam found herself envious of the little girl. Nan was able to enjoy the companionship of her Amish family while still living a typical English life.

"You'd better get yourself cleaned up, dearie," Nancy said, gesturing toward Miriam's faded work dress and the kerchief over the mussed hair that pulled haplessly out of her loosening bun.

Miriam couldn't find the words to speak and only shook her head.

"Surely you don't mean to wear that

dress? I've seen how pretty you look on Sundays."

"I'm not getting married today." Miriam kept her eyes far away from Nancy. She worked her hands quickly so she could excuse herself.

"Isn't Henry leaving tomorrow?"

"Yes." The simple word came out as no more than a whisper. She swallowed hard.

"Then, what about Henry? You're just going to let him wait for you at the courthouse? He deserves an explanation. It's only right."

Miriam paused her work. Her lips pursed, holding in her emotions. *Henry.* Her eyes closed. She pictured him standing there. She shook her head when she realized that for the first time, she imagined him in his soldier's uniform instead of his Amish clothing. When had her mind begun to see him more as a soldier than an Amish carpenter? She shuddered.

"I'll write him. I just know I can't go today. I need to go inside to prepare lunch. You are welcome to stay."

She picked up the empty basket and walked away.

Miriam excused herself after supper. Falling exhausted against the back of her bedroom door as she shut it, she slid her body to the floor and finally let herself weep. She cried for her mother's physical pain and her own heartsickness. But mostly she cried over the image of Henry, waiting at the door of the courthouse for her. Did he stand there alone, or did any of his friends come to witness? She imagined the sun shining off of the buttons of his uniform, making him look even statelier. What had he thought when she was late? How long had he waited? She hated herself for hurting him. She knew she should have asked Nancy to give him a message, but what a position to put her neighbor in! It wouldn't have been fair to Nancy.

After emptying herself of tears, she gathered her nightgown and bonnet and underclothes. Her parents would be in bed soon, and she wanted to take a long, cool bath, hoping to scour away the misery that had embedded itself into her being. She pulled out her journal and recounted the day's events and the circumstances that she found herself in. Once there was a long silence from the first floor, she put her journal under the floorboard and stepped quietly downstairs.

After preparing the bath, she dipped her toe in. The temperature was perfect. The air in the kitchen where the basin of water sat was thick with heat, and her skin was moist to the touch. With only one lamp flickering in the room, she gently lowered herself into the bath. She sighed as she settled her body deeply into the water, wishing she could stretch her legs out completely.

In the coolness of the bath, she felt clarity come into her mind. The events of the week washed over her. She squeezed a cloth of tepid water over her head. Water traced down the sides of her face, then her neck, pooling into her collarbone. Why had God let her life spin so far out of control?

The water in her cupped hands poured over her hair and face, and she relished in the escape from the heat. She pulled out her hairpins and let the length of her hair fall into the water. In the flicker of the lamplight it didn't look strawberry blonde, nor did her skin appear so fair. Things weren't as they appeared, and she imagined her life as someone else. Maybe an English girl who wore green and lilac-colored dresses. Her hair would roll in curls and waves and her lips would pucker like a rose. She pictured herself on Henry's arm wearing a long white dress, like in photos she'd seen. That was when the storybook fantasy stopped. Would she ever have the chance to marry Henry now? The war could take his life, but even if it didn't, he might never forgive her.

After a lengthy soak, Miriam dried herself and pulled on a long, white cotton night-gown. It was billowy and the air floated around her, invigorating her senses. She combed her hair in the reflection of the window that faced Nancy's house. Usually she did this upstairs, but with the window open slightly the breeze felt so nice she didn't want to leave. The night had drawn a black curtain without allowing even the glimmer of light to penetrate through. She could see nothing, making the window almost as good as a mirror.

Eventually, she saw a beam of light, slowly bobbing through the darkness, and her heart boomed in her chest. It was getting closer, and Miriam picked up the lamp, bringing it closer to the window. She was sure it was Henry. Who else would it be? His shoulders were slumped, and his gait was slow. Without a thought, Miriam set down the lamp on the table and quickly padded her way to the front door, grabbing her own flashlight that always sat there. Her toes curled around the cool grass as she walked to the edge of the lawn. She waved her beam of light, hoping he would see her.

Her eyes focused on the small round light as it stilled. Her eyes adjusted, found the outline of his tall stature breaking through the blackness of the night. She tipped a toe onto the gravel drive in front of her, wishing she'd worn her house slippers. The small stones pushed into her feet as she stepped slowly toward Henry. Her foot curled, and she winced against the jagged edge of a rock. She rubbed away the pain before placing her foot back onto the gravel. Standing erect again, she looked ahead for the light and found only blackness. Her eyes panned from left to right. There were no lights on at Nancy's house, either. Her lungs filled with air and held it, pausing in the moment. Henry was gone.

Weeks went by without word from Henry. He consumed Miriam's thoughts. When she was kneading dough, Henry was the softness in her hands. When hanging laundry on the line, he was the cool breeze that caressed her. His smile was reflected in the eyes of every baby, and his voice was in her own soft breath when she was between wakefulness and sleep.

She stood behind the table, serving food. This time she was serving slices of ham next to Ida May, who handed out grilled chicken with one hand. The other she had at her back, balancing her large belly. She was due to have a baby in a matter of weeks. It seemed no one wanted Miriam's ham as they passed her by without notice, choosing Ida May's chicken instead.

"Ach, it seems no one has the taste for ham today," Miriam commented, leaning over to Ida May.

Ida May's smile wavered and didn't reach her eyes. "I guess so," she responded, equally quiet.

Her reaction made Miriam furrow her brow. Ida May's usual boisterous personality seemed to have disappeared. Miriam's eyes trailed down to her cousin's large protruding belly. Ida May was just tired. Miriam's heart twisted. Would this ever be her? Had she followed through with her plan to elope, would they have been able to consummate their marriage, and could she have conceived so quickly? She felt her body grow warm with the thought of that kind of intimacy with Henry. Did she want to marry him merely to become a mother? If that were the case, why didn't she just marry Eli?

No.

She wanted to marry Henry because she loved him. No doubts. But the reality was that she had left him waiting at the courthouse and he hadn't contacted her since.

She couldn't blame him, naturally.

"Miriam, don't you know?" Ida May's voice cut through her melancholy.

"What?"

"Everyone knows." Ida May was speaking in such a low whisper Miriam could barely decipher her words.

"Knows what?" Her voice cut her own tongue with its edge.

"Everyone knows what happened." Ida May's hand squeezed around Miriam's arm and pulled her away from the serving table. Their eyes met. "Everyone knows what happened between you and Henry and your *Mem.* Did you think you could keep such big news a secret? Come on, Miriam, you know how news travels."

Miriam's mind flashed back to how empty the church bench had been around her and her mother. Fannie had been whispering to her group of friends. It occurred to her that she had not been invited out to the quilting the week before, though she'd passed it off as an oversight. Then Mark and Barb's baby Jonas was born, and she hadn't been asked to be the maid. She heard that Fannie's oldest daughter had stayed for a few days and the baby cried continuously. All of these small details trained her focus. It all could mean only one thing.

"Excuse me," she said. She leaned over and dropped her fork in the hill of ham and walked away from the serving table.

Her shoulders hit several men as she sought the door. She winced when a baby's cry sharply entered her ears. Her hand curled around the wooden screen door, its screech a welcomed noise. Long strides turned into running through the great backyard, past the large red barn. Her breathing was ragged.

The air blew through her *kapp* and the ties danced. Her eyes grazed over the field in front of her, and she let her lids close. She needed to feel God talking with her, and the stifling constant stir of people made her insides scream. If she was going to hear God at all, it couldn't be amidst the noise. Before now, had she given God more than a moment's thought? Her guilt spoke — yelled — so loudly inside of her. Wasn't that God? Wasn't He the guilt within her?

A voice echoed repeatedly into the soft rolling land. It wasn't until her hands were green with stain that she realized she was on her knees in the grass, weeping. Her own voice traveled in the wind. A wave of embarrassment traveled through her, and she righted herself, brushing away any signs of her caving to weakness. She dared not turn around to see if anyone had witnessed the scene, though part of her didn't care anymore. She had put so much effort toward doing what she was told was right. Wasn't it enough that she had missed her chance to marry Henry in order to remain faithful to her responsibilities? Still, the community — her friends — were avoiding interactions with her. What was next — a talk with the *Aumah Deanuh*, the head deacon?

"Well, half the house inside heard you, in case you wanted to know." Eli strode up with his usual arrogance. "Feel better?"

"Yes, actually, I do. And I don't care who saw me," she half lied. "I'm so —"

"You're so sad that you didn't marry your soldier-boy." Eli's voice lilted and rang like a joke. "You're scared that your Yankee Doodle Dandy's going to get shot, and you missed your chance at becoming his widow?"

Whack! Miriam slapped Eli's face. Her hand stung as they both stood startled.

"My love for Henry has never been a secret," she said, waving a finger at him. "I have never told you any differently. Why would anyone think that just because he enlisted, my feelings have changed? Why would the church think that I'm such a terrible person for wanting to marry the man that I love? You answer me that, Eli."

"Well, with all the necking a month ago, you could've fooled me."

"Leave me alone." Her lips snarled as she walked away from him.

Eli let out a familiar laugh. Her blood boiled.

"You sure talk big, Miriam. But I know you waffle more than you care to admit." Eli loudly tossed back burning words. "By the way, how's your *Mem*? Have you had to run any more errands since her accident?"

CHAPTER 17

August 1944

The summer not only brought on the heat outside but a heat inside of Miriam that could not be quenched. Those around her were punishing her for merely loving Henry. For the sake of her family, she had not married him when she had the chance. This was what obedience brought her? Her mother was healing well from using a special salve a woman in their community made. While this was a comfort to Miriam, the fact that her mistake with the gas and kerosene was never again spoken about fortified the guilt that had built around her heart.

Her feet stepped with surety out to the mailbox as she mailed her first letter to Henry. She pleaded for his forgiveness and told him that she would wait for him, if he would have her. Every day she would march out to the mailbox with the hope that a letter would be waiting for her. And even when weeks went by without word, she continued to write.

It was midday, and the ticking of the clock during their silent mealtime prayer was broken by the sound of the mail carrier. Her head snapped up, and she watched the mailman place a small stack of mail inside the box. The butterflies in her stomach began forcing their way up her throat. She sat on her hands and forced her head to bow. The rickety chair she sat in creaked with even small movements. Her eyes squeezed shut, and she inhaled through clenched teeth, making a raspy sound. Her father cleared his throat.

How much longer could this prayer be?

Her father cleared his throat again, louder this time, and shuffled his feet, the customary way he declared the prayer to be completed. Her parents wordlessly went about buttering bread and spooning chicken and noodles onto their plates.

"I'll be right back." Would they even notice that she had gotten up from the table?

The air was chilled and there was dampness in every gust of wind against her. It was so cold for August, but it was Delaware. The weather was known to be changeable. She picked up her pace and her hands rubbed against the goose bumps that rose on her arms. Usually a short-sleeved dress was perfect for this time of year. The two houses, hers and Fannie's, shared the rusted black-and-white tin mailbox. The door creaked open, and she flipped through the stack.

A letter for Fannie from a friend who had moved to Canada.

A bill from a buggy company in Pennsylvania. Her oldest nephew was getting his first buggy.

Her mother had three cards that were likely for her upcoming birthday.

Then, on the bottom, was a beaten-up and weathered envelope. The return address showed Henry's name. A chorus of angels sang in her ears like she had never imagined before. Tears of joy reached her eyes instead of the bitter ones she had wept for weeks, months even. Did it contain the hope of his forgiveness? Did he still love her?

Her hand carelessly stuffed the other envelopes back inside the mailbox and clasped Henry's letter to her chest. She paced herself slowly as she walked toward the house, alternately kissing and breathing in the letter and clutching it tightly. Warmth filled her against the chill of the breeze. The kerchief she wore pulled away, the pins tugging at her hair, but she didn't care enough to fix it. When the rain began dotting the earth around her, she let it fall on her upturned face.

Her feet barely touched the ground as she floated into her house. With the letter in her hand, she returned to the table. She smiled as she buttered and honeyed her bread. Honey dripped onto her hands, and childishly she licked it up while stuffing the homemade bread in her mouth. She giggled.

"I love when Andy gives us the piece of honeycomb and not just the honey," she said absently about the local beekeeper.

"Did you get a letter from Henry Mast?" her father's voice boomed, filling the kitchen.

"Yes, I did," she said, smiling and lifting her chin. "I have been writing to him for weeks, and I've been waiting for a letter in return."

"Did I not tell you that you are not to have any contact with that boy?" Her father slapped a hand on the table, causing everything on it to tremor.

"Melvin, don't get yourself too upset. Your heart, remember." Rosemary put a hand on his arm, but he yanked it away.

"She is blatantly disregarding my rules. I looked the other way when I heard that she was meeting him at night when he was visiting. She was being foolish with him right under our noses and almost married him."

"How is it that everyone knows what is my personal business?" Miriam's heart raced at the words that pushed against her father. "I am a grown woman, and I love Henry. I'm not ashamed of it, either."

"You and your young man are careless. Any number of people knew your goings-on. I thought you had put it behind you until now. Foolishness."

"It's not foolishness, *Dat,*" she said with her voice rising in excitement. "I didn't marry him because I didn't want to disappoint you both and the entire family. But that does not mean that I don't intend on marrying him when he returns. If he'll have me."

"If he'll have you? You will not lower yourself to marry such a boy. No daughter of mine is marrying a soldier."

Miriam brought her hands down onto her lap and clutched Henry's letter. How would he want her to handle this situation? He would want her to be sure of herself but also be respectful. Her eyes remained on her hands as she decided what to say.

"I'm sorry I've upset you. I am not going to lie to you about my intentions with Henry. I won't turn my back on him, not while he's at war where he could lose his life, and not when he returns." She raised her head and looked at both her mother's and her father's eyes alternately. "I am going to stand by him."

Her mother's eyes filled with tears and her father grunted. He pushed his half-eaten plate away and left the table. Miriam heard him let the screen door slam and knew he was off to be with Truman and the cows. That was always where he went when something upset him. He would try to work off his anger. But in his old age and in his frail physical condition, any work wore him out.

"Can't you understand me, *Mem*?" she said desperately. "Would you have let your parents keep you from marrying *Dat*?"

She didn't answer. She just sat there with most of her plate uneaten.

With the lunch put away and dishes washed, Miriam finally had the courage to open Henry's letter. She could see Nancy's house through the window in front of the desk in her room. An image of Henry walking up the steps into that house trailed through her mind. The last night, when he left her standing in the darkness with only the single beam of light, troubled her.

She took the letter from her apron pocket

and traced his perfect handwriting. It felt intimate to touch where he had written her name only recently. She turned the envelope over in her hand and carefully cut it open with her letter opener. The single paper inside was thin.

My Dearest Miriam,

You broke my heart. Nancy came and told me what happened and that you would not be coming, but even still I waited until the courthouse was closed. I prayed you would change your mind. Then, finally, I walked back to Nancy's. I saw you that night when you walked out in your nightgown. Your hair was long and loose in the breeze. You looked beautiful, like an angel. But I could not bring myself to go to you. Even though in my heart I think I'd already forgiven you. I can't explain why exactly, except that I know nothing but my love for you and God's love for me. I miss you and your nearness and the peace and comfort of being home.

The energy and emotions here are hard to describe. We will be heading "over there" soon. By the time you get this, I may already be on the ship. Thump and I often sit quietly together and pray. Our prayers comfort me. But sometimes I get lost in thought in the midst of the crowded hustle of men and machines as we prepare to head into the unknown. Some of the guys, like Johnny, seem to be excited about the prospects of killing but I've never been so scared. Thump and I have memorized Psalm 9:10. I know the Lord will not leave me.

Of course, you are forgiven. Will you wait for me? But, most of all will you pray for me?

I love you,
Your soldier, Henry

It comforted Miriam to know that he still loved her. His pleading for prayer, however, turned her heart into clay, molding itself around the fear that had taken residence next to it. His words stood with a confidence in God but shook with a distress that frightened her.

Prayers from her memory charged through her.

. . . fill our hearts with heavenly comfort and joy, so that we may be cheerful and satisfied under all circumstances . . .

Thou has taught us that we are nothing of ourselves.

Help us to overcome our own sinful nature,

268

as well as the world and the evil spirits.

The words soaked into her mind as she silently spoke the prayers. She'd never spoken these words aloud alone, only amidst the voices of the church. Truthfully, she'd never spoken any prayer aloud. She was just a single voice. Would God hear her with the loud world around her?

CHAPTER 18

August 1944

Dearest Miriam,

I never imagined I would ever have to leave you. Leaving you for CPS work was difficult enough and this is much worse. I wish I could understand why God called me to fight. Why would he want me, an Amish carpenter, to leave everything I've ever known and become a soldier? Though I can't understand this, I don't question the strength that I know only He provides.

Often, as I fall to sleep, I imagine your face in my mind. Your gray eyes that can see into my soul and your fair skin that I long to touch. Then I count the freckles across your perfect nose. You have forty-three. Yes, forty-three lovely little kisses from the sun. I'm jealous of the sun. How I miss you, my Miriam.

We ship out tomorrow. I'm scared, but I'm ready. Pray for me.

Yours,
Henry

As Miriam put the letter back in the envelope, she noticed something else inside. It was a picture of Henry. It was just like the pictures of James and Vic that Nancy had framed, only it was small enough to fit in her wallet. She stroked it and smiled at his serious expression. After looking at it for several minutes, she almost thought he would wink or smile at her. She pressed it to her heart and inhaled deeply.

With the picture propped up in front of her, she wrote him. She realized her own paper supply was low and reminded herself to buy more when she was out with Kathryn to get their rations. In those moments her heart was full, and her fear was great, but she felt more enlivened than ever. She put Henry's envelope to her nose, taking in the scent of the paper, and then pressed it against her cheek. Henry's hand had held it, and now, this was his way of holding her. She read the letter again, along with the first one, before storing them secretly under the floorboards.

"Miriam," she heard Fannie calling from

downstairs, "we need to go."

Miriam stuffed the envelope in her packed overnight bag. Ida May had delivered her baby, a boy they'd named Jesse Junior. She was going over to help for a few days, as they'd always planned. Ida May's mother had young children of her own, and Miriam would be able to provide a great help to her friend and cousin. After carefully picking up the blueberry pie and loaf of bread to take along, she climbed into the buggy, where Fannie waited.

They arrived at Ida May's house quickly, and Miriam was glad. Her relationship with Fannie was steadily declining. As the oldest child in their family, Fannie had always been opinionated, direct, and downright bossy. She often treated all the younger ones more like children than siblings. Miriam usually didn't mind, but when it came to Henry, her emotions ran sensitive and deep.

"Come on in, Fannie," Lucy May, Ida May's mother, said. "Did you bring little Irene?"

"No, the girls are watching her."

Just as she said that, three young children ran in circles in the living room. They were Ida May's youngest siblings. Lucy May was closer to Fannie's age than their own mother's age, even though they were cousins. Ida

May's youngest sibling was four and had already been an uncle for a few years.

Miriam waited patiently for Lucy May to say hello to her and offer to take her pie and bread to the kitchen, but before she knew it, the older woman was walking toward Ida May's bedroom door. She opened it, letting them in.

"Congratulations, Ida May," Fannie said, nodding. "I hope he's a good baby. None of mine ever have been."

"Well, I hope so, too." Ida May looked down at her baby as she swayed back and forth.

"Hello, Ida May, I'm finally here. I meant to get here sooner," Miriam said, forcing her way around Fannie, who stood right in her way. She put the pie and bread carefully on the dresser and her bag on the floor before approaching the bed where the new mother sat.

Ida May's face turned white. Miriam was surprised to see Bertha Miller sitting in the room. Bertha and Ida May exchanged looks, unnerving Miriam. Since when had Bertha and Ida May ever been good enough friends to exchange looks? Bertha was a little younger than them both, and they'd never been close. She'd gotten married last fall also and appeared to be due for her first child.

"Are you feeling okay?" Miriam touched Ida May's forehead with the back of her hand. "You're not hot, but you're as white as a sheet. Is Suzie coming back tonight to check on you and little Jesse?"

"I feel fine," Ida May said. "It is a little hot in here though."

Miriam opened the bedroom window. She had to stretch over Bertha, who sat at a chair near the window and didn't appear willing to move. Bertha held her chin at an arrogant angle and cleared her throat when Miriam accidentally brushed against her leg. She put both arms around her belly protectively, infuriating Miriam further.

"Well, let me get a look at little Jesse," Miriam said. She pushed away her irritated thoughts about Bertha, not wanting to take anything away from Ida May's first day as a mother.

"They aren't calling him Jesse, they are calling him Junior," Bertha said, her voice barging into Miriam's excitement over seeing her best friend's first child.

Miriam sat on the edge of the bed to catch a glimpse of the squirming baby.

"May I hold him?" Miriam felt sheepish to even ask, since Ida May had been her closest friend for nearly her whole life. "Then, I promise to get started on whatever you want me to do."

Bertha cleared her throat again, and she felt Ida May stiffen next to her.

"What's wrong, Ida?"

"I thought you knew."

"Knew what?"

"I asked Laura Miller to come stay and help." Ida May's voice was quiet and warbled nervously.

"Laura Miller?" Miriam questioned. This did not sound like Ida May. Laura was Bertha's sister-in-law and only fourteen. Miriam could run circles around her.

The silence was deafening and wrapped its muggy, hot arms around Miriam.

"Well, I didn't know that Laura Miller was hiring herself out as a maid."

"Oh, I've been hearing good things about Laura," Fannie added, and Miriam spun around to look at her sister.

Fannie knew that Laura was working for Ida May and hadn't told her? No one had told her. She shifted between hurt and anger, unsure of where her heart would land.

"She does a great job," Bertha said. "Everyone's talking about her. I am going to hire her, and I heard that Lucinda Byler and Mary Graber are both fighting for her since they are due around the same time." A smile, like a façade, formed across Bertha's face.

It was obvious to Miriam that Bertha's excitement over Laura's newfound work was purely to spite her. And why wasn't Fannie defending her? Miriam had always been the coveted maid to hire after a baby's birth. Not only was she an amazing baker and a fast worker, but she had a natural knack with babies. They attributed this to her mother's inability to bake much in recent years, leaving all the baking to Miriam, and she'd had so many brothers and sisters having babies, there was always one to nurture.

Miriam decided to change the subject. "I brought you a loaf of bread and your favorite, blueberry pie."

The uncomfortable silence wove itself like a basket between the women.

"Did your *mem* make it?" Ida May stuttered out.

"Of course not," Miriam almost laughed, "you know with her poor eyesight *Mem* can hardly bake."

Fannie, Bertha, and Ida May passed glances.

"They won't need any more food," Bertha

interjected. "Besides, Laura is excellent in the kitchen."

"But it's the crumb crust, just how you like," Miriam said weakly, picking up the pie and showing her.

"Well, I know your *dat* loves it, too." Ida May's words came out broken and no louder than a whisper. Her face was still a sickly white. "I'm sure he'll enjoy it tonight after supper."

Miriam's heart fell through her stomach. This was about Henry. She nodded in agreement to her friend, then sat in a chair in the corner. The three other women went on to talk about babies and any other gossip they could think of. The room closed in on her.

CHAPTER 19

September 1944

Miriam opened Henry's letter, overjoyed to find a small wooden heart inside. It was somewhat crudely whittled, nothing like the expertly crafted items he usually made, but he'd done this for her. She put the small piece of wood to her heart and kept it there as she read his letter.

Dearest Miriam,

We've been over here for more than a month. I cannot tell you about our arrival. I'm not sure I could ever speak of it. Having to relive it even in my mind would be too much to bear. We lost Buck already. My mind can't grasp that, but Thump reminded me that on the ship over, Buck learned of Christ's love for him, and He accepted Him as his Savior. Buck is in heaven. For that, he is better off than me. All that I see around me is hell.

Your Henry

After reading his letter several more times she placed the wooden trinket on her nightstand, wanting it near her every morning and every night. She prayed it would not be the last gift she would ever receive from him.

Miriam understood so little about the war effort and what it even meant that he was in the 80th Infantry. She felt safer in her ignorance, but as the days passed into weeks she became more curious. Whenever possible, she began spending more time with her sister at the Pooles'. Ralph was able to explain a little about how the front was moving. It was still like a foreign language to her, but knowing Ralph understood it comforted her. The radio provided only limited information, so, truthfully, the war was a mystery to the entire country.

When her parents spoke to her, which was seldom, they were kind. They asked nothing about Henry, however. Even their interaction with Kathryn was stilted during her frequent visits. She was due any day and had decided against having a hospital birth. She'd had Nan at home with the same midwife many of the Amish women used,

Suzie Kline.

When her labor quickly began early on a warm September morning, Nancy ran over, calling for Miriam. A layer of dusky mist hovered above the grass. It was quiet except for the muted sounds of her brother-in-law, Truman, and her nephews beginning their morning chores. Her arms wrapped around herself, her teeth chattered. She was still wearing her nightgown.

"Are you sure she said she wants me?" Miriam was confused as she and Nancy hustled over.

"Miriam, you're her sister and the closest friend she has right now." Nancy's voice peeled away some of the insecurity she was feeling. "You understand her better than anyone else."

Her shoulders rolled back some as she entered the house. Kathryn needed her. No one had truly needed her for so long, besides Henry. With him she often felt so helpless. But today — now — Kathryn wanted her and needed her. This great responsibility heightened her senses.

Ralph was pacing the living-room floor with his hands wrapped around a mug of coffee. His grimace was deeper than Miriam had ever seen. He paused his walking for a moment, then looked up and nodded at her, his scowl speaking volumes. His mere acknowledgment of her presence was an improvement over the months she'd been visiting, and surprisingly, the radio was turned off.

"Don't be worried, Grandpa, everything is going to be fine," Miriam said with a smile.

He grunted in response, and then continued pacing.

"She's upstairs. She and Nan stayed here last night, because she wasn't feeling well." Nancy led Miriam up the narrow, closed staircase. At the top, she could see Nan curled up sleeping. They turned to the left and found Kathryn leaning over the bed in James's boyhood room, breathing deeply. Her hair curtained her face.

"Miriam, is that you?"

"I'm here." She pulled Kathryn's hair back away from her face.

Kathryn began weeping and turned toward Miriam, collapsing against her. The weight of her body startled Miriam, and she helped her sister sit on the bed, keeping her arm around her. Her breathing was rapid as she cried harder. Her clothing was already damp all the way through, as was her hair.

"Miriam, I can't do this without James," she said between sobs. "I'm so afraid."

Miriam rubbed her back as she'd seen midwives do. *Think, Miriam, think.* She went on her knees in front of her sister and put her hands firmly on her shoulders.

"Kathryn, now listen to me," Miriam said, trying to mix tenderness with toughness. Kathryn needed both. "You need to stop crying first. Then I'm going to get you into clean clothes. I need you to listen to me."

Kathryn's red, puffy eyes met Miriam's, and she nodded and allowed Miriam to help her up. They carefully took off her nightgown and underclothes, replacing them with the only other set inside her small overnight bag. As the contractions came and went, Miriam gently helped her sway and breathe as she'd seen Fannie do with her earlier labors. With her later ones, she would do similar swaying and breathing while baking bread and pies and making meals. She said the activity kept her mind off the labor pains.

Kathryn sat on the bed between contractions, and Miriam smoothed a comb through her hair and braided the long auburn strands in a single long plait. The nostalgia of this act reminded her of the years they shared a room and how they often braided and combed each other's hair before bedtime. Their sisterhood had been so important to Miriam. Tears burned against Miriam's eyes.

"Do you remember how much we did this when we were young?" Kathryn said.

"I was just thinking about that myself."

Miriam helped Kathryn up as a pain began, and she leaned against Miriam with her hands on her shoulders. She swayed and breathed.

"This reminds me of the one time James took me dancing," Kathryn whispered. "I had never been, so I didn't know how. He just told me to hold him. So I did."

In a few hours, the contractions were strong enough to call Suzie Kline. This gave Miriam the chance to return to her house and change out of her nightgown and into a dress. Before leaving the house, she asked her mother if she wanted to come for the birth.

"I should stay." Her mother's eyes flicked over to her father, who had stopped writing his letter. His ear was leaning in toward the two women.

"Kathryn needs you." Miriam was wringing her hands.

"De Mem blapt doh." Her father insisting that her mother stay made Miriam tense.

Miriam knew better than to press the issue. She couldn't help but wonder how it had happened that her mother had attended Nan's birth. Perhaps her father had agreed in a weak moment? Or was it possible that her mother had put her foot down? That was highly unlikely. She hesitantly moved over to the door, unsure if she should say anything.

"I'll come let you know once the baby's born," she finally said, hoping it was safe enough to say.

She waited for a moment for a response, but when nothing was said, she walked into the bright sunlight. September's golden hue soaked into her face, and she imagined taking a walk with Henry. Where was he? What sky was he under?

A baby boy, James Melvin Poole, arrived before supper. He had a loud scream and a hungry belly. He looked just like his father, with a shock of bright auburn hair from his mother. Kathryn was courageous throughout the labor and crooned in her baby's ears, telling him within minutes of his birth how much his father loved him.

When baby Jamie and his mother were taking their first nap together, Miriam walked over to tell her family the news of the bouncing baby boy. Without considering the risk, she gave her mother a play-by-play of what a good job Kathryn did laboring such a large baby while knowing she didn't have a husband ready and waiting to hold the new child. Her father abruptly stood and left the house. His mood concerned Miriam, since it had seemed for months that he was accepting Kathryn back in limited ways. Her situation with Henry and poor standing with the church clearly was taking a toll on both her parents. It seemed neither she nor Kathryn was very welcome here anymore.

Dearest Miriam,

Since I don't get the chance to be alone, I imagine taking a walk through the woods behind my house. I did it so often when I was a boy. Sometimes I pretend I'm watching the sunrise again in that tree house. I always feel lonely until I see you walking toward me. Your image in my mind brings such peace to my heart. That's when I remember that I promised myself to be honest with you in my letters.

I am afraid. I am afraid that I might not be brave enough to do what God has asked me to do. What if I let my fellow soldiers down, or worse, what if I let you down?

Psalms says, "Though a host should encamp against me, my heart shall not fear: though war should rise against me, in this will I be confident." I know my hope is in the Lord, and if I am to give my life for this cause I pray I will be noble in it. I also pray that you know how much I love you, and I promise that I will do whatever I can to return to you.

Yours,
Henry

While the sun shone brightly, bringing encouragement to Miriam's heart, her shoulders suddenly carried the heaviness of the sky falling down upon her. What was holding Henry together was his love for God and for her. She would not let him down.

A buggy made its way into the drive behind Miriam as she reread Henry's letter, walking back in from the mailbox. Tears streamed down her face. During the second read, her insides moved from ice to the warmth of the daylight that wrapped around her. She walked over to the side of the yard as the buggy passed. When it stopped in front of her house and an old friend, Adam Gingrich, hopped out, she was surprised.

She squinted her eyes, furrowing her fore-head.

Why was he here?

Adam was in his thirties and handsome, with dark hair and bright blue eyes. He had been the best of friends with several of her older brothers and for years he been like another brother to her. Just over a year ago the lots had been cast, and he had been chosen to be the *Aumah Deanuh*. This made him the deacon in charge of scripture reading, service organization, and church discipline. It was difficult for Miriam to get used to the idea that a boy who had once pulled her covering ties and sneaked out with her brothers at night was now in such a crucial church position. His wife, Amanda, was a sobering woman. She looked downcast most of the time but was very respected, since she'd already given Adam five sons.

Miriam smiled and waved as she trotted up to him. He nodded and diverted his eyes.

"Hello," Miriam said, as she got closer. Concern rested on her forehead, matching Adam's. "Would you like to come in? *Mem* and *Dat* are probably awake from their nap." When he failed to respond, she continued talking. "How's Amanda?"

"Sie ist gut." While still avoiding Miriam's eyes, he confirmed that his wife was well.

"The boys keep her busy."

"Well, yes, if they are anything like you were when you were a boy," Miriam chuckled.

Adam did not. He poked at the ground with the toe of his shoe.

"Did you hear Kathryn has a baby boy? She calls him Jamie." Miriam inadvertently pointed across the street to the Pooles' home.

"No, I didn't hear." His voice faded as his gaze lingered where Miriam pointed.

"I think we have some cherry pie. I'm sure *Mem* and *Dat* will be glad to see you." She invited him in a second time but instead of waiting for a response, she turned toward the house and expected him to follow.

When Adam's hand touched her forearm, she stopped. Her heart pounded. She turned and met the young deacon's eyes.

"No one's glad to see me anymore." His hand fell to his side, and Miriam could see sorrow between the lines of his face.

She sucked in a breath. Where was the young boy who had teased her? Was he somewhere inside?

Miriam didn't know how to respond, so she only turned and walked toward the house. He followed silently. Her mother was preparing tea and didn't seem surprised at the unexpected company.

Adam took his hat off and began wringing the brim. His head dipped low as he approached Miriam's parents, and he grasped their hands with a strong single shake. By the time the other three were seated, Miriam's hands were moist with sweat and her heart was pounding. She realized that while to her the visit appeared unannounced, it wasn't. Her parents seemed prepared.

"Have a seat, Miriam," her father said unapologetically. He made a chewing motion with his mouth, something he'd started doing recently that reminded Miriam of someone really old. He was significantly older than her mother and was already in his mid-seventies.

Miriam pulled a kitchen chair out and took it into the living room. She sat on the edge of the chair, nervous. She tried to calm her heart by considering the Psalm that Henry had written in his letter. She couldn't remember the exact words but recalled that it had said something about when there was trouble around, she shouldn't be afraid but be confident in the Lord.

Only, whose side was He on? Her heart fell. She clasped her hands to keep them from shaking. She had witnessed the *Aumah Deanuh*'s visit in the past, the one before

Adam, though had heard nothing of the conversation. The vision of a girl in a yellow dress, an English dress, penetrated her mind. The girl was Kathryn, young and newly baptized. She was sitting across the table from the deacon in charge of the discipline. How frightened such a young girl must have felt! He was an old man and Miriam had peered around the staircase, frightened of his stern eyes and black birthmark that stole all the attention away from a face she could never recall exactly. Just then, she could hear her father's voice.

"Miriam," her father snapped. "Adam asked you a question."

"Oh, I'm sorry," she responded. The girl in yellow, her only friendly companion, faded from her mind. "What did you ask?"

Adam swallowed hard and appeared reluctant to repeat his question.

"Do you know why I'm here?"

She didn't know how to answer. Sure, she had an idea of why he was there. She'd openly been supporting Henry for several months. She spent most of her time with Kathryn and Nancy, and though not officially against the *Ordnung,* it didn't help when piled atop everything else. Also unconventional was her not attending the Singings anymore, which almost surely further

290

declared her allegiance to Henry. She had met with Henry in secret, even traveling into town to arrange their marriage. Was she to list all of these things? What was she supposed to say? She knew that while none of these things alone warranted a meeting with the deacon, together they spoke loudly of what was in her heart. The community would see her actions as rebellion against the church.

Her silence must have spurred on Adam's responsibility.

"Miriam, you are playing with sin by having one foot in the church and the other in the outside world." Adam's furrow was so deep and wrinkled around his forehead, he appeared decades older than he was.

"I can't just stop loving him, Adam," she said as gently as possible, knowing that words spoken in any other way could come across as defensive and disrespectful. "It's Henry. You and he are friends — or *were* friends."

"Henry is living in the outside world." Adam paused. "He's so deeply involved, there might be no hope for him. But there is still hope for you. You'll need to leave the past behind and move on."

"Move on?"

"I've learned that you don't even attend

the Singings anymore. You should really consider the opportunity for a girl like you to go to the Singings." Adam's eyes turned down. The sadness he appeared to feel for Miriam weighed like a stone in her stomach. Was he so disturbed by her actions?

"Opportunity? As in, dating?"

"It would be wise for you not to be so involved with those from the outside world more than those from our community. It is the wrong influence on you."

There was a thudding deep inside of her. She had just gotten Kathryn back. How could she turn her back on her own sister?

"Your parents are concerned and feel that if you don't make some changes, you will continue to follow in the footsteps of others who have turned away from the church."

Were her relationships with Kathryn and Henry in effect forcing her to turn her back on her parents? Could she not be loyal to all of them? The thought of losing any of these people made her stomach turn over several times. Her eyes snapped between the three in front of her. Her mother's aged gray eyes had fallen onto the handkerchief in her tightly wrung hands. For the first time, she realized that her mother's mouth was lined with more frowns than smiles. Her father's eyes appeared to resist hers, locking on something over her shoulder. His jaw caught a strained underbite.

Adam was the only one who met her eyes. The blueness of his eyes seemed the only thing left of his boyhood. He pursed his lips as their eyes closed in on each other for several long moments.

Her eyes then peered through the window across from her. She could see a reflection of herself look back. The blurred image didn't provide much more than a simple outline, forcing her features away. Suddenly the hollowness from the inside forced itself out. Miriam stood, painfully overextending her knees. The back of her chair made an angry slap against the floor.

She tried to excuse herself, only to find herself running out of the house a moment later. Her hand caught a splinter on the outhouse door a moment before she heaved everything in her stomach. She retched several times and was forced to use her apron to wipe her mouth. She leaned against the thin wooden wall and slid down until she was sitting on the floor with her knees pulled up to her chest. How had this become her world? She imagined staying in there until nightfall. She usually did everything possible not to go to the outhouse alone in the dark, afraid of what was on the other side of its blackness, but now she was sure it couldn't be worse than the darkness inside her.

She heard Adam's horse pull his buggy out of the drive about ten minutes after her escape. The sound of the horse's hooves and the large round wooden wheels grinding against the gravel took a small bit of weight away from her shoulders, enough to help her stand. How could she enter the house again? The look of disappointment she could see in her parents' faces nearly forced another heaving into the toilet.

Hard, unrelenting knuckles pounded against the outhouse door. It shuddered under the heavy hand.

"Ja, ich bin fadeach." She told the person outside that she was finished. It was unusual for anyone to knock on the outhouse door. They were all family and would just call through the door if they had an emergency.

When she opened the door, she came face to face with Fannie. She held a dish towel in one hand and a wooden spoon in the other. Though her sister's sharp expression was the only thing that struck Miriam, she imagined she could feel the sting of the wooden spoon on her backside nonetheless. Fannie must have been drying dishes when she saw Miriam run out of the house.

"Vas nah?" What now, she asked Fannie. She didn't even try to resist rolling her eyes. Fannie's scolding was getting tiresome.

"So, the *Aumah Deanuh* came to see you?" Miriam nodded.

Fannie looked around Miriam's shoulder and into the outhouse. Her eyebrows raised and her lips snarled up. The scent of her vomit seemed to weigh down the fresh September air.

"Did you vomit?"

"Yes, I did, Fannie," she said, sighing heavily.

"Don't you get snippy with me, Miriam. You were just *auh gretah,*" she said, rebuking her for the official warning Adam had given her. "This is happening too much like Kathryn, who also refused to listen to me. But you are going to listen. Do you hear me?"

Hearing the phrase *auh gretah,* a veil was lifted from Miriam's eyes. She suddenly recognized the meeting for what it was, an official warning by the head deacon. Her knees wobbled. She inhaled and held the air tightly in her expanded lungs. Her eyes blurred.

"Hock anah," Fannie said, grabbing her by the arm. Fannie pulled her, and Miriam felt the plop of her body being pushed down to

sit on the glider swing.

"Now, you listen to me. *Mem* and *Dat* can't handle going through another heartbreak like they did with Kathryn. You are playing with fire by not forgetting about that Henry and just moving on. Eli Brenneman would have you, and I'm sure there are a few other boys who would too if you just made yourself available. But you're so stuck on Henry that no one else has a chance. And for what? For a boy who left you, his family, and the church? Do you really want to marry a man like that?"

"You don't know anything about —"

"I'm not done. You're being selfish, Miriam. If you think all of this affects just you, you're wrong. If *Mem* and *Dat* end up sick or dying, it's on your shoulders. You and Kathryn think you can have it both ways, have our parents around your pinkies and the world by the tail. But you can't, Miriam. You just can't."

Fannie stomped away without giving Miriam a chance to respond. Her soul was drowning amidst her unshed tears, and her heart was burrowed deep in the dirt beneath her. She felt so distant from the world around her. She had nothing to say. What could she say? Everything her eldest sister said was true. She had no right to put her family through the pain of her rebellion. She knew that she was walking a tightrope, choosing to write Henry and support his decision when her parents were adamantly against it. But to have the church involved now, with her being *auh gretah,* officially warned; this wasn't what she wanted for her life.

She'd lost her heart again tonight, not to love, but to utter shame. The only way she would regain it would be to break another heart in the process — a heart at war that she delicately held in her hands.

CHAPTER 20

October 1944

Normal life did not resume after the meeting with the *Aumah Deanuh*. Church services were like needles being pushed into her back because of the eyes that were on her and the eyes that were turned away. Babies were born without even a thought to hiring Miriam as a maid, and she was never asked to come and greet the new babe. She wasn't even officially banned, but the bitter taste of it was heavy on her tongue.

She received a letter from someone who didn't even have the courage to sign his or her name, telling her to leave and spare her parents the agony of watching her grow in sin. Eli walked by her without saying hello. He diverted his eyes from her when they accidentally caught hers at church. She was asked not to serve the food anymore. She often ate alone on a back porch away from the community of people who were so hurt and confused by her irresponsibility.

Her parents spoke to her only when necessary and hadn't even tried to understand the war that was being fought between her mind and heart. Those she felt most loyal to through her entire life were treating her like a stranger. Her unlikely companions had become a nervous neighbor who loved unconditionally, her shunned sister, and an outcast, her almost-husband who was thousands of miles away, fighting a bloody battle. And what was he fighting to come home to? A community that pretended he didn't exist. She now only lurked in the shadows of the church. She had learned the look of the backs of her former friends and family; faces no longer existed. What choice did she have? To confess meant to forget Henry for good. The mere thought brought tremors to her hands, but the alternative forced the same reaction. She had no good options.

Jamie is growing so quickly. He has rolls on his rolls. Kathryn says that when he looks at her, it's almost as if she can see James peering through the babe's glassy blue eyes. Nan became a little mother overnight, and Nancy is overcome with joy. Since little Jamie was born in their house, I think the attachment is even greater. Even Ralph cuddles and croons at the baby, though the radio seems to be on for days at a time, without a break. We are all so worried. Are you safe while you read this letter? Are you fed? Do you have a warm place to lay your head? My dear, how I long for you to be home. I love you.

Her pencil stopped as she considered telling him about her visit from Adam and the warning from the church, but she didn't have the heart for it. She didn't want him to be concerned about anything but staying alive. She just needed him to come home and make things right so they could all move on with their lives.

Her eyes landed on the small suitcase that lay open on her bed. Two dresses and pairs of stockings were inside, neatly folded against her nightgown and night bonnet. Stationery was placed on top, along with the picture that Henry had sent to her months earlier. His face comforted her, and after soaking in his image, she closed her eyes and struggled to see him wearing a simple cotton shirt and pants with suspenders. She pictured him with his chiseled jawline and strong brows that framed his deepset eyes. His closely cut hair made her see even more how handsome he was.

Rebelliousness. The word caught her off guard and the flash of a girl in a yellow dress crossed over her mind. She looked down at herself. She wore a faded *fadauks rohk,* a chore dress, nothing she would wear to church or even out to a grocery store. She was not leaving with the same flair as her sister, remembering the swing of the yellow fabric of her skirt.

But I'm not really leaving.

She brought her focus back to the letter she was writing to Henry. She decided to tell him that she was going to be staying with Kathryn for a little while, maybe just a few weeks. She told him that Kathryn needed help with the children, which was true, but her reasons went so much further than that. Everyone needed a break from the burden of her choices. After a few weeks away, perhaps things would look better. Maybe she and her family would gain some clarity, she hoped. She gave Henry the new address and then closed the letter, folded it, and placed it in the envelope with a kiss. She put it in her purse, then closed the small suitcase that lay on her bed. Her hands shook when she put on her black cape and bonnet. Her purse weighed down her shoulder like it never had before. She took several deep breaths in and out to regain her composure before leaving her room.

It's only for a few weeks, she repeated to herself.

Each step down the stairs weakened her knees, and her suitcase grew heavier. Her courage was slipping away. She was walking into the unknown future ahead of her rather than the down same old staircase she'd descended for years.

She put her suitcase down and stood in the kitchen. She'd written a letter to her parents explaining that she would be spending a few weeks with Kathryn. She pulled the sealed envelope out from her purse. She turned it over in her hands a few times, unsure if she could really do this. A long exhale, greater than a sigh, escaped her lungs. Her mother was busy with Fannie. Would she even find the letter? Her father would likely find it first. Who would stay with her parents? Fannie's oldest daughter? Or would one of her brothers finally pitch in and send one of his daughters? Surely, someone would come. They couldn't stay on their own.

She squeezed her eyes together, knowing these were plans she should have made before making such a rash decision. A yoke of carelessness wrapped around her shoulders. How long would her burdens hold her in bondage? She didn't want to live this way.

She looked up and imagined her letters in the floorboard of her room. A shudder wracked her body, almost forcing her to go back upstairs and take them with her. She forced her feet to be firm. It would be too permanent to take them now.

I'm coming back.

She slid the white envelope onto the kitchen counter, then picked up her suitcase and walked through the mudroom. The damp October air made her bristle. Goose bumps formed on her arms. Though there wasn't a long line of church members watching her as she stood there holding the suitcase, she felt watched, observed, and judged.

With a jolt, she realized her father was walking to the mailbox. She had thought he was with Truman in the barn. He usually was. She could see he had envelopes in his hand and likely had just realized that he'd forgotten to put them in the mailbox earlier this morning. It was the routine he kept. After breakfast he would mail his letters and then go find his son-in-law and grandsons working in the barn.

How would she face him? What a coward

she was. She had hoped to do this silently, without having to look anyone in the eyes. Realizing the error of her judgment, she inhaled. If this was truly the choice she was making, she had little option. He hadn't seen her standing there, but if she hurried back up the staircase she would know for certain she was a coward.

Henry was facing gunfire and bombs. She could face her father. Couldn't she?

She watched him, her feet rooted to the ground, as he pulled out contents from the mailbox and then stuffed his late mail inside. He pushed the flag up before he looked down and thumbed through the mail. He paused for a moment and even at the distance, Miriam could see him bite his lower lip and his shoulders sag slightly. He looked up, his eyes scanning in front of him, appearing to look for nothing, until they fell on Miriam. His head cocked to one side, and Miriam inhaled. She could see his eyes move from her face to the suitcase she carried. No words would be needed; he knew exactly what she was doing. Her free hand moved to cover her mouth as a sob escaped.

Suddenly, her father grabbed his left arm and fell. A dagger moved through her gut. She dropped her suitcase and ran to his still form. With great effort, she rolled him over onto his back. The mail was already muddied by the damp dirt and gravel of the driveway. She shook him.

"Dat!" she yelled repeatedly.

She looked into his eyes and recognized the unseeing nature she saw daily in her mother's. His face was slack. Her head fell to his soundless chest. He was gone.

After her father was moved, Miriam stayed. Her knees were uncomfortable against the indention of gravel from the driveway, but it didn't matter. There were footsteps, tire tracks, and flashes of voices that remained with her, along with the mail scattered on the ground. Each envelope wore the scars of boot prints and scrapes against the stony drive. Miriam, still stunned from watching her father die, felt responsible for his death. She finally managed to gather together the pieces of mail.

She stuffed the envelopes into her apron waistband, remembering in the following moment about her own letter to her parents. Was it still on the kitchen counter where she'd left it? She twisted her ankle as she ran to the house. She grabbed her suitcase and went inside. The kitchen was filled with her nieces and nephews from next door, but it was Fannie's stone-solid expression that consumed the room. It could not be ignored. She had a hand on her mother's shoulder. *Mem* sat on a chair at the kitchen table, her face stoic and frozen.

Miriam's awkwardness in holding the suitcase drew everyone's eyes to her. Her chest was rising and falling rapidly. She was glad that no one could see her knees wobbling. Fannie's eyes met hers, and she held up the letter with her free hand. Miriam sucked in a breath.

"I was supposed to go and help Kath—" Her lungs deflated.

Nothing else was said about it while plans were made for the funeral. Fannie continued to lead the way, making all the arrangements for their father and the family. No one questioned her judgment or plans. She knew exactly which preachers should do the service and planned for her brothers to make the casket instead of the typical casket builder. She decided on the person within their community who would direct the three-day mourning that would be held at the small *daudy haus*. Fannie chose the designated family members who would be sitting with the body at all times and put herself in charge of making sure the candle next to it was always lit. The Amish never let the body lie alone or without the glow of a candle or oil lamp.

Fannie bullied her way through, making almost all the arrangements. She ruffled feathers in the ensuing days, but Miriam wondered what their family would do without her.

These days were a constant blur in Miriam's mind. It was as if she were living outside of herself. She could hear her mother and feel Fannie's condemning eyes on her, yet she did not have the sense that any of this was real. She had learned to numb the pain when Henry left for basic training, and now numbness had become a full-time feeling. She reveled in it.

The community, as typical, set aside their regular routine of life to bind the frayed pieces into a new pattern of living for the family. There wouldn't be a lot of heartfelt conversation about Melvin, but the available support and hope for the future was apparent. There would be unending and selfless work done for the family, along with support and companionship. Miriam marveled at the generosity of the community and longed to be among them herself instead of on the outside.

Fannie continued to move without hesitation, even when there were other women to pick up her duties. She still baked, cooked, and tirelessly served everyone as well. Several ladies came to help and supported Fannie's efforts, but there was no disguising who was leading. Meals were cooked and served from Fannie's kitchen to feed their entire immediate family, as well as any visitors, whether from the community or from afar. Miriam could not understand how Fannie could keep going as she usually did. All Miriam could do was stare off into nothingness and not just relive the days that were long spent but imagine the days to come. In all those days she would never be given the chance to make things right with her father. How could she live with that guilt for the rest of her life?

The traditional three-day mourning moved into the three-hour funeral service. Two preachers took their turns expounding on how to live a godly life and reminding the community that rebellion can drive you into an early grave. They both agreed in their rhythmic preaching chant that Melvin Coblentz was a faithful Amish man, but he did have two daughters who were wayward. Miriam felt Kathryn squeeze her hand and swallowed back tears. No one spoke harshly to her but graciously shook her hand and gave her the typical long-faced, mournful look. She watched with restrained sorrow as the pallbearers strapped the casket onto the flatbed buggy that would lead everyone to the gravesite.

Miriam was put into the last buggy for family members, since the buggies to follow the casket were in order from eldest to youngest. The rest of the community followed behind the family, with Kathryn also in the rear, because she was shunned. She knew she was blessed to be allowed to attend at all, so she didn't mind. As they rode on the rutted dirt roads, Miriam looked out the small buggy window. The long line of black buggies appeared like ants trailing after one another. She'd seen the image many times over the years for funerals, but it never ceased to make her heart swell with pride. They were a community who mourned together. Everyone helped everyone else. Nobody was left on the sidelines. Even she had gained more sympathetic looks from friends than she deserved.

Miriam's eyes squinted at the sun as she turned to look up ahead. After getting out of the buggy, she followed the crowd toward the graveyard that sat on a small hill. The glare from the sun forced her eyes shut. Why did the sun need to be so bright on a day such as this? Shouldn't it be raining, or shouldn't the sky at least be gray? Her eyes fell upon her black shawl and dress. Her heart sagged in her chest and took the weight of each beat with dread. The muscles in her legs felt the rise of the hill as she considered what the next day would bring. By then her father would be buried, and life was supposed to be continuing. What did that even mean?

One of the preachers prayed. Miriam listened to every word, pleading for comfort from the guilt that wrapped around her heart.

"Strengthen us in Your power. Assist us so we may resist the devil. Keep us from the world. Help us overcome our own sinful nature. Precious Holy One, give us the grace to be prepared every hour to leave this sinful world and enter the joy of Your presence.

"And finally, Holy Father, when our last and final arrives, provide us the power to finish our fight of faith in Your honor and glory, so we may win our awaiting reward. Till that day, may we look forward to the glorious return of Your Son, Jesus Christ our Lord. Thank You for redeeming us through the power of His blood, Amen."

Am I redeemed? Am I really forgiven? The thought lingered in Miriam's mind.

The grave that was dug invited Miriam to dive in and cover herself up with the cold dirt and hide away. Would anyone notice? The casket was moved from the flatbed to two sawhorses near the grave. The pallbearers unscrewed the top of the casket one last time for the immediate family's final goodbyes. Miriam stood back and waited for her turn. Everything usually went in order of age, unless you were shunned; then you went last. As the brother ahead of Kathryn passed by the casket with his wife and children, she felt a light nudge on her back and turned to find Kathryn.

"Go ahead, Miriam," she said with weepy eyes, "I'll go after you."

Miriam's head turned back to the casket. It was plain wood, strong and solid. The crowd was set apart from the casket; no one stood nearby. Could she make her last goodbye alone? The vision of Henry standing next to her, holding her hand, came to her mind. He was so far away. He didn't even know that her father was dead. He didn't know that her heart crumbled a little at a time every minute. She needed him now more than ever. The grass knitted around her black shoes, holding her in place. She was paralyzed.

"Miriam?" Kathryn touched her elbow.

"Are you okay?"

Without saying a word, Miriam grasped Kathryn's hand and took a step, but Kathryn's feet were immobile. Miriam turned to look at her older sister. She was wearing a black pillbox hat and her hair was styled simply, pinned back much like Miriam's beneath her covering. She noticed for the first time that day that Kathryn had even gone without rouge and lipstick. The face of her sister from years gone by was staring back at her.

"Please, come with me. I can't do this alone," she pleaded in a whisper.

"I'm supposed to wait." Her eyes were glassy.

"We don't have anyone but each other. Please."

Kathryn bit her lower lip, a nervous trait that many in the family had, then clutched Miriam's hand tighter and took a step. They linked arms as they walked the few more steps up to the casket. Their hold on each other tightened as Kathryn wept for their father. Miriam reached out and touched the suit that she had so often carefully ironed. She couldn't bear to touch his cold skin, wanting to keep the memory of his once warm body. Her tears choked her, but she could not let them fall.

"I love you, *Dat*," Kathryn said. "I won't forget all the lessons you taught me."

Miriam's eyes fell on her sister, who was looking on their father so lovingly. She could find nothing in her expression that begrudged the shunning she was under. Tears streaked down her face and landed in the crease of her nude lips. She could see in every action Kathryn took that she was a woman of character, and Miriam wished she could be like her.

"Tell him, Miriam," she said, sniffing but keeping her eyes on their father's face. "You need to tell him, so you can move on."

"I don't know how."

"Just pretend he's asleep."

Tears burned her eyes. Could she let them fall? She'd only let her emotions break through when she was alone, afraid of completely losing control in front of others. She swallowed, forcing her eyes dry. Her head shook as if breaking away from the tent of sadness that hovered over her.

"I can't," she whispered.

Kathryn's body shifted from a heavy sigh. Her sister placed her fingers on their father's cheek and told him she loved him once more. She took a step away, pulling Miriam with her. She wasn't ready to go, but with one more look at her father, she followed

Kathryn back into the crowd of family. She watched the pallbearers return the top portion of the casket, lower it into the ground, and start moving dirt on top of it. Each shovel of dirt made a hollow jolt against the wood below. Her heart shuddered each time. When the sound became round and dull, she knew dirt was falling on dirt and her father was really gone.

The mournful day was a new square in the quilt of Miriam's life. This new block was being patterned against fabric from the past. As a needle would weave in and through fabric, up and down, she felt the pain of piecing the new reality against the old. It was reality, however, and the weight of guilt was heavy on Miriam. Was Fannie right, had her rebellion been the cause of her father's heart attack? Had God chosen to discipline her father for her misdeeds?

A week later, she hesitantly walked to the mailbox. The disappointment of not receiving any news from Henry broke her heart daily. She pulled three envelopes from the mailbox and took a deep breath before looking at them.

One was from her brother who lived in Iowa. The second appeared to be a doctor's bill. The third forced her stomach to cave in. It was a letter addressed to her father from Henry. *Her* Henry. The contents hidden within were a mystery. Miriam's eyes followed the familiar handwriting. Her heart fell on the gravel where she stood. Henry had written to her father.

She rushed to her room and to her desk. She held the letter like a weight in her hands, nervous to open it. The sound of the envelope being torn open hit her ears in the quiet dimness of her room. Her hands shook, and she dropped the letter opener.

Dear Melvin,
 I greet you in the name of our Savior. I pray for your health and that of your family. May the Lord shine His light upon you.
 Thank you for your honesty with me in your letter.

Miriam inhaled. Her father had written to Henry?

 I am unsure of how to answer you, though I felt you deserved a response as soon as I was able to write. I understand why you would like me to end my relationship with Miriam. It is very difficult for me to consider, despite my respect for you as her father. I will take this matter in serious prayer to the Lord. He will provide me with the answers I need. I assure you that however He leads me, I will follow.

Sincerely,
Henry

Miriam shook her head as the letter fell from her hands. How could such words fall silently when they screamed so loudly in her ears? The truth that her father had written Henry insisting that he leave her alone was difficult to swallow. Henry's response was so very Henry; he would pray over the matter. Why did that frighten her so? What if he heard from the Lord that her father was right? What if after everything, he decided to move on without her? What if she never saw him again?

She picked up the letter and her eyes went to the corner of the paper. It was dated a month ago. It suddenly occurred to her that she hadn't heard from him in two weeks. In a rush she moved to the floor, opening up the floorboard to the mass of letters. Without caring how she disturbed the stacks, she pulled out the most recent letter and tore it from its envelope. The last letter she'd received from Henry was a few days older than the one he'd written to her father. She hadn't received a letter since. What if her father had changed Henry's mind? Or, worse, what if Henry was already dead?

Her eyes squeezed shut. The image of the prayer book broke into her thoughts, but she couldn't make out any of the words on the page. All those years of memorizing and nothing came to her mind. The words weren't the only thing that escaped her. The very sense that anyone, even God, was with her in the moment had vanished. The consciousness of her desperation squeezed the breath out of her.

She jumped up from the floor and into the chair by her desk. She riffled through the drawer where she kept her paper. Her fingers stung with the slice of paper against her skin. She winced as she slapped the paper onto the desk. Her hands continued to shake as she pulled out a pencil, breaking the tip as she tried to write.

Her grip loosened on the pencil, and she let it fall out of her hand. It hit the desk and rolled off the edge. Miriam took a deep breath in to calm herself. Her eyes glanced over at Nancy's house. Would it be easier to just walk away from this life? Just start over. Kathryn was at peace with her choices and her life. Though she missed her husband dreadfully, she carried a clear confidence that Miriam couldn't understand.

Laughter from her nieces and nephews running around chasing each other in the yard below her caught her attention. They were children from several of her siblings, all cousins, all so comfortable with each other. Would Nan ever be accepted as one of them? Did it matter that she spoke their dialect perfectly, or would her outward appearance and the church she attended keep her apart? Was it fair to put children in a position to be outsiders among cousins and even grandparents? Though her heart would still clearly choose Henry, she felt her eyes roam the clouds, wondering if God in heaven at this moment was telling him otherwise. To let her go. To agree with her deceased father, that he was no longer good for her.

Her breath quickened. To whom could she go? She could not run to Nancy and expect her to fix it with cookies and tea. Kathryn's peace was beyond Miriam. There was no one else. Her knees hit the floor and her face fell against the wooden seat of her chair.

"God! God!" she yelled. Her fingernails dug into her skin as her hands balled together. "Why are you doing this? Why?"

Her cries scratched against her throat,

clawing it raw. Her sobs echoed in the corners of the room. Loudly they bounced back, piercing her ears. After several long minutes her breathing became more regular, and the air was lighter around her. Her body relaxed. A whisper spoke in her ears.

Miriam, what are you doing?

The words were so clear in her mind, she paused from her grieving. The words were familiar, and her eyes landed on the open letter near her.

The letter from Henry she had opened lay nearby. Her arm stretched out slowly and she picked up the paper. She sat up straighter and scanned the letter, finding the words that were such a comfort to her.

Thump and I have been reading about Elijah and are comforted by how God never left him. He ran away into the wilderness but God was there with him. But Elijah couldn't find Him. He wasn't in the powerful earthquake or fire but only in the still small voice. In a whisper. He needed to be still in order to recognize God's voice and hear His instructions. And when he did, God shared with him what he was to do. Now, even though there's chaos around me and peace is so far away, I strive to keep my

319

heart still so I will recognize God's whisper, and I won't miss His plans for me, no matter what they are.

Written in Henry's scrolled handwriting, the words sunk into her mind and slowly wrapped around her heart. Was Henry's letter God's way of being there with her in those moments? Henry was ready for God's plan, no matter what it might be. Her gaze moved upward and she could even sense the clouds and blue sky beyond the ceiling.

"I'm ready to be still."

CHAPTER 21

November 1944

The crisp dead leaves ushered in the end of autumn. In the cold morning even when the sun was shining, the smell of snow floated through the air. People stopped coming around to pay respects to Rosemary Coblentz over her husband's death. Fannie's older sons took over the small chores his grandfather had left behind. It was almost as if he had never been there. No one spoke of him anymore even though bills still arrived in his name.

As commonly occurred, as a soul left the world, another would soon be arriving. Fannie was expecting again, though her figure didn't change between babies anymore. There was a mere passing conversation that made it clear she was due sometime in May. While no one said anything, Miriam expected that if the baby was a boy, his name would be Melvin out of respect.

She did have another nephew in his teens named Melvin, as well as one who lived far away, in Iowa, also named after his grandfather. He was about eight or nine. Having a third Melvin wouldn't be unheard of.

Miriam had continued to avoid all interaction with the other singles, retreating either quietly to her room while her mother spent most of her wakeful time at Fannie's or spending time with Kathryn at Nancy's house. She never did make it over to Kathryn's home to help with the children, but her sister spent most of her time with Nancy. They kept a constant vigil for James, the Pooles' other son, Vic, and Henry.

Miriam held a hot mug of tea in her hands as she sat at her father's old desk near the woodstove. She was reading the letters her mother had recently received from distant family. Fannie's daughters had been assigned to handwrite their grandmother's letters for her. It seemed that with the shock of Melvin's death, Rosemary's sight had worsened yet again. She saw little more than shadows and glimmers of light now.

A knock at the door woke Miriam out of her solitude. She placed her tea on the kitchen table as she went to answer it. The window through the front door framed a bleak view, with Eli's face in the center. His eyes showed a kindness that Miriam hadn't seen in months. Since their altercation after church in the springtime, they'd avoided one another. He had been dating Henry's sister Sylvia ever since, and seemed more settled than she'd ever seen him.

"Eli?" She opened the door and stepped outside with him.

There was a sudden comfort in standing next to a friend from her past. It was the world she was still a part of, even though she was more separate than ever. He appeared nervous as he shuffled his feet, which surprised Miriam. When had he ever been anxious in anyone's presence?

"Hi, Miriam." His eyes met hers with gentleness.

She was pleased to see a glimmer of a smile on his face. She noticed he held a paper bag in one hand.

"What brings you by?"

He handed Miriam the brown bag, and she opened it up, pulling out a pieced quilt. It had all her favorite shades of green, blue, and yellow. She recalled admiring it when she was helping with the twins. The fabrics were patterned exactly how she would piece them, if she were good with detailed work like that. Her eyebrows laced as she felt the unfinished quilt between her fingers.

"Ich faschtay net?" She told Eli that she didn't understand.

"Mem wanted you to have it." His voice warmed the air around them. "She remembered how much you liked it. She had planned on finishing it and giving it as a wedding present to you — someday. But . . ."

"But what?" Miriam matched Eli's softness.

."But with — everything . . ." He shrugged a shoulder. "She was afraid . . ."

"She was afraid she wouldn't have the chance to give it to me because of Henry. And that maybe I wouldn't be getting married here — or at all."

She paused for a long moment, considering what to say. Such kindness stunned her.

"I can't tell you how much this means to me." She looked into his eyes.

The two were silent, holding each other's gaze. A steady, cool breeze brushed against the ground, pushing the dead leaves, the quiet rasp the only interruption to the stillness around them.

Miriam looked inside the brown bag again. The gift spoke to her heart, as did Eli's matured demeanor. Perhaps Sylvia Mast's influence over him was helping him change his ways.

"How is he?" Eli broke the silence. "Henry. How's he doing?"

Self-righteousness hit Miriam like a gust of wind. Eli had no right to suddenly be concerned about the friend he'd abandoned. Her eyes were still on the bag with the quilt, her fist clenched around the sewn pieces like a silent scream.

"I know I have been a terrible friend, Miriam," he continued, "to you, to Henry. I can't tell you how sorry I am — for everything."

Miriam's eyes snapped up to meet his. He was serious. He meant what he said. Maybe he did care about what happened to Henry. Or was he doing this just to get back into her good graces?

"I don't know how he is." The words fell out of her mouth before she had the chance to pull them back. "I haven't heard from him in well over a month. I don't even think he knows what happened with *Dat.* I don't even know if he's —"

"Don't talk like that." Eli voice grew intense, and his hand touched hers. "He'll be back."

Their eyes held one another's for another long moment. Miriam wanted to ask him so many questions. Where had this new Eli come from? Why was he reaching out now, after so many months of ignoring her?

"How do you know?" She knew he didn't — he couldn't — but his confidence would maybe breed some in her.

He shrugged and kept his eyes steady on Miriam's.

"He has the best reason in the world to come back." His voice was husky, and he suddenly diverted his eyes.

The air warmed around them.

"I'd better go."

"Please don't." Her words surprised her. She took a step toward him. "I've — I've missed you."

His lips posed in a provocative grin. They both laughed for a moment, and then the seriousness of their meeting heaved one last blow.

"I really did love you, Miriam. I never meant to hurt you," Eli whispered.

"Eli —" Like a worn path, her brow furrowed.

"I know you love Henry." He sighed heavily but he smiled.

"What about Sylvia? I thought the two of you were . . ."

Miriam's voice faded, unsure of what to label the couple. His Adam's apple bobbed dramatically as he swallowed. Her heart was tender toward him. Even if he loved her only half as much as she loved Henry, she knew his pain was real.

"I'll be seein' you, Miriam," he said. His shoulders were hunched low as he shuffled to his buggy. A part of Miriam wanted to follow and do anything she could to relieve his sadness. Knowing the pain she herself was in, her tolerance in seeing it in others was low. There was no way she could do this for him, however, not without forsaking her real love. Eli would have to work out his path, as she was doing. He would need to find his own whisper from God, as she was determined to do.

Her covering ties blew in the wind and against her face as she watched him leave in the buggy. Less than a week later, she heard that Eli had been drafted. Before she had the chance to even see him, he was whisked off to a CPS camp far away. The community was shaken with another young man gone, and for it to be one of the most popular . . . There would be great trepidation over the influence he would have as he served and returned. If he returned at all.

Eli's leaving brought a cold spell to the community that compounded the effect of the winter weather. The thought of a joyful Christmas turned Miriam's stomach. It had been over two months now since she had heard from Henry. The prospect that he was dead smothered her. Surely if he were wounded he would have gotten word to her. She knew there was what the Pooles called protocol when a soldier was wounded or killed. Typically the next of kin would receive a telegram through a Western Union messenger. Surely, Henry's family would have told her if they'd received such news. When she wanted to cry, she prayed. When she longed for his letters, she would reread his old ones. She continued to write him several times a week. All the while, the only people who understood her anxiety were the Pooles and Kathryn. They, too, waited.

Across the road, Kathryn's car pulled into the driveway. The horn sounded for several long seconds, prompting Miriam to drop the potatoes she was peeling and go to to the window. The horn stopped, and Kathryn fell out of the driver's-side door. The exhaust from the rear of the car showed that it was still running.

What was happening?

Miriam threw on her coat and headscarf and rushed out into the knee-deep snow. Ralph and Nancy reached Kathryn first. Miriam couldn't see Kathryn, who had stumbled on the snowy ground, but when she heard Nancy wail, she knew. Kathryn had received word.

James was dead.

The news that James had been killed in action struck the family with a force they couldn't have anticipated. A son, husband, and father — dead; Kathryn was a widow. The children were fatherless. Ralph's large, weathered hands covered his face as he wept; Miriam released another round of her own tears.

The hours to follow moved like long days. Nan wouldn't leave Kathryn's side, and Ralph wouldn't leave Nancy's, his strong arm remaining gripped around his wife's shoulders. Kathryn or Nancy alternately held baby Jamie, who was oblivious to the state of his world. All Miriam knew to do was to cook and clean. So that's what she would try to do for as long as they needed her.

After several hours of mourning, Ralph began making phone calls. In the meantime, Miriam had made simple sandwiches and had let Fannie know of James's death. Miriam was amazed when Fannie brought over a hot dish, and over the next two days almost a dozen Amish families made their way to the house to pay their respects and drop off a dish of food or bread or even pie.

Over half of the families were her and Kathryn's own siblings or cousins. All the sisters who visited cried with Kathryn, except for Fannie. They'd also shown Miriam sympathy in the midst of the tragedy. Perhaps all of them were thinking the same thought: Henry was next. If James Poole died — tough, large, strong, determined James Poole — how would sensitive, thoughtful, compassionate Henry survive?

After two days of wearing the same clothes, having no time alone, and watching her sister walk through the depths of a hell on earth, Miriam finally returned to her home.

"Miriam?" There was a tenderness in her mother's voice that hugged Miriam's soul.

"Yes, I'm here," she said and sighed. She walked up to her mother and knelt in front of her rocking chair and cupped her hands over the aging wrinkled ones. Her mother's hands at first stiffened with the uncommon gesture before they relaxed under Miriam's touch.

"How's Kathryn?" The old woman's brow furrowed and her head tilted. Her eyes looked through Miriam's own, never finding an anchor.

"A little better than yesterday." Her voice was weak, but for the first time in months, she felt unrestrained in front of her mother and relished the comfort in it. "She has a strength I cannot explain, *Mem.* She's hurting, and there are times she seems to just stare off, and I wonder if she's thinking of the past she had with James or her entire future without him."

A heavy sigh escaped Miriam's mouth. Her mother's mouth turned down and her chin quaked. Suddenly, she gripped Miriam's hands tighter than before.

"I had your father for over fifty years." Her voice warmed in reminiscing as her eyes landed where his chair sat empty. The old woman reached a hand out, and after missing the first time, grasped the arm of her husband's chair on the second try. "I lost him as an old man after a house full of kids and grandkids. I wasn't ready to see him go, but I also feel very blessed that God gave us a long life together. So many years . . ."

Her voice faded away, and she brought her hand back to her lap and on top of Miriam's. She could see in her mother's eyes that she was thinking of how to go on.

"Poor Kathryn had so few years. Such a young man, young children — a young wife." She brushed a tear from her eyes. "I know God knows best, but these are the times where I can't help but question why."

Several trails of tears rippled down her wrinkled face. Her back hunched over and she wept into Miriam's chest.

"And poor Nancy," she eventually continued, surprising Miriam. Her mother hadn't spoken so many words to Miriam in months. "It's unnatural for a child to go before his parents. Just doesn't seem right."

"Will you come to the memorial tomorrow? I know Kathryn would appreciate you being there." Miriam inhaled.

Rosemary's head sunk to her chest and shook.

"I can't," she whispered. "I'm sorry. But I'll go over to Nancy's when you all return. Maybe I can hold Jamie for a little while."

Miriam patted her mother's hands. She understood her mother would not want to give the impression of anything questionable, such as attending a soldier's funeral. It wouldn't be wrong of her, but it would stir up talk that she knew would be difficult for an elderly widow to handle. She felt bad for her mother, knowing her heart wanted to be with Kathryn. "I think she'd love that."

All she could think about for the rest of the evening was how nervous she was to attend James's memorial. It was being held in the Baptist church that Kathryn and the Pooles attended. She'd never been in a real church building or to an English memorial. Ralph said it would be sparsely attended, because the weather was very poor for traveling relatives. A military chaplain was planning to give a eulogy to James, and the church ladies offered to put together a small reception for them.

On the morning of the funeral, Miriam woke to a freezing chill that pressed against her as she lay in bed. Frost streaked the windowpanes like icy fingers trying to pull her through into the frozen world. She pulled the quilt tighter to her chin and curled her legs up to conserve her warmth. Her eyes landed on the wooden strawberries in a bowl that Henry had whittled. Recalling how that summer strawberries had been difficult to come by, she craved them even more. Her mouth couldn't help but curve into a smile. Strawberries in winter; she could almost taste them. Next to it sat the small rugged wooden heart.

Where are you, Henry? Come back to me.

She dressed carefully that morning. She would be the only Amish person at the funeral and she wanted to be sure everything was in place. Her black dress felt too familiar on her willowy frame. She made her way down to help make her mother's breakfast, but Miriam herself couldn't eat.

Her stomach coiled and recoiled.

She rode with the Pooles and offered to hold Jamie, hoping the distraction of the baby would help her nerves. Kathryn gladly handed him over since Nan needed more of her attention over the next few hours. The little girl was stoic as a statue. Her lively and cheerful ways seemed to be a distant memory.

Jamie's smiles and charming blue eyes offered Miriam a measure of comfort. By the time the car lulled to a stop in the church parking lot, his eyes drooped, and Miriam wondered what it would be like to be free from the pain of the day. Would she soon have her own day, similar to this? Though all she had was a billfold-sized picture of Henry, and not a large one like the photo Kathryn was having displayed in the front of the church. And she wasn't Henry's wife. She'd left him at the courthouse waiting. A stab of pain circled in her heart. How could she have done that?

As they walked into the church, Miriam couldn't help but take in the scene. A small room for coats and what looked like the pastor's office were off to the left. As they hung their coats, only the dull ting-ting of the metal hangers against the metal rod could be heard. Everyone was silent, even baby Jamie, as they moved farther into the church. The flat carpet was navy blue with flecks in a paler blue. The walls were a plain white. A long bench with a back, unlike the backless Amish church benches, lined the wall. She heard someone call it a pew.

Ralph led the group to the left, into the main part of the church. Miriam wasn't sure what the English called it. It was full of the same pew-style benches and carpet, but her eyes immediately swept over the tall, steepled ceiling in a natural wood. It curved beautifully around the height of the building. Her eyes then fell on the stained-glass window in the front: the vivid picture of a cross. The winter sun beamed through the top of the cross, shedding light on the pulpit. For a split second, she basked in the beauty of the church and envied every person who attended. How would it be to arrive every week to such beauty that was specifically designed for Christ and His followers?

A low rumble caught her attention. She turned and realized that the church was already half full. Several people smiled tenderly at her, and no one was staring in a way that bothered her. She was not accustomed to being around such a crowd of English people. Her head spun back around

335

as she saw Nancy take a framed photo from Kathryn and place it on a front table. She placed three other framed photos of James taken over the years. The first was a baby photo. In the second one, he wore shorts and smiled with a toothless grin. He was a teenager sitting in a truck with Ralph in the third. She remembered the Pooles' blue truck and how Jamie and Vic learned to drive it, and the racket that it made across the road. The recollection of wishing she could learn to drive flashed through her mind. She pushed it away, feeling guilty for thinking of anything but the funeral.

Funeral.

Kathryn, her sister, was a widow.

CHAPTER 22

December 1944

The old superstition that deaths came in threes prodded her anxiety. Her father and James had already left the world. Would Henry be next? Would she hear about it today? Tomorrow? Next week? Would there ever be an end to the agony that held her heart captive? The guilt for having not married him when she had the chance weighed heavily on her. She told no one of her regret. Kathryn was the only person who would understand, and she was in the midst of coping with her own crisis. It would be unfair to burden her with more.

In an effort to fill the void from not hearing from him, she reread one of his last letters.

Know that you are forgiven. I never should have asked you to marry me in such a rush. I understand now why you couldn't. Know that leaving you was the hardest thing I have ever done, but having your love makes everything else bearable. I will be brave and when my time comes . . . I will be ready to die knowing that I was serving my God and country. I will be ready, knowing that I have loved you.

The same wave of fear she got when she read it the first time washed over her. How could he say he would be ready to die? He couldn't say that. She recalled writing him back and fairly scolding him, reminding him that he needed to return to her and that it wasn't his time to die. Then after that, she apologized for her admonishment and told him that, if she could do it over again, she would marry him in her nightgown if she had to. Would she live with this regret for the rest of her life?

An early December wedding had brought Miriam out of hiding. The community had pretended not to be shocked by the announcement that Sylvia Mast would be marrying Mark Brenneman, Eli's younger brother. He was handsome, yet a slightly smaller, less charming version of Eli. Mark was a good, quiet, and humble young man. Miriam believed he would make an excellent husband, and the rest of the community likely agreed. Miriam knew, however, that the question on everyone's mind was whether he would be able to handle Sylvia, and what had been the rush for them to marry? Mark was twenty-one and Sylvia was nineteen; waiting until spring should not have been a great problem.

While the suspicion of their quick marriage lingered, the last thing Miriam wanted to do was cast any more negative attention upon the Mast family. After harboring so much guilt over Henry's rebellion, she could think to do nothing but provide some encouragement.

The snow whitened the ground and everything it could land on. It was so heavy and thick on a Sunday morning that nobody ventured out for church. Snow rarely kept people away, but it was dangerous for buggies to be out on the icy roads with motorized vehicles. The day would be spent quietly, of course. Rosemary didn't even walk over to Fannie's home. She remained contentedly rocking and napping off and on in her chair. Miriam had already finished her baking for church, but since it was canceled she decided to take over a pie or two to the Pooles after lunch. They had more than enough.

Kathryn had moved in with the Pooles just before Christmas. She had gotten a job, but it did not provide enough income to keep her home. Ralph and Nancy insisted on the new arrangement and on taking care of the children when she worked. She was on the cleaning staff of the hospital. She eventually wanted to go on to become a nurse but needed to save some money before she could start school. Even though it was just a cleaning job, Kathryn was becoming more independent and serious about her future, which made Miriam so proud. There was something about the new Kathryn that she envied: her independence and strength. Miriam imagined what it would be like to go to school to be a nurse, and her heart thudded with just the thought. It wasn't for her. All she had ever wanted was to be a wife and mother.

She'd barely made it over to her neighbors in the blustering wind when her sister bounded down the stairs in her cleaning uniform. Her hair was pinned up under a hat. It reminded Miriam of old times. Kathryn rarely pinned her hair up, as she liked to let her auburn waves move freely, but now she looked more like the Kathryn she remembered, minus the red lipstick she still wore. Her grieving seemed to come in waves, but she always pulled herself up and continued to be the strong woman Miriam admired.

"Off to work in this?" Nancy complained.

"Hospital still needs to be cleaned," she said. "Don't you worry, I'll be fine."

"Don't ask me not to worry, Kathryn." Nancy went quickly to the kitchen and began pouring hot soup into a thermos. "Give me just a minute, and I'll add some bread and coffee to this."

Kathryn smiled at Miriam. "She doesn't let me do anything for myself anymore."

"It's nice, though, isn't it?"

"Better than nice." Kathryn's old smile zinged across her face. "I am finally seeing that there may be life after James. But Ralph and Nancy will always be like parents to me, no matter what."

A knock at the door startled everyone. The three women looked at each other and then each turned to look at Ralph. No one answered knocks anymore but him. It was too frightening to find what might be on the other side of the door. Vic hadn't been accounted for in too many weeks.

Ralph cleared his throat and made large strides toward the door. He stood in the doorway, blocking the cold air and snow blowing and also the visitor that stood there. Miriam heard him invite the person inside for coffee or tea but was refused. When the person left, she could see the back of a uniform moving down the stairs of the porch. Her heart stopped. Not Vic, too. This couldn't be.

"Ralph?" Nancy's chin quivered. "Vic?"

Ralph turned, holding a telegram that was so much like what Kathryn had received. He looked down at it and as his muscles relaxed in his jaw, Miriam found her hand loosen its grip on Kathryn's. She didn't even know she was holding it. She looked at Kathryn for a moment, then back at Ralph.

"Ralph, please," Kathryn scolded.

"He's coming home," Ralph said, his voice faltering and breaking. "He's been wounded, but our boy's coming home, Nancy."

"Our boy's coming home!" Nancy squealed and began bouncing up and down. "My baby's coming home."

"When?" Miriam asked amidst the celebration.

"How was he wounded?" Kathryn asked just after Miriam.

"Slow down — let me read this again and get the details." Ralph went closer to the lamplight and replaced his smile with the scowl he usually wore when concentrating.

"He'll be home in a month and," he paused and sighed, "he's lost a leg."

"A leg?" Nancy repeated.

"Yes, dear, he's lost a leg." Ralph pinched his lips together. "We'll make do."

"We sure will." Nancy jutted out her chin.

"What a joy it'll be to have Vic home!" Kathryn's eyes sparkled.

Vic and James were so alike and had always been such good boys. Miriam expected Kathryn would find some portion of comfort in having her lost husband's younger brother home. He would return a hero.

In a whirlwind, Kathryn kissed them all and was out the door. Miriam stayed for another hour, discussing and rediscussing the news. They had all needed good news, and two legs or one, Vic was alive. The steady weight that always stood on her heart had shifted. They had been in a constant vigil over their soldiers. What about Henry? What fate would he meet? What fate had he already met?

Vic was home in less than a month, and Miriam watched as he hobbled on his crutches, still wearing his uniform proudly. Nancy and Ralph could not have looked more pleased as they all exited the car. When Nancy tried to take his arm to help him up the walk, he insisted he could make it up the front porch steps without help from anyone and using only his crutches. Nancy couldn't help but put her arm around his back and Ralph stayed close as he walked slowly. The wintry scene had given way to slush and mud, an ugly scene in which to bring home a wounded warrior. Fannie's kids lined the hill across the street as they watched him exit the car with one pant leg pinned up far above where his knee used to be. The kids couldn't help but stare and point.

Miriam chuckled as Vic turned toward them when he made it to the top of the porch and said in perfect dialect, *"Ich komm gricht dich,"* teasing them that he would come and get them. They all squealed and ran into the house. Vic had always been interested in their language, unlike James, and had learned quite a few words and phrases. He winked at Miriam when he turned back around, and she chuckled in her hand.

"He's the same old boy, isn't he?" Nancy said in question, but seemingly more to convince herself than anything else. The poor woman's brow was furrowed. "Both my boys are safe now. James is in heaven, God rest his soul. And I have my Vic back. My boys are safe now." She repeated the last phrase several times.

"Oh, how proud James would be," Kathryn wiped fresh tears from her eyes, but a few still mingled in the corners of her upturned lips. Such bittersweet moments could not be lost on a war widow.

"Kat." He winked at his sister-in-law. They hugged for several long moments.

"I'll always be here to help with the kids, you know that, right?" Vic said sincerely.

Kathryn nodded her head but wasn't able to speak.

"Miriam," Vic said, turning his attention to her. "I brought something for you."

Vic winked as he handed Miriam a rolled-up newspaper. Her brow wrinkled in confusion. She followed her neighbors inside and they all gathered around the kitchen table to a meal Kathryn and Miriam had insisted on preparing, even though it was hours before supper.

"Where are my niece and nephew?" Vic said. "I want to see James's kids."

"Here you go." Kathryn handed Vic a wiggling Jamie. "He's big and chubby, just like your mother said you and James were."

"Oh my," Vic took the boy, who instantly

grabbed his hat and nose simultaneously. Everyone laughed. "He looks just like him."

"James?"

"No, like Dad," Vic laughed. "Bald and fat."

Vic was back. He had lost his leg, but he had not lost his sense of humor. Miriam, however, was still poring over the newspaper. It wasn't current but from December. There were numerous photos of children smiling with a few soldiers and gifts in their hands, mostly small dolls and trucks. Apparently, some of the soldiers had found ways to bring gifts to some of the children throughout the Christmas season.

"Vic, I don't understand. This is an old newspaper."

"Once I got to the hospital, I got all of the letters Mom and Kathryn wrote. That's where I found out about James." He patted his mother's hand quickly amidst wrestling a roly-poly Jamie in his arms. "Mom also told me about your Henry. Have you heard from him yet?"

"No, not since October."

"Did you see the date of the newspaper?"

"Yes, it's from December."

"Didn't he whittle? I remember him carving up all sorts of stuff. He made me a truck once. The wheels even turned."

"Yes, but I still don't understand."

"Look at the picture on the next page."

Miriam laid the newspaper out on her lap and flipped the page wide, displaying several more pictures of children.

"Read the caption."

" 'American soldiers offer gifts to German children who return to rebuild their homes and cities. One young boy says he watched a young private he called Hank whittle him a truck using his own pocket knife.' " Miriam's face grew warm and hot tears formed in her eyes. She looked up at the family, who appeared as struck with the words as she. "Henry?"

"Look at it." Vic pointed at the picture. "It looks just like the truck he made for me a decade ago. A little more rustic maybe, but it's gotta be him."

"He did whittle a small heart for me a few months ago." She paused for a long moment. "But then why haven't I heard from him? Wouldn't he have written?"

"All I can say is that when a division is as busy as the 80th, he's not going to have a minute to write, or any way to get letters to you even if he did write. There's no way you can understand how it is over there without being there."

"But he had time to whittle? He couldn't

have written?"

"I can't really explain it, Miriam. It's easy for us to question that, but in the moment with these children amidst the ruin of their homes, these children were probably more important."

Miriam just studied the picture. Could Henry have carved this truck? The little boy held the truck high in his hands, directly in front of the camera. Henry's friends had called him Hank. It could be him, which would mean he was alive, at least in early December. The knowledge comforted her. But, still, was he alive now? When would she know?

"Thank you, Vic." Miriam's voice was barely a whisper as she reached her hand out. He took it gently, not like a handshake, and she gripped it. "You've given me hope."

Just then, the door began to rattle with incessant knocking. Before anyone could open it, a young blonde woman bounded through it. She was as breathtaking as any woman Miriam had ever seen. Her appearance seemed unaffected by the ugliness of the season. Her perfect red lips landed on Vic's own before anyone knew what was happening.

Vic's eyes widened, and everyone stood shocked. Then he let Miriam's hand go and pulled the girl onto his lap and kissed her thoroughly. Once they were through, he smiled, red lipstick smeared over his own face, though somehow the blonde's lips remained immaculate.

"This is Victoria. We met at the dance hall before I shipped out. I call her Queen. We're getting married as soon as possible." His eyes never left Victoria's face.

CHAPTER 23

January 1945

In January, it was Truman and Fannie's turn to host church at their house again. Miriam found herself in a precarious position. As she walked past the outhouse next to her home after the Sunday service, she heard a woman weeping inside.

She knocked lightly against the frozen wood.

"Musht hilve?" she asked, seeing if the woman inside needed help. "I can help, or I can get someone for you."

The crying suddenly quieted, but Miriam could still hear the quick breaths of grief inside. She knocked again.

The latch from the inside came undone, but the door didn't open all the way. Miriam carefully opened the door farther, allowing a sliver of light to enter the small building. The brightness revealed the woman in front of her, who held her head

in her hands. She was wearing their customary clothing — a white covering, indicating
she was married, and a royal-blue dress,
meaning she was likely a young wife.

Miriam was puzzled. She latched the door
behind her and turned back around. The
small space had just enough room for a
person to stand if the other person sat. The
young woman sat next to the toilet opening, weeping.

"Vas ist letz?" She put a hand on the
woman's thin shoulder and asked what was
wrong.

The woman looked up at her, and Miriam
did her best not to register her shock. Sylvia
Mast, or rather, Sylvia Brenneman. What
was Henry's sister doing sitting in her
outhouse crying? It was then that Miriam
noted the pool of blood on the floor next to
her.

"Sylvia, are you bleeding?"

While neither said anything, it was known
that Sylvia was expecting. The talk of it had
spread through the community in a matter
of weeks, and Miriam's heart hurt for the
young couple. She knew well enough what
it was like to be talked about in such a
scandalous way.

"Now you can gloat, Miriam Coblentz,"
she spat. "Now you know the rumors are

true, and you can spread more because I think I just lost both of the people that I love."

"Sylvia," she said gently, but her voice could not hide her surprise. "I would never spread talk about you, true or not. Are you sure you've lost the babe?"

She shook her head. "No. Not for sure. But I was hurting all through the service and when I came in here I realized I had blood down the back of my dress and everywhere else." She began weeping.

"Even if you lose this baby, you're not going to lose Mark. You still have him. You haven't lost him."

"I wasn't talking about Mark." Her voice started out raspy, almost yelling, but ended weakly. "I married Mark because I had to, and now I've lost this baby."

Miriam didn't know what to say. As Sylvia wept again, she did the only thing she knew to do and reached out to hug her. Surprisingly, Sylvia clung to Miriam and wept into her middle. Miriam let her cry for another minute before she pulled her away.

"Let me see your dress."

Sylvia stood and turned around. The red blood showed well enough, since the dress was royal blue. Miriam's lips pursed as she decided how she could help. The Amish dresses were made in a way to become smaller or larger based on how tightly you wrapped the skirt. She and Sylvia were virtually the same size but for the small bulge that couldn't be hidden beneath the unforgiving Amish skirt.

"Come to my room, and you can wear one of my dresses."

Without argument, Sylvia agreed. Miriam walked closely behind the younger girl so no one who might be nearby would notice the bloodstained dress. Luckily, they had only to walk a small way to the side door of Miriam's house. No one seemed to notice. Miriam then led her to the upstairs room. She helped Sylvia sit in the chair at her desk.

"How are your cramps now?"

"They've gone away a little, but I feel a bit weak." She paused. "I'm scared."

Miriam sighed. "I know you must be."

Miriam paused before opening the closet door and looked Sylvia in the eyes. Why didn't she go to her mother? She had no older sisters like Miriam, and maybe the embarrassment of expecting before she was married made approaching her mother for help too difficult. The Masts couldn't handle any more scandal, but here they were, with another blemish on their family's name.

"Do you think there's any chance the baby's still alive?" Sylvia asked weakly.

Miriam considered how to answer this. In her years of helping women after birth, she'd learned a great deal. She knew several women who bled through much of their pregnancies and still delivered healthy children.

"I think there's a good chance your baby is fine."

A look of relief washed over Sylvia's face. "I think if I have this baby, Mark and I might find a way to be happy. But without this baby —"

Miriam knelt next to Sylvia and held the young woman's hands in her own. Like never before, her heart nearly burst with the desire to offer help and encouragement. Where was this love coming from? Sylvia had never been anything but awful to her.

"Oh, Sylvia, I wish I could say something that would help."

"I am ashamed when I'm around him. Because of what we did before we were married." Her voice swelled with emotion.

Miriam remained silent.

"What woman gives her body to a man she's not married to? He'll always know what kind of woman I am, and he could never love me. I'll be ashamed for my entire life."

"Did you ask for forgiveness?"

"What do you mean?"

"Have you asked God to forgive you?"

"I can't face the church like that."

Miriam was reminded of all that Henry had been teaching her in his letters. Dead or alive, his words permeated her soul, and now she could relay God's message of grace when this woman needed it most.

"You know, Henry taught me something through his letters. Something that I just never really understood before."

Miriam had Sylvia's attention unlike ever before.

"He told me that he was only accountable to God. He wasn't accountable to the church or anyone else. Not his family. Not me. Not the bishop. If we do something wrong, if we have dishonored our relationship with God, we answer to Him. He is the only one who can really cleanse us from our sin. He's the only one who can wash away the guilt, bitterness . . . the shame."

"But the church —"

"The church has a set of standards and rules that aren't bad, and our actions can hurt those we love and our church. But that guilt cannot consume us or we will never be whole. We can confess to the church, the bishop, our parents, but it would mean nothing without first confessing and pleading with Christ. Does that make sense?"

"Sadah." Sort of, she said, and nodded her head.

"Do you want me to pray for you and your baby?" The words fell from Miriam's mouth before she had the chance to pull them back. Her heart hammered inside her chest. What had she just offered to do? Pray out loud? This wasn't their way. Wasn't it prideful, or drawing attention to herself rather than God? Prayers were between the person and God and didn't need to be heard by others. What was she doing?

"You would pray with me?" Sylvia's soft and warm question helped Miriam realize that she had said exactly the right thing.

She nodded her head, in a near panic over what she would even say.

Sylvia simply nodded.

Miriam felt heat rise to her face as Sylvia gripped her hands. She silently pleaded with God to give her the words to say. Something she'd never done either. One of her hands opened and she placed her palm on Sylvia's abdomen. Tears dripped on her hand from the broken woman who sat in front of her.

"Father in heaven." She thought starting

with words similar to the Lord's Prayer would be familiar to them both. What should she say next? The pause remained heavy. "I ask — Sylvia asks for help. For this baby. Help the baby. And Mark —" Her voice shook and she paused abruptly, her heart pounding. "Help him and Sylvia." Did she need to say anything else? "Amen."

The silence that followed whispered to Miriam, calming her, comforting her, healing her. She had just broken her own boundaries. This was what Henry was talking about in hearing the voice of God. How real He became to her in those moments. She wondered if Sylvia had experienced the same comfort. She looked up. Sylvia's pained eyes carried brightness behind them that wasn't there before.

"I've never prayed out loud before," Sylvia said, interrupting the silence.

"This was my first time, but I know Henry does it all the time."

Sylvia sucked in a breath and let it out evenly as she spoke.

"He's not very Amish anymore, is he?"

"I don't know what Henry is except himself. He is still the same person, only closer to God and stronger — courageous even." Miriam felt the sting of tears in her eyes.

"How is he?"

Miriam shook her head, tears falling on her cheeks. "I don't know. I haven't heard from him since October."

"October?" she gasped.

Miriam nodded but was unable to speak.

"And you're still so loyal. You love him so much. And your strength." The girl's mouth was agape. "You are so strong, Miriam. I'm so weak. As soon as Eli got his draft notice he said he wouldn't marry me, and he didn't want me to wait for him, either. I was so angry, I went to Mark. Now look at me. Mark and I made a huge mistake."

"I'm not so strong. I've had my weaknesses too," Miriam said.

"With Eli," Sylvia didn't question but stated.

Miriam nodded. "He's a good man, but he's not for me. I could never love anyone but Henry."

"I was so angry with you, because I knew Eli would never love me like he loved you. But I didn't think you deserved Henry, either."

Miriam didn't say anything. She wasn't sure how to respond. Not only had Sylvia known that Miriam had been tempted with Eli, but also that he had loved Miriam. Had all of that been so obvious to everyone?

"I was wrong to be mean," Sylvia said.

Silence settled between them for several long moments.

"Mark says that he loves me." Sylvia smiled. "He was after me for years, and I kept turning him down. I had my eyes on Eli, when Mark would do anything for me. But all I did was disgrace him."

"I think Mark was just as involved in all of this as you. Why don't you talk with him about how you're feeling, and I bet you'll learn a lot about your husband."

"Husband." A shy smile crept over her face. "It still sounds strange to me. Even though I like the idea of being married, I just haven't been able to enjoy it yet."

"You shouldn't hold onto this guilt forever." Miriam was holding onto guilt also. Guilt over disappointing her father. Her heart stirred. The laughter of kids playing out on the lawn brought her back.

"So, let's find a dress for you. Take that dress off, and I'll give you a paper bag to take it home in." Miriam opened her closet door and began rifling through the few dresses that she owned. She was wearing her best Sunday dress now and, as far as winter Sunday dresses went, had only one other. She pulled out the black dress and handed it to Sylvia. "I think this will fit."

Sylvia's eyes enlarged.

"What, you don't think it will fit? I'm a little taller, but I don't think it'll be too long on you."

"No, It's just that several people made comments today about how pretty my wedding dress is, and that it's nice to be able to wear it again and again." She looked down at her stained dress. "I'm afraid it'll be obvious if I go back out there wearing black."

It didn't take long for Miriam to know exactly what she should do. She reached past her covering boxes and pulled out a brown paper package. She took it over to the bed and untied the string. She pulled out the different pieces that made the entire dress and laid them carefully on the bed.

"Wear this one," she said quietly, yet with resolve. "It's the dress I made for my own wedding. It's the same material, because we had a late-autumn wedding planned. I don't think anyone will suspect."

"You're going to let me wear your wedding dress?" Sylvia seemed close to tears again.

"Yes, I am. Someone should get some use out of it."

"But, what about when Henry comes back?"

Miriam paused before she spoke, her

360

hesitation half out of contemplation and the other half resisting what she felt was true. "I haven't heard from him in months. At this point I don't feel like I'll ever hear from him again," she whispered.

"Don't lose hope, Miriam." Sylvia gave her a shy smile. "Please. If you do, then I will, and then I know I won't be able to go on."

Miriam thought of the newspaper picture. She and Sylvia hadn't even spoken more than a few words together before today, but suddenly they were talking about such personal things. While it was strange, it also felt right to her.

"I want to show you something." She went to her desk and pulled out the newspaper. "Vic, the neighbor boy who just came home, gave this to me. Look at this picture."

Sylvia took the paper and narrowed her view of the truck. Her lips pursed and her face grimaced.

"Surely he's not going by the name Hank, is he?"

Miriam nodded, and Sylvia studied the picture again.

"I think it really could be." She nodded. "I'm sure there are a lot of men that can whittle as well as Henry, but this does give us reason to hope. Especially with the mention of that awful name Hank."

Miriam sighed. "It just has to be proof that he's alive."

"This was back in December, though," Sylvia reminded her. "Early December, even."

Miriam nodded. "I know. But if something were wrong, your parents would've had a telegram delivery. There hasn't been anything like that, right?"

Miriam instantly noticed Sylvia's body stiffen and her hand went up to her mouth.

"From Western Union?"

"Sylvia, what? You need to tell me." Miriam sat at the edge of her chair. Her breath quickened.

"Sometime late in December I was over at *Mem* and *Dat*'s and a Western Union man came to the door. *Mem* went to the door, and when I asked what a man like that was doing at the house, she just said that *Dat* was waiting for a telegram about a buggy he wanted to buy. I asked why they didn't just write a letter, and she just said that it was more urgent than that because their buggy was getting really rickety. Even though she said it was about their buggy, I still found it odd. *Dat* never used Western Union before. Now, I'm wondering."

"Would your *mem* do that? Just not say

anything?"

"I was so caught up with my own problems, I just didn't scrutinize it more." She paused. "I need to find out more, don't I?"

"Please, Sylvia, if this would give us some information about Henry. If he's —"

"He's not dead, Miriam." Sylvia took Miriam's shoulders. "He's not. I just know it. We need to hope together," Sylvia offered. "And pray?"

"Yes, and pray."

She promised to check with her mother as soon as she was able and to let Miriam know.

By the time the two returned to the church crowd, Miriam saw Mark frantically searching for his young bride. He ran over to them, his face awash with relief.

"Syl, where were you? I was getting worried. I thought maybe —" He paused and looked at Miriam, unsure of what more he should say.

"She knows everything. I think we need to go to the doctor to have him check on the baby, and maybe on the way we can have a talk." Sylvia took Mark's hand and then looked back at Miriam and smiled.

Miriam watched as the young couple walked away, Sylvia still slightly hunched in her physical weakness and Mark instantly putting a protective arm around her and taking the brown sack with his other hand. She watched as they stopped for a moment, and he looked inside the sack. His eyes enlarged as they met his young wife's eyes. Even though Miriam couldn't read lips, she was sure she saw him say that no matter what, they would make it through.

Those distant words alone whispered to her soul. God would pull her through, no matter what.

CHAPTER 24

January 1945
Miriam squinted in the darkness and was caught off guard by a uniformed man limping toward her. He walked with the use of a cane. His hat was tilted just right. His brow furrowed as he looked at her. Emotion wracked his face, which was scarred but still handsome. His hand reached for her, and Miriam walked toward him, then ran. Just when she got close, their fingertips almost touched and he was sucked back by the darkness of the night.

"Henry!" She sat up in bed, sweating. The chill around her crudely stroked her dampened neck, and she clasped at her heaving chest. The dream was too real. Henry was trying to get to her and couldn't. Would there be news today?

She rolled around the possibilities in her mind, working out the scenarios and what her reaction might be. Anytime she considered his death, her heart recoiled and she pushed away the sensation of vomiting. Surely, even in the darkest of moments, his mother would not hide that fact. But what if he was missing? Or injured? Next to death, the worst scenario would be that the telegram had nothing to do with Henry and they would all remain in the dark.

It wasn't until nearly lunchtime that she saw a buggy turn into the drive. Sylvia was driving it, and Miriam ran outside.

"Mervin," she called over to her nephew, "take the horse in the barn to stay warm. Unhitch him, too."

The young boy did his job without a word, and when the horse and buggy moved, Miriam was shocked to see Linda, Henry's mother, standing on the other side of it. She had come with Sylvia. There would be news today.

"Linda," she said without thinking, "you've come also."

The older woman nodded, then looked down at the ground as she slowly made her way toward the door. Miriam quickly led the way through the mudroom and into the kitchen. She put out three mugs with hot tea. Fresh warm bread in thick slices joined the honey already on the table before Miriam finally sat with her company.

No one spoke for what seemed like hours,

but it couldn't have been more than a minute.

"So, I asked *Mem* about the Western Union telegram she got a month ago," Sylvia began. "She wanted to come herself to tell you."

Miriam inhaled and held her breath.

Linda reached into the fold of her waistline and pulled out a folded and crumpled telegram. It seemed impossible that it was only a month old. The older woman's hands shook as she tried to unfold it. Tears formed in her eyes and trickled down her loose-skinned face. Her lips quivered. Sylvia's hand reached out to touch her mother's for a moment.

"It's okay, *Mem,*" she said gently, "Miriam's a friend. She'll understand why you didn't come sooner."

Miriam and Linda's eyes met, and sympathy traveled between them. Linda's head tilted to one side as she handed the still folded telegram to Miriam, her hands quaking.

"I'm sorry," the older woman said quietly.

Miriam couldn't contain her need to know the truth and wanted to snatch the paper from the woman's hands in one hasty action. But she realized that it had taken great courage for Linda to come to the house, and Miriam didn't want to disrespect her in this way or put her in greater discomfort. She slowly lifted her hand, and for a moment both women held the telegram, their eyes still connected. When Linda finally released it, her hands clasped together in her lap and her eyes retreated downward.

Miriam's own hands trembled so terribly, she was afraid of tearing the telegram while unfolding it. Its edges were discolored from being held in sweaty hands. How often had Linda read and reread this note, unfolding and refolding it? Her eyes scanned the date and time and moved to the message below.

THE SECRETARY OF WAR DESIRES TO EXPRESS HIS DEEP REGRET THAT YOUR SON PRIVATE HENRY MAST HAS BEEN REPORTED MISSING IN ACTION IN GERMANY SINCE DECEMBER STOP IF FURTHER DETAILS OF OTHER INFORMATION ARE RECEIVED YOU WILL BE PROMPTLY NOTIFIED STOP

Miriam looked up at Linda. Her own tears, pouring from her eyes, tasted bitter.

"He's been missing for almost a month and you didn't tell me?"

Linda then pulled out another telegram and handed it to her. This time Miriam didn't move slowly. She grabbed the telegram unashamedly and didn't cringe when she made a small tear in the fold of the paper when opening it.

THE RED CROSS HAS INFORMED THE SECRETARY OF WAR THAT YOUR SON PRIVATE HENRY MAST WAS FOUND SERIOUSLY WOUNDED IN ACTION STOP IF FURTHER DETAILS OF OTHER INFORMATION ARE RECEIVED YOU WILL BE PROMPTLY NOTIFIED STOP

A hospital address followed.

Miriam looked up, meeting Linda's eyes, then Sylvia's. Just before January, Henry was alive, but seriously wounded. He had been missing for only a few days.

"Why didn't you tell me?" Her words were barely discernible as she began to cry in earnest. "Why?"

"I wanted to, but when I showed Amos, he said it would just cause undue worry and more bad attention." She sniffed and swallowed hard to keep from crying. "I am sorry, Miriam. I truly am."

Miriam wanted to be angry, she wanted to be furious, but knowing that she now had news was enough for her to move past the reasons why she wasn't told. She would write to the hospital immediately and see what more she could find out. Why hadn't Henry written since he was at the hospital? She discussed this with Linda and Sylvia before they left, and none of them could come up with a good answer.

"I have held these telegrams with me almost constantly ever since. I miss my boy," Linda said. "I just don't know what to do."

"I'll take care of it, I promise, and as soon as I know anything, I'll let you know. Can I keep these telegrams, at least for now? I'll probably need them to find him," Miriam asked the older woman, who nodded weakly. Linda had been agonizing alone about these telegrams for weeks. Miriam understood the depths of pain in that, as she had been distressed over not receiving news for months.

Sylvia hugged Miriam tightly before leaving the house. "I know it's going to be okay. Mark and I have begun praying every night together specifically for you and Henry."

A breath hitched in Miriam's throat. She didn't wait until their buggy pulled away from her drive before she ran to the desk to pull out stationery. As she grabbed for a pen, she stopped in her tracks. She ran over to the window and saw that Kathryn and Nancy were both home. Maybe she could send a Western Union telegram herself and ask for information.

Before an hour had passed, Miriam had sent a telegram back to the Red Cross field hospital, and all she could do now was wait. How long would this wait be? A week? A month? Who would finally respond to her? What would the news be?

As Miriam waited for a response, she did everything she could to keep busy. The two weeks she'd already waited had made her more impatient than ever. Kathryn and Nancy proved to be her stalwart pillars of comfort. When she wasn't doing her chores, she spent nearly all her time with them.

Miriam sat at Nancy's table, bouncing Jamie on one knee, as the Poole family talked over Vic and Victoria's wedding, which was coming up that weekend. The family had fallen in love with Victoria as quickly as Vic and forgave them for their secrecy.

Victoria was every bit the queen that Vic had nicknamed her. Her father, Carleton

Jones, owned several large businesses in Dover, and their wedding would lack for nothing. What Victoria wanted, Victoria's daddy provided. Vic was quickly able to get a management job at one of the factories owned by the Joneses, and he was as happy as a man could be. The Pooles absorbed the surprise well and still reveled in the fact that their son was safe.

This world was so vastly different from anything Miriam had ever observed. She couldn't help but be attracted to Victoria's charismatic personality. Victoria doted on Nan and Jamie as if they were her own and insisted they call her Auntie already. There was no slowing down Victoria.

"Miriam, look." Nancy nudged her, and her excited tone of voice hushed the entire kitchen.

Miriam knew everyone could see what she just saw: a uniformed Western Union man walking toward her front door. She turned to find Nancy and Kathryn's eyes round. She imagined she was mirroring the same expression.

"Go, quickly." Kathryn grabbed Miriam's coat and stuffed her in it. "And come back right away."

She didn't take the time to close her coat, though it was a chilly February day. The snow had come again, but not in a blizzard this time. She barely looked down the road as she ran across it and waved at the uniformed man as he knocked on the door.

"I'm Miriam Coblentz — the telegram is for me."

The young man looked down at the telegram and nodded. "Yes, it is."

She took it from his hands and opened it.

PVT HENRY MAST IS NO LONGER A PATIENT HERE STOP WE REGRET FURTHER RECORDS AT FLD HOSPITAL UNCLEAR STOP

Her heart dropped. Records unclear? What did that mean? That they weren't sure whether he was dead or alive? Was he discharged? Was he out there fighting again? Where was Henry?

Chapter 25

March 1945

Miriam watched as Fannie waddled to the mailbox. She had started calling it her daily exercise when her midwife told her she should be careful about how much weight she was gaining with this pregnancy. Fannie had laughed when she told their mother. Miriam hesitated to join in. Fannie had never been a small woman and after having babies in the double digits, the last thing she admitted to being worried about was her figure.

"Nah, Fannie, you should try to be healthy," Rosemary chided.

"Who has time?" Fannie shoved her mother's comments aside with the wave of her hand. "And don't you look like that at me, Miriam. You're so skinny a slight wind could carry you away. But you just wait — someday, when you have babies, you'll understand. You'll end up as fat as me."

Miriam laughed at the conversation even now, weeks later. She and Fannie had struggled so severely with their sisterhood, and that had been the first open door she'd received from her eldest sister. Though she still hadn't heard any further news about Henry, she had slowly begun to regain her sister. She also enjoyed her new friendship with Sylvia. Kathryn proved to be more independent than ever and continued to face her new life with courage and strength. Her children were thriving, as they lived with their grandparents and had their Uncle Vic to wrestle with. Miriam's mother was becoming more open and sympathetic, with Miriam even asking after news of the community every so often. The mystery around Henry was what seemed to keep her life at a standstill.

She looked up when she saw Fannie waving a letter. Before she knew it, she was outside.

"Is it from Henry?"

"How should I know?" Fannie said, huffing and puffing.

With her hand out, Miriam made it to her quickly.

"I don't like it, you know," Fannie said, holding the letter just out of reach. "You getting letters from all over the world. Gives my kids strange ideas. It's not good."

"I'm sorry, Fannie." Miriam did her best to keep her voice even and soft. "I really don't mean to do this to hurt anyone."

Fannie handed her the letter and began shuffling toward her house when she turned toward Miriam.

"I hope he's okay, you know," she said.

"Thank you, Fannie." Miriam smiled. "Thank you."

Miriam examined the envelope, finding nothing identifying the sender. She ripped open the letter and instantly noted the mid-January date.

Dear Miriam,

I know you don't know me, but Private Henry Mast is my patient at a field hospital in Germany. I'm an American nurse with the Red Cross. I don't often write a soldier's loved ones, but felt I needed to write you.

We found Private Mast carrying a soldier over his shoulder. Both were seriously wounded. Since he only spoke what sounded like a dialect of German, he was immediately isolated and investigated, which is why his family may have been told he was missing. Because I speak German, I was his attending nurse throughout the week he was in isolation until they confirmed that he was indeed an American and not a spy. By then we also learned about you from the private whom he saved, Private Johnny Rossum. He told me all about Private Mast's background. I wanted to write to you myself, as I understand he has been unable to for quite some time. Private Rossum told me of your engagement.

I am not going to lie, Private Mast's wounds are serious. For the first several days he was often incoherent and constantly mumbling in your Amish dialect. I could understand very little except that he continuously repeated your name — Miriam — and often his ramblings resemble prayers or Bible passages.

He was often difficult to control, his injuries were causing him great pain and frustration, and he kept asking for you. I finally found your address in a letter that arrived for him. He does not know that I'm writing.

Please know that we will do everything we can to make sure that your fiancé makes it home to you. He'll likely be transferred out to a military hospital in France, but I'm unable to share the specifics. I hope he will be able to contact you himself very soon after.

Pray for him, Miriam. He needs it now more than ever.

Sincerely,
Marie Spencer, Red Cross Nurse

The letter was written almost two months ago, and it came from the hospital she'd telegrammed. Marie Spencer was her only link to finding out where Henry might be and if he was still alive. She wrote the nurse right away, but knowing that the letter would sit in the mailbox until Monday morning was agonizing. Tomorrow she would have to sit through church and pray for the focus she needed. She would wait to hear the whisper from God within the message, in the breeze, in the trill of the songbirds that would arrive soon.

As she walked back to the house from the mailbox, a buggy entered the driveway behind her. She moved out of the way as she continued to her front door. She wasn't expecting anyone and assumed that it was someone for Truman and Fannie.

"Miriam," a low, booming voice said behind her.

"*Ja?*" she said.

She turned around as she spoke and found herself looking into the sympathetic face of Adam Gingrich, the district's *Aumah Deanuh*. Her hands balled up and her fingernails penetrated her skin before she breathed a prayer to calm herself. He was here for her. *Aumah Deanuhs* didn't make casual house calls.

"Hi, Adam." Miriam sighed when she spoke his name, her voice resigned to the discipline she was sure to receive. She knew she'd deliberately gone against the church's *Ordnung* and that her time of confession had come. How much longer could the church's leadership wait before providing her the opportunity to confess to the congregation members her wrongdoings?

"Miriam," he said with a nod, his eyes just barely meeting hers. His shoulders hunched when she saw him inhale and exhale deeply, his face red. "I think you know why I'm here?"

Miriam nodded. Until Adam had warned her a few months ago, she'd never had as much as a hair out of place in her entire life. This series of events felt like a bad dream. This wasn't her. This wasn't what she'd imagined her life to be. Only a few weeks prior, she had endured watching Mark and Sylvia confess their sins before the church. Miriam felt her heart crush as Sylvia knelt in front of everyone, her large belly a focal point for all to see. They'd done their penance with such dignity, knowing what they did was wrong. She longed for the grace that Sylvia had exhibited.

"We've given you months to examine your ways and to show your obedience to the church. I'm sorry to say that you've failed to prove your willingness to obey." His voice faltered and broke as he continued. "You have been found eating at the same table with Kathryn and riding in her car. You know this is against our ways since Kathryn is shunned. Your contact with her has crossed over the church's boundaries."

There was silence except for the noticeable spring breeze that had been gracing the landscape for the past few days. The scent was sweet to Miriam's nose, and she could almost hear the buds growing, bringing new life. They stood in the golden light of a warming sun, and the slush and gloom of the fading winter had given way to dry earth.

She knew that while the sin that she was being asked to confess was eating and driving with Kathryn, her support of Henry was the real problem. She hadn't gone against the rules of the church by writing and loving him, but the appearance of her carrying on with a man who was openly disregarding the *Ordnung* was distasteful. Emboldened, she wanted Adam to admit that the real problem was Henry. She wanted to hear him acknowledge that as truth.

"And Henry? Adam, you know me — we grew up together. You know I can't turn my back on Henry." She spoke quietly but effectively, suddenly realizing that the things he spoke of appeared so minor when putting words to them. But they were against the *Ordnung* that she had vowed to uphold. At first, it had struck her that she was doing something she knew was wrong, but it had, over the course of months, seemed to happen often enough that it stopped fazing her. "You know that I wouldn't purposely go against the church. Don't you want Henry to return? What if you knew that Amanda was —"

"This isn't about Henry," he interrupted, then cleared his throat. Miriam watched as the corners of his mouth quivered. She had heard of the sensitivity of *Aumah Deanuh*s and that in especially difficult cases they were known to be emotional. In this case, Adam had been a chum of hers, as well as Henry's. She imagined how difficult this had to be for him. And how difficult it would be to be expected to live not just up to the standards of the *Ordnung* but above them. She did not envy his pressured life. "He will be required to face his own sin. His sin is not yours. If he returns." His voice hiccupped and he stopped.

"When," Miriam helped, softening her voice. "When Henry returns."

"Yes, when." He inhaled and attempted to bolster his chest only for it to fall again, along with his gaze. "We — I — will meet with him then. But you must confess your own wrongdoings to the church. Your relationship with Kathryn has broken your standing with the church; a confession is required."

His humble demeanor should have pillowed the words hitting her heart, but they did not. Her standing with the church was in question. Tears no longer hung in her eyes but fell. She did not hide them as she tried to meet Adam's downcast eyes. She knew he was doing his duty, and that she must do hers.

"I understand." Her tears strolled along her jawline and down her neck. She sniffed.

Adam finally allowed his gaze to snap upward. A thick hand went to his face and he covered it, heaving several sobs. The horse stamped its feet, and Miriam wondered if the intuitive animal recognized the sadness that traveled between the two old friends. Adam pulled out a white hankie and wiped his face before blowing his nose. Then, while his eyes remained sad, his face grew tense. Miriam could see him clench and unclench his jaw several times.

"You will be called forward for your confession next Sunday. The following church Sunday after that is *Gross Gmaey,* everything must be made right by then; otherwise you may be asked to not attend both of those services." He didn't meet her eyes until the last few words.

At his mention of *Gross Gmaey,* her heart shuddered. It was a twice-a-year all-day event. They would read their standards and rules to the entire district one Sunday, then they would partner for foot washing and a holy kiss before taking communion the following church Sunday. All breaking of the *Ordnung* had to be made right by then or, as he said, all who had broken it could be asked to not attend, which could lead to being shunned. She had one Sunday to ensure that her path was following the same narrow road of the church so that when she attended *Gross Gmaey,* there would be no question of her heart.

"Of course," she said, nodding, trying her best not to allow more tears to flow. She fought against the natural urge, believing she didn't deserve such grieving when she knew all along that her lifestyle had not been serving the community properly. She was now humbled and ashamed.

Their eyes didn't meet again. He took a few long, deliberate steps to his buggy and was out of the driveway in less than a minute. She remained there and didn't move until the clip-clop of his horse's hooves couldn't be heard. The drum of them calmed her heart, forcing it to beat regularly. It was then that she noticed her mother sitting on Fannie's front porch. Her unseeing eyes were distant, but Miriam knew her mother's ears were never deafened to any sound. While she couldn't have caught every word, the intention of the visit was not lost to her.

Miriam controlled her steps as she returned inside the house only to let her knees fall when she reached the closed staircase. In the silence, she wept. How had she let her life move in this direction? It seemed that only a moment ago she was concerned over Henry's shorn hair, so trivial to her now. Now, she was on the verge of her own shunning, all because of the love of a young man.

CHAPTER 26

March 1945

Miriam watched as the mailman pulled out the letter to the nurse on Monday forenoon. She sat on the front porch alone. There was nothing else she felt stirred to do. The house was so easy to keep clean with only her and her mother living there. There was no baking to prepare for, and she already had their laundry on the line. The breeze was light today, and the clothes mostly hung flat.

She hugged herself, warming her arms against the slight chill that lingered in the early-spring air. Usually it was much colder, but perhaps God was giving them a reprieve after such a difficult winter. Or was the winter only difficult for her? She often wondered if anyone felt life as acutely as she did.

She had kept Linda Mast informed of everything she was learning of Henry, though there was so little. On her most recent visit, Miriam saw how her house was in perfect order, her children impeccably dressed, her demeanor as jolly as usual when anyone else was present. But when she and Miriam were alone, she could see the true anxiety Linda faced. The fear that gathered in her eyes was reflected in Miriam's own.

The rest of the week moved as slowly as that morning. She watched water boil, dough rise, and chickens peck at their feed. The new white spring clouds appeared shiftless in the blue sky. The birds nestled longer with their hatchlings, leaving even the worms to relax. Was nothing willing to move at the pace of Miriam's pounding heart? So April was ushered in, quietly, softly; it was far too beautiful. She didn't want to bother anyone with her anxiety about the Sunday approaching and what she must do. She was frightened to confess her wrongdoings in front of the community she had always known, even though she'd felt such peace with it over the week of praying and casting away her cares. The refreshment of forgiveness would outweigh the embarrassment of the act, she hoped.

Sunday morning's dawn was as familiar as the creak of an old door. Miriam had often woken at dawn, finding herself praying for peace in the midst of waiting for news. Today was no different.

Lord, will I know today where my Henry is? Let him be safe. Let him come home to me.

Those were the words she spoke today. The words changed with her waking mood. Sometimes she woke in tears and her utterings could not be spelled out. Other times she woke with the sensation of the angels kissing her eyelids, reminding her that she was never alone. So often, she woke with the purple hue of dawn only to have it hidden by winter storm clouds that wouldn't be prayed away. The spring brought on a new sense of hope, as it always did. But when would this nightmare be over? How long had it been since Henry was drafted and sent to the CPS camp? Was it only two and a half years ago? Had Henry ever lived among them, or was it all a dream?

She dressed in black. Confessing was a mournful responsibility. She noted that the pin marks on her waist were changing. Her waist was smaller than it had ever been. Despite her thinness, breakfast would go uneaten. She clutched her stomach at the thought of it. She knelt in front of her window and clasped her hands. This would be her stance in front of the church. She bowed her head and whispered.

"Ich bekan es ich kfeld happ. Fashpaht Got und de gmaey, hatslich geduld aw, fanna hee bessah sige drah." She had been practicing the traditional memorized confession she would be expected to say.

The words penetrated deeply within her.

I confess that I have failed. I promise God and the church, in humbleness, from here on out to make better choices.

Would she? Would she really make better choices? While she knew she could avoid meals with Kathryn and riding in her car, she felt that Adam had given her an unspoken message. In her heart she felt the church was telling her it was time to leave Henry behind — to move beyond her waiting. Her acceptance of his life as a soldier was hurting the community. Her heart ached for herself, for her church, and for Henry.

A harsh knock on the door startled her from her practiced confession. She stood and noticed a black truck in front of her house. It was shiny everywhere except for around the wheel wells. She didn't know much about vehicles, but the truck looked newer than the ones she was used to seeing. Logan's Auto Services was written on the door, with a phone number. The engine was loud. How had she not heard it drive up?

Another rapid knock followed. She couldn't see the front door from her window, so she grabbed her black covering and shoved it on her head. By the time she got to the top of the stairs she could hear her mother's shuffling steps moving through the kitchen.

"I'll be right there," her mother's voice sang sweetly.

Miriam was sure her mother had heard the loud idle of the car, but she spoke her words as if she were expecting a grandchild waiting at the door ready to sneak a cookie. Miriam knew that her mother knew every time a cookie went missing from the smirk on her face, but the grandkids took full advantage of her blindness and thought they were really getting away with something.

She stopped midway down the staircase when she heard the conversation at the door.

"Is Miriam Coblentz still living here?"

Miriam couldn't place the strangely familiar voice.

"Yes," her mother said, sounding confused. "May I ask who you are?"

"Yes, ma'am, I'm sorry, ma'am," the voice said quickly and confidently. "I'm Private Johnny Rossum. I'm a friend of Henry's."

Miriam didn't remember stepping down

the stairs or walking through the mudroom, but the next thing she knew, she was staring into the eyes of a young man she had met with Henry almost a year earlier. Johnny was the one she'd disliked for his brashness. He had embarrassed and irritated her. But now, here he was, a breath of fresh air.

"Johnny," she blurted. At her voice, her mother twisted, confusion written across her face. Miriam spoke in dialect. "*Mem,* it's okay, he's a friend. I'll deal with it. It's okay for you to go back inside."

Miriam tried not to notice the hurt on her mother's face. She didn't want to dismiss her rudely, but at the moment there seemed nothing more important than talking with Johnny in private. Surely he would only come if he had news about Henry.

"Johnny." Miriam turned back to face him, noticing the pinned-up left sleeve where his arm used to be. He had pins and medals all over his starched uniform. She didn't know what any of them meant, only that they hadn't been there before. His face was scarred but handsome. She hadn't noticed how handsome he was when she'd met him in the summer. "Do you have news about Henry?"

"I need you to come with me." He turned and pointed at the truck with his good arm.

"I have to get the truck back tonight. I'm only borrowing it."

"Slow down." Miriam shook her head. "Go with you? Where?"

"To get Hank," Johnny said, quickly. "It's time you brought him back. He's going to be discharged and has nowhere to go."

Johnny's one body turned into two as the world spun. Miriam braced herself against the door frame, then felt a strong hand on her forearm. Once she felt steady, she opened her eyes. Johnny's thumb rubbed against her thin dress, soothing her. Her hand covered his and their eyes met.

"Are you okay?"

"Where is he? I don't understand."

Johnny took this moment to help her descend the few steps and stand beside him on the grass next to the stony drive. He rubbed her arm before he brought it back to his side and resumed his explanation.

"Henry thought you knew that he'd been injured."

"I did — I mean, I do know that. But we haven't been given information in months. The last I heard, he was at a field hospital in Germany and was seriously wounded. I —" She shook her head, feeling relief and anger twist inside of her. "Are you telling me he's here? And he's alive?"

"He's at a convalescent hospital in Maryland. I need to get the truck back this evening, so we need to go now. You'll see Henry today, Miriam."

Johnny's smile beamed. Miriam guessed he realized what a relief his news was to her. Her hand went to her heart. She began weeping and laughing all at once. Then she threw her arms around the one-armed army private who had just given her back her life. Her grateful tears turned into deep, sorrowful sobs. After all the months of not knowing, the prayers that had gone unanswered, the agonizing sleepless nights, now she would see him. Henry was alive.

She would go to him today.

Today.

Today, she was supposed to give her confession to the church. To make her heart and her standing right in front of her community and her leadership. Without this confession, her presence would likely be excluded from *Gross Gmaey.* The pit she was already in was growing deeper and deeper with every heaving sob onto Johnny's shoulder. Was there no true relief for her?

"Miriam? Miriam? Is Henry —" Fannie's nearby voice was laced with fear.

"No, he's alive." Miriam lifted her head to

see Fannie's hand cover her own mouth. Her mother wept as she stood in the door frame.

Nancy and Kathryn jogged to her from across the street.

"He's alive!" she yelled at them. She finally let go of Johnny and ran to her sister and neighbor. "Henry's alive and is in a convalescent hospital in Maryland. Johnny is driving me there today."

The small crowd cheered, jumped in circles, and wept.

"Glory be," Nancy said, lifting a palm to the heavens. "Our prayers have been answered."

"He's alive, Kat," she said, clasping her sister's forearms. "He's alive."

"I couldn't be happier for you, sister." Kathryn's words moved through Miriam's ears and like velvet, wrapped around her soul. Her sister's eyes carried joy, but the furrow of her own grief couldn't be mistaken. "I am so thankful."

Their glassy eyes met. They smiled and hugged for a brief moment.

"You can't go today, Miriam," Fannie interrupted. Miriam broke from Kathryn's embrace, noting her eldest sister's red face and glassy eyes. Her voice didn't sound condemning but concerned. "You have your confession to make today."

"Why didn't you tell me?" Kathryn asked.

"I've made peace with the fact. There was no point in telling anyone," Miriam simply said to Kathryn. Then she faced Fannie. "I know." She sighed.

"Look, Miriam, I don't exactly know what that means, but can it be postponed or something?" Johnny said, pointing to the truck. "I can't wait much longer. Besides, do you really want to make Henry wait?"

Nancy spoke up. "I would say I'd take you, but I would be a nervous wreck driving that far. Maybe I can ask Vic?"

"You need to go today," Kathryn said, clutching her hand. "This is what you've been waiting for."

"Kathryn, don't tell her what to do," Fannie interjected. "I think she should come to church and make her confession first."

"Girls, *shemet ahich*!" Rosemary suddenly broke up the arguing, telling them they should be ashamed of themselves. She divinely made eye contact with each of them. "Miriam must find her own way. None of us can tell her what she knows she must do. Whether the church be happy or not over her decision, it would be least-of-all happy over a quarreling family. Now, Miriam, you make your decision and be at peace with it."

The silence hovered around the small crowd that was growing larger, with Fannie's older and younger children joining them on the porch. Even Truman was standing there, witnessing the scene.

Miriam looked at Kathryn, then Fannie, and finally to her mother. Her eyes lingered on her mother's dearness the longest. How long had her mother had confidence in her youngest, steadfast girl? And now, she would give her the greatest of disappointments.

The pieces of her life were meeting in the wrong places. Johnny and her mother were from two different worlds. Kathryn was a widow, and she'd just found out that Henry was alive. The celebration both drained and exhilarated her. Saying yes to Henry meant saying no to her confession. It was all mismatched; it never should have happened this way. The peace in her heart, however, told her that God had chosen for each of the clashing circumstances to be part of her life. He found beauty in His plan for her. Would her mother ever see that same beauty?

"I need to go to Henry — today."

Fannie went to her mother and walked her gently to the large house, shooing in her children. Miriam watched as her mother turned once before entering and lifted her arm to wave; then, with hunched shoulders and a rounded back, she went into Fannie's home.

Nancy's hand went to her heart. "I feel for your mother, dearie," she said to Miriam and Kathryn. "There's no pain like believing your children are lost to you."

"I will make things right," Miriam said, swallowing down her doubt. "But I must go to get Henry first."

Twenty minutes later, Miriam was packed. Henry's roughly whittled heart caught her eye as she was leaving. She went back to grab it and tucked it into her purse. It was the last thing he'd given her and she didn't want to go without it.

After a quick stop to tell Sylvia the news, the two unlikely travel companions were on their way. Miriam sat rigid in the seat next to Johnny, wondering what they would find to talk about. She clutched her black purse until her knuckles hurt, she didn't often travel long distances and her nerves rattled inside her. She'd taken a moment to pack a small bag of clothing, unsure of how long she would be away, and she also packed some pie, bread, and meat. Even before they arrived to catch a ferry to cross the bay,

Johnny had devoured a healthy portion of what she'd brought. She ate only a few bites. Secretly she wanted to save everything she could for Henry. The entire process of waiting for the ferry, boarding it, having the truck brought aboard, and waiting for the truck to be driven off seemed endless. Now she understood why Johnny was in such a hurry.

Once on the road again, Johnny sung with the radio when they could pick up a station or by himself when they couldn't. He had stripped off his broad-shouldered uniform jacket, and his right arm rippled with muscles as he gripped the large steering wheel. She looked away when he caught her noticing.

"I was a skinny bag of bones when this happened," he said, gesturing to his missing arm. "But I figured, well, I guess I can get double the muscles in my right arm to make up for it."

"I wasn't . . ." She didn't know how to say that she wasn't gawking, when she was. Her face grew hot.

He grinned but didn't say anything.

"How did it . . ." Each word came out slow and uncertain.

"How'd I get my arm blown off?" He said it so happy-go-lucky that Miriam started laughing.

"Yes, I suppose you could say it like that." It occurred to her during this conversation how comfortable she was with him. A year ago she would never have been comfortable talking with an English man for so long, or alone. She'd never been alone with any young men except for Henry and Eli.

"We'd been fighting for what felt like months, but it was really weeks, this time around." He licked his lips as his fingers drummed on the steering wheel the beat of the song on the radio. "Henry and I are all that's left of our little group that came out to see you."

"Henry told me about Buck, but Abe?"

"Yeah, good ole Thump didn't make it. Killed in November."

A reverent silence fell between them.

"Anyway, we got caught in an explosion from those Krauts — I mean, those Germans." He winked at her. "Blew my arm clean off and knocked Henry right off his feet. We lost a lot of fellas that day. Next thing I know, I'm dangling off Henry's shoulder being slung into a Jeep, and then on a bed at a nearby field hospital. From what I'm told, your Hank had been carrying me a while. I was told later he was half out of his mind when they finally got him to lay down in a bed."

Miriam's hand went up to her mouth, pinching her lips. She looked straight ahead down the darkening narrow road. She squeezed her eyes, forcing herself not to live through the experience in her mind. To imagine the pain, the fear, the unknowing.

"Man, it hurt like nothing I ever felt before." Johnny was silent and pursed his lips. His eyes appeared blank for a moment, like his mind was somewhere else. Her hand reached to nudge him back to reality and to the road, he snapped back. "But I'm okay now. Never been better." His smile was so genuine, she believed him.

"And Henry?" she finally asked. "I got a letter in March from a nurse who was taking care of him in January. She said he was seriously wounded."

"Oh, Nurse Spencer, right? She was my favorite. She was a looker. I did anything she told me to do." He seemed lost in his own memory for a moment before he began again.

"So, Henry, well, he should've died, that lucky grunt." He winced. "Sorry, that probably sounds crude in front of a nice lady like you. I've been trying real hard to use better language. It's tough when you're out there, you know. It's hard to have the right frame of mind to even try to talk good. It's hard for me to believe that I'm not still there, so the language just kind of sticks with me."

"It's okay, Johnny." She meant what she said. "I'm just glad you made it back."

"So Henry's a tough one. The docs say he has a brain injury, whatever that means. All I know is that with a brain injury, it's hard to say how bad it is and how long the problems will last."

"Problems? What does that mean?"

"Well, for him it meant being really confused and in pain for weeks. He hardly spoke any English, and that caused some issues. You know, with the whole German thing and all. He was pretty bloody because of some shrapnel, but that was the least of his problems."

"So, he was confused? How is that a serious enough injury to scare his family and me half to death?"

"You'll understand when you see him. It's hard for me to really explain. I think he'd rather have you see for yourself. What I *can* tell you is that I owe him my life."

He met Miriam's gaze for a moment before turning back to the road.

Miriam smiled, then looked forward again. She closed her eyes and forced herself to realize the truth that Henry wasn't overseas anymore; he was alive and she would see him soon. A reality she couldn't fully grasp.

"Do you think it was some type of miracle? How even as confused as Henry was, he found me and got me to help?"

Miriam opened her eyes and looked at him. She nodded her head a little. "What else could it be?"

"Well, you've got me there. I never believed in all that stuff before. But I'm starting to think that maybe Hank and Thump were on to something with all their praying. I started praying myself when I thought Henry might not make it." He nodded his head several times. "Yep, I did. He prayed for me a lot, it was the least I could do."

Miriam smiled at him and nodded, unsure of what to say. She had never talked to an English man about her faith.

"So, what will you and Hank do?"

"What do you mean?"

"When you get him home." He hesitated. "I don't really know how all of this Amish stuff works, but, does he just go back and be Amish again or what?"

She paused, considering his question. What would they do? She'd often imagined him coming home, imagined marrying him, but she'd tried not to dwell on the process of being allowed to marry. She had just skipped her own confession. What did all this mean for them?

"He'll have to confess to the church. I don't exactly know how that will go. I want to marry him," she said simply. "That's all I really know."

"Well, that's good, because he wants to marry you." Johnny chuckled.

A rush of adrenaline coursed through her. The anticipation of seeing him suddenly made her nervous.

"If he weren't so stubborn, you would already be together and maybe already married. You can get married at the courthouse just about any day. Or I'm sure you could plan a big wedding, but then you'd have to wait. All I know is Hank has talked about two things the whole time we were away. God and marrying you."

He smiled and winked at her. She returned his smile, but she couldn't find anything else to say.

They stayed silent after that for some time. Miriam leaned her head back again, and this time, she did let herself fall asleep. Her dreams wavered between the feeling of falling and being pulled up. Back and forth. She would fall, and just before she'd hit whatever the bottom was, she'd be pulled up. The comfort she received in being pulled up and protected was worth the fall every time. It seemed only minutes before she heard Johnny's voice awaken her.

"We're here."

CHAPTER 27

April 1945

As ready as she was to acknowledge that Henry was alive and that she would see him, her nerves made her want to vomit. What if he was changed? What if he didn't want her anymore? He had never fully answered her father's request about quitting her. He hadn't written to her in months. Why didn't he write while he was in the hospital?

"Come on." Johnny opened her car door. He picked her small suitcase up from the parking lot and led her toward the brick building in front of them. "Follow me."

She gathered her wits and righted her covering, wondering if she looked as disheveled as she felt. They walked into a reception area and Johnny was greeted with smiles and nods by a few orderlies and the nurse behind a desk.

"Private Rossum," the woman said in a flat, nasal voice, "no visitors right now."

"I have a little favor to ask," he said, leaning into the desk toward the young nurse, whose crooked smile didn't appear affected by Johnny's swagger.

"Another one?"

"Now, wait," Johnny protested, putting his hand out, "when I asked for an extra helping of potatoes, that was not a favor. Have you seen how skinny Hank is?"

The mention of Henry made Miriam's nerves rattle.

"Private Mast will beef up all on his own." The nurse looked down again. She appeared to be organizing some forms on her desk and hadn't even noticed Miriam standing behind Johnny.

"Well, I think this is a request you won't be able to refuse." He put the suitcase down and turned to pull Miriam up to the desk.

The nurse stifled a gasp, then looked at Johnny with confusion written across the furrowed lines on her forehead.

"This is Hank's girl," he whispered.

"Miriam," the nurse stated. Her voice broke from its monotone and sounded almost feminine.

Miriam watched as the nurse stood and looked her up and down. She didn't feel scrutinized, but she was uncomfortable nonetheless.

"So, you're the girl he can't stop talking about but won't write."

"What? He doesn't want to write me?" Panic rose in Miriam's heart.

"That's not what I said, sweetheart," the nurse clarified, coming around the desk. She clicked her tongue a few times and went from looking at Miriam to looking at a list of something on the desk. "Well, you're in luck that our own little Nazi orderly isn't here right now."

"She's talking about Helen Crowley. She's not really a Nazi but she's a battle-axe, and no one breaks the rules on her watch."

Miriam was immediately afraid of this Helen Crowley. Her hands gripped her purse tighter in one hand and the brown bag of food in the other.

"Follow me," the nurse said, out of the side of her mouth. "By the way, I'm Nurse Flannigan."

"Thank you, Nurse Flannigan," Miriam said as she followed the tall woman down a dimly lit hall.

"Wait here."

Miriam's heart pounded and her breath was rapid. Johnny didn't seem to notice this in the least, and it seemed an eternity before the nurse returned.

"He seems pretty hard asleep right now.

406

But, as long as you don't tell anyone, you can wait until he wakes up," she said, whispering. "He said not to wake him for supper, but I'll let you do that."

"Really?" Miriam swallowed nervously.

"Listen, sweetheart, I know what it's like to not see your soldier, for years even." Her voice, though carrying a tough eastern accent, still felt soft around the edges. "That's why I'm a nurse, as a matter of fact. No one can say I don't have a heart after this. Now, go on in and see your soldier boy."

Before Miriam could even say thank you, the nurse walked away.

"Do you want me to wake him?" Johnny asked.

Miriam thought for a moment. "No. I think I'll go in alone?" She didn't want to say it as a question, but she didn't want to sound harsh in asking to go in alone after all that Johnny had done. "I can't say thank you enough, Johnny."

Johnny blushed and then shrugged. "I think a little kiss would do nicely."

"Johnny!" she scolded.

"It was worth a shot," he said, laughing. "I have to get that truck back. I'll stop by sometime tomorrow and see how you're doing and if you need anything." He set her suitcase down next to her.

"Thanks again." She squeezed his hand, and he winked in return. Then he turned and walked away.

She put her hand on the doorknob and turned it soundlessly. Opening it only halfway, she set down her purse, the food bag, and then her suitcase. Then she closed the door. There was a curtain blocking Henry's bed from the door, and she took a deep breath before moving beyond it.

The vision of the strong, thick-necked young man in uniform came to mind. But when she pushed the curtain aside she found a thin, pale frame, a version of Henry, but not him. Her hand went to her mouth to stifle her gasp.

His head lolled to the side as he slept soundly. His hair had grown longer, though not as long as it had been in his Amish days. A long scar ran the length of his jawline. Next to his bed was a small stand with stacks of letters. She silently moved over to them and recognized instantly that they were all of her letters. But why hadn't he written back?

She turned to pull a chair over, making sure it wouldn't scrape against the floor and startle him awake. He was thin and still convalescing; he apparently needed all the rest he could get.

"Miriam?" His familiar voice caressed her ears.

"Henry." She stopped and turned around. He opened his eyes for a moment before they closed again. He was still asleep.

She pulled the chair closer and just sat and watched him. Occasionally his arms would startle, almost like a baby's, and he would shudder for several long moments, then return to a restful sleep. After more than an hour, Miriam finally rested her head on his mattress and let herself fall asleep.

"No, no!" Henry yelled and sat up in bed. "Don't leave me behind."

Miriam startled. She stood and put her arms out toward him, unsure of where to touch or grasp. His arms were raised and making wavy, shaking movements. Miriam saw panic in his wide-open eyes.

"Henry, it's all right," she said. Though he had spoken in English, she spoke back to him in Pennsylvania Dutch. "I'm here now."

He looked around the room, breathing deeply. Then his eyes landed on Miriam's face. He looked at her for long moments, but his arms didn't rest — they quaked as if still in shock from his nightmare. His eyes went from confusion to recognition.

"Miriam?" he said, instantly crying. "Miriam, you're here?"

All she could do was nod.

He wrapped his arms around her, nearly crushing her. Her head found the familiar spot in the curve of his neck and shoulders. He was bonier, but she could take care of that in a matter of weeks with her cooking. He was alive. That was all that mattered. She sat on his bed and they held each other, weeping for several long minutes.

"Johnny came and got me this morning. I've been here" — she looked at the clock, — "well, a few hours."

"Why didn't you wake me?"

"You need your rest," she said, tracing a finger along the scar on his jaw. "You're awake now. And I'm here. Everything is going to be all right now."

Though they held one another, there was so much left unsaid, and Miriam didn't know how to broach the questions she had. Why hadn't he written her? What had the war been like? Why was he still convalescing when he didn't look injured?

"Knock, knock," a man's voice said from the other side of the curtain before pulling it aside.

Miriam was alarmed to see the man walk in while she sat on Henry's bed, in his arms. The impropriety made her face warm, and she began sweating.

"I heard you had a visitor?" the tall older man in a white doctor's coat said. He had a smile on his face when Miriam jumped from the bed and stood next to it instead.

"G'evening, Doc, this is my girl," Henry said, pulling at Miriam's waist, bringing her as close as possible. "This is Miriam."

While Miriam enjoyed being called his girl, she considered it to be such an English expression. The tempo of Henry's speech had changed. His Pennsylvania Dutch accent had diminished, but there was something else. She listened to his words again in her mind. Was it the way he phrased them or his inflection that had changed? Was it just that he spoke faster? She wasn't sure. The desire to hear him speak more was mixed with the grief that there might be small pieces of the old Henry that were lost to her forever.

"We're all glad to see you here, Miriam. I'm Doctor Allen Bryant." The doctor smiled, putting a hand out to her.

Miriam shook the doctor's hand but was still nervous to meet his eyes, knowing she'd broken the rules.

"I see you have plenty of food for him to make up for missing supper tonight." The doctor motioned to the pie carefully sitting atop her overnight bag.

411

Miriam felt her face warm. "Yes. I hope it's okay that I'm here. I certainly didn't mean to break your rules."

"We've needed a morale booster for this soldier to get him up and outta here. I think you and your pie might be just the thing." He laughed. "He's been reluctant to be discharged, but his big day is coming up."

"Really, he can leave soon?" she asked, unashamedly.

"Yes, his therapy is going well, and I think he can leave later this week." He looked at the file he held.

Miriam looked at Henry. He clenched his jaw.

"Has Henry explained his injuries to you?"

Miriam looked between the doctor and Henry. Henry's face fell.

"No, he hasn't."

"Henry, may I?" The doctor raised his eyebrows. "I need your permission."

Henry nodded and turned away, looking out the window.

"Henry sustained a traumatic brain injury. You can't see the scars on him, but inside of his brain there are scars from the damage. There's part of his brain that is having a hard time telling his muscles how to work. We've noticed significant improvement over the past month since he's been here, and I think the next thing is for him to return to his regular life. Sometimes that's the best therapy for situations like this."

"So, what does that mean? Besides how thin he looks, he looks fine. I don't see what the problem is."

"Henry?" The doctor walked over to the bed and put a hand out toward him. "She needs to see."

Miriam was petrified at what this meant. What did she need to see? She stepped back to give him room and watched as he moved to get out of bed. He reached two arms out to take the doctor's hand and couldn't keep his own steady. They shook uncontrollably, and it took several tries for him to grasp the doctor's hand. The doctor helped him out of the bed and even as he stood straight, his hands quaked at his sides.

"Pick up a letter." The doctor pointed to the stack on his bedside table.

"Doc," he said before sighing. "I can't —" Henry's voice was gruff, and he spoke through clenched teeth.

"Henry." The doctor put a hand on Henry's shoulder. "Pick up a letter."

Henry turned toward the stack and inhaled, then exhaled deeply. He lifted his hand and the tremors began. Try after try, he could not control the shaking enough to pick up an envelope. Finally, he flung his arm and cascaded the letters all over the floor. Miriam jumped back, amazed at his frustration. She had never seen him lose his temper. He breathed deeply, in and out, his teeth slightly bared. His face was shining with beads of sweat after what appeared to be very little exertion.

"Henry's brain is having difficulty communicating the right message to his arms, hands, and fingers. And, believe it or not, his tremors have improved significantly."

"So, does that mean that eventually he'll be cured?" She spoke cautiously, afraid that Henry would find her question intrusive. Her heart thudded when his face turned away. "Henry, I don't care about the — tremors. All I care about is that you're alive and you're coming home."

When she touched his quaking arm and the muscles in it tensed tightly, she pulled her hand back as if she'd been burned.

"Henry?"

Henry's eyes glassed over and he turned away from her and stared out the window. His breath slowly returned to normal as the doctor and Miriam continued to speak.

"I believe that he will make a full and complete recovery, if he chooses to," the doctor said evenly and began picking up the letters. "He can walk now, which is the biggest improvement. When he was transferred here from overseas he was just barely doing that much."

"Is this why you wouldn't write me?" The thought suddenly occurred to her, though she wished she'd kept this part of the conversation for a private moment instead of in front of the doctor.

"Write you?" his voice fairly barked. "I can't even eat by myself."

"Henry, you can't eat by yourself *yet,*" the doctor said emphatically but not with the anger that laced Henry's voice. He turned back to Miriam. "Miriam, he needs you to help him move on. A daily routine and some small therapeutic exercises we will teach you to do with him will be the best way to help him continue to improve."

"I'm not ready to leave. I need more time."

"No, my boy, you don't." The doctor put a hand on Henry's shoulder. "You need to get on with your life. Leave everything else on the battlefield and move forward."

Henry roughly pulled his shoulder away from the doctor's touch.

The doctor raised his eyebrows at Miriam. He had wanted her to see that it was more than just the quaking. Henry's anger needed curing more than anything else.

"Well, Miriam," he said, putting out a hand again. "It's a pleasure meeting you, and I'm certain you can get this soldier back into shape." Then he turned to Henry and nudged him slightly with his elbow. "Henry, behave. That's an order." He winked at Miriam before leaving, then added, "As you can see, he has a bit of a temper."

Miriam didn't want the doctor to leave and would have done almost anything for Nurse Flannigan, Johnny, or even the rule-following orderly Crowley to come into the room. She didn't know what to do or say. Henry didn't want her there. After all those months, all she could think about was to be with him, and it seemed all he could think about was not having her see him in this state.

He surprised her, however, and turned around. He sat on the edge of the bed and sighed.

"I'm sorry," he said simply.

"For what?"

"For all of this." He gestured with his head to his hands. "For getting angry. I really did want to write you, but I was so angry that I just couldn't. I was afraid of what you would see when you found me like this. I'm still afraid of what you think about me."

"You're alive, Henry. We didn't even know

that much for months. That's all I care about. You're alive. And I'll help you. Whatever it takes. I'm not going anywhere without you."

He inhaled and lifted a frantically quaking arm and reached for her. She moved toward him and took his hand. He wrapped his arms around her and wept, and she let him embrace her for a long time.

When he pulled away he met her eyes. "I was right, Miriam," he whispered.

"Right?"

"About God calling me to enlist."

She cocked her head. He had said all along that this was right, despite how wrong it appeared. What did he mean?

"God wanted me there to save Johnny's life so that He could save his heart."

Over the next few days, Miriam learned that when Henry rested he didn't tremor. With large movements he did fairly well. It was fine movements, such as eating, picking up small objects, or even scratching his face, that he couldn't make. Miriam had taken up the difficult task of feeding him. It was difficult because Henry complained of his handicap through every meal. After a good scolding from Miriam, however, he began to stifle some of his self-deprecating comments and forced himself to smile and say thank you at the end of the meal.

Miriam refused to feed him an apple, and he had to eat it on his own. She told him if he threw it she would stay away the rest of the day. He ate it, grumbling the entire time, but Miriam was smiling. The entire nursing staff continued to encourage her, telling her they hadn't seen his attitude improve until she came. Even Orderly Crowley told Henry that Miriam was the best thing that had happened to his therapy. Johnny had convinced another nurse to let Miriam board in the nurse lodgings for the week. Miriam offered to sleep on the floor if needed. She was given a bed, however, and was thankful for it.

She also telephoned Nancy, giving her enough information to let her family know that she was safe and would be coming home with Henry by week's end. The squeal on the other end of the phone nearly deafened Miriam's ears.

"Where shall he stay, dearie?"

"I'm not sure," she said. "I doubt he will feel comfortable at his parents', and I just don't know if his *dat* would allow it."

"Don't say another word. He can stay in Vic's old room."

"Thank you," Miriam said, relieved. "I

just can't thank you enough."

They arranged for Ralph to pick her and Henry up at the bus station that Saturday evening, and all that was left was a few days of gathering what remained of Henry's courage to make the trip. What a pair they were, a wounded soldier who couldn't feed himself and an Amish woman. The nurses and staff at the hospital saw them off as if they were both brave warriors and insisted they would never forget their Amish soldier. Miriam believed them.

"You haven't told me much about how it's been for you," Henry said a few hours into their bus ride home. "How is everything at home?"

Miriam sighed. She hadn't told him anything about the difficulty she'd had; she didn't want to burden him unnecessarily. But now that they were nearly home, she was glad that he'd asked, since it would not only be her problem, but both of theirs. It would be good for him to know what her standing with the church was. Over the next several hours she told him everything. Everything from her anger with Eli to his apology before leaving for the CPS camp to her father's and James's deaths. She left the visits from the *Aumah Deanuh* until the end.

"All because of me," he said, looking

down at their entwined hands. "I never meant for you to go through so much, Miriam. I'm sorry."

"Don't apologize. Adam insists it's because I ate and drove with Kathryn," she said, gently. "I made choices, just like you. I know they haven't liked that I've openly supported you. It gives the young people the wrong idea. But what was I supposed to do? Forget you?"

Henry squeezed her hand and swallowed hard.

"I could never forget you," she said.

Miriam knew there was so much left to be discussed. Their future was unclear and it frightened her. But God had not let her down, and she knew He wouldn't now. Their future was already planned and ordained by Him. She chose to trust in Him.

When they arrived at the bus station they were greeted with happy tears. Ralph, Nancy, Kathryn, and the children were there waiting. Henry's smile was wide and bright as he thanked everyone. Miriam noticed how Henry looked over everyone's shoulders and the way his jaw muscles tightened. Was he disappointed that his family hadn't come to welcome him home? When would these hurts heal? When would they end?

"Let's get him home," Nancy said and took one of his arms, leading him to the car.

It was difficult that night to leave Henry at the Pooles' and walk over to her own home. She was unsure what kind of greeting she should expect from her mother. She decided that as easy as it would be to wait until her mother was asleep before returning, it was the cowardly way. She returned to find her mother rocking in her chair.

"Hello, *Mem,*" she said.

"Miriam." Her mother's voice was gentle and she smiled. "How is Henry? Kathryn told me about his — problem."

Miriam paused, pleasantly surprised.

"He's doing better every day. But he needs a lot of help still."

"I see."

There was a great pause between them. Just as Miriam was about to say good night, her mother spoke again.

"So, you two are planning to marry still?"

"Yes."

"With the church?"

After several long moments of pause, she forced a yawn. "I'd better get to bed."

She couldn't help but see the confusion cross over her mother's face at the question left unanswered. How she wanted to answer that question and bring relief to her mother's heart, but she knew tonight was no time to make promises she wasn't sure could be kept. The truth was that she just didn't know what was in her future now that Henry was home.

With that, she retreated to her room. She slept soundly for the first time since before the draft notice arrived over two years earlier. Henry was across the street. No matter what happened, he was alive and safe. They were together.

CHAPTER 28

April 1945

Over the next week, she saw that the doctor was right. Henry's spirit improved greatly. He wore his old clothes again and looked more like himself every day. He was beginning to fatten up with Nancy and Miriam's cooking and baking. Ralph had him help around their property with small things that kept him busy. He still shook and couldn't feed himself most foods, but he was patient with himself and, more than anything, he began to realize that being still was not a bad thing. In his still moments he would read his Bible and pray. No tremors. No erratic movements. Turning a page in the Bible proved to be some of the best therapy any doctor could have recommended. Miriam was overjoyed as she watched him grow and change so quickly.

"Tomorrow is *Gross Gmaey*," she told him after a week at home.

"I'm not ready," he said quickly. "I don't think I can face everyone yet."

Miriam nodded, unsure whether she was disappointed or relieved. Going alone after skipping her confession would be difficult enough. Having a changed Henry at her side might be unbearable, though she longed to see him back in the fold and protection of the church that she loved.

"All right. Well, I'm going to go, if they'll let me, and I'll be back later tomorrow." She tiptoed up and kissed him quickly on the lips, then began reaching for her coat. "Now, don't give Nancy a hard time."

A hand went around her wrist and pulled her closer.

"Henry," she said, smiling, "that's the best you've done yet. I didn't even see you coming."

He smiled and gave her a real kiss.

The church was far more gracious to her than she had anticipated. Adam Gingrich caught her eye and approached her before the service began. He admitted his disappointment in her not coming to church on the day she was supposed to give her confession.

"You will be welcome to attend the regular service, but once *Gross Gmaey* begins with the reading of the *Ordnung,* you'll have to leave. This will happen right after lunch." He met her eyes, and Miriam saw in his a genuine burden for her. "You actually might be more comfortable leaving before lunch."

Miriam nodded, understanding that her communion with the church had been broken. Though she was not shunned yet, eating alongside the other members would cause discomfort for everyone. This felt just to Miriam. She hadn't met with the standards of the church and would be required to pay penance for her wrongdoings. She understood this and couldn't argue with it. *Gross Gmaey* was held during the two Sunday services in April. She would be allowed to bring her confession to the church in May. She wondered if Henry would be ready to attend services by then. Her heart squeezed tightly at the thought of missing *Gross Gmaey.* While the reading of the *Ordnung* was daunting at times, there was something refreshing about the act of foot washing and the self-reflection on your deeds and faith.

Sylvia found Miriam before she left after the regular Sunday service.

"I got your letter. How is Henry?"

"He's getting better every day," she said. "He wasn't ready to come today."

"I expected that. Tell him I said I'm glad he's back and that *Mem* wants to see him this week."

"Will your *dat* allow that?"

"I think so," she said. "Maybe you could bring Henry to my house. It might be more comfortable there. We'll do it between meals, too."

"Thank you, Sylvia." She wasn't sure whether Sylvia meant this because of both her and Henry's church standing or because of Henry's tremors and inability to feed himself. Either way, she was thankful.

"I'd better go."

She saw her friend join the crowd to help serve the lunch. There was a sting in leaving her community, and she tucked her head down into her chest as she walked away.

"Miriam!" Ida May's voice called.

Miriam stopped, surprised.

"Please tell Henry that Jesse and I are glad he's home. Jesse sure has missed him. Maybe you can both come over," she paused as if trying to find the right words, "soon? I've missed you."

"Oh, Ida May." Miriam hugged her cousin, careful not to squish baby Jesse between them. She pulled away and met Ida May's eyes. "I hope that we can come over soon as well."

Miriam understood what "soon" meant. As soon as her and Henry's standing with the church was righted and all fences were mended. It couldn't happen quickly enough for Miriam. She received several more happy waves and smiles. It appeared that there were many people glad that Henry was safely home. Her heart and mood were lighter as she walked the rest of the way to her buggy.

As she drove home, she thanked God for the hope He had brought to her life. A warm breeze carried the scent of growth and the sounds of new life. Spring was here, and with it arrived wedding season.

Henry was nervous as they walked into Sylvia's home the following day. He held onto Miriam's hand tightly.

"Stay next to me," he said when they got to the door. "I know I can do anything with you at my side."

"I won't go anywhere."

But the moment they walked into the house, Henry left her side and ran to his mother, who stood there waiting, already crying. They hugged for what seemed like an eternity. It wasn't until they pulled away that she noticed his father had entered the room from the back living room.

"Son." He put his hand out.

Henry, almost as if he'd forgotten his handicap, went to take his father's hand and couldn't. Miriam could see the panic in Henry's face as his parents eyed each other. She went up to him and took Henry's hand gently and placed it carefully in his father's. Miriam noted his father's glassy eyes as they shook firmly.

They all sat in the living room, and it was silent for some time before his father finally spoke up.

"What should we expect now that you're home?"

Henry looked at Miriam, and she nodded for him to continue.

"I know Miriam and I both have things we need to make right with the church," he started but faltered. "I know I've caused a lot of pain. I'm sorry for that."

"Do you see now why what you did was wrong?" He waved at Henry as if gesturing at his tremors.

Miriam winced.

"I still believe I was following God," he said quietly but confidently as he looked into his father's eyes.

Miriam felt both pride and anxiety swell in her. She could see her Henry in his words, and his quiet confidence was returning. Yet if he still believed that he was following God, he would have a difficult time confessing in front of the church.

"But you are coming back — right?" His mother's eyes were red and puffy from crying.

"My intention was never to leave the church, but in order to follow God I had to move beyond the church's standards." Henry's voice grew stronger with every word. It seemed that his actions being challenged was all he needed to regain his strength in them. With deliberation, he grabbed Miriam's hand as they sat near each other on the couch. There were no tremors in his movement.

"I don't want you coming around the house, Henry," his father said, sticking his jaw out, "gives the others the wrong idea. Influences them the wrong way. Sylvia's married; Mark can decide for them. But unless and until you make things right with the church, you can't come home."

"I understand," he said respectfully. His eyes turned away from his father and settled deeply in Miriam's.

The summer heat came early with the arrival of spring. Fannie's baby also arrived several weeks early. Everyone looked into the babe's eyes, ready to see the eyes of the Coblentz patriarch. Baby Melvin was declared to be the spitting image of *Daudy* Melvin.

Later in the week, a familiar face on Nancy's front porch forced the topic of Miriam and Henry's future.

"May I speak with Henry and Miriam?" Adam Gingrich said as Nancy answered the door.

Miriam was at the house almost constantly now. She didn't feel right about leaving Henry's care to Nancy. Her mother was always with Fannie. Except for breakfast, she took all of her meals with her eldest daughter as well. Miriam felt no need to sit at home alone.

The two walked out onto the porch and stood with Adam. He put a hand out to Henry. With concentrated effort, Henry's hand moved out toward it. The quaking had improved some, though he still had a long stretch of healing ahead of him. But he was able to take Adam's hand and gave it a firm shake.

"As you know, Miriam is making her confession in front of the church in May once *Gross Gmay* is finished," he began. "I'm glad to see that you're home and doing well. But you've been home for almost two weeks and haven't initiated anything about your own confession. The church wants to acknowledge that you have your own wrongs to right. You know your enlistment was not our way. And I know you want to get married." He turned toward Miriam, then back to Henry. "With your confession, you could."

Miriam's heart stopped beating at these words. She was one Sunday away from having what she'd wanted her entire life. What she'd been patient to wait for while Henry was at the CPS camp and then at war was so close now. She and Henry could be married, and soon.

"I understand," Henry said, gently.

The furrow in his brow broke Miriam's heart. It didn't matter how sure Henry was that what he had done in enlisting was right; the guilt over the pain he caused his family weighed so heavily on him. She hated watching Adam pile more fault and shame on his shoulders. She was not ashamed of him; she was proud.

"Adam, do you know what he's been through?" She surprised herself with speaking up. "He's a hero. He risked his life for others."

Adam didn't say anything but only looked wide-eyed at Miriam. Of course he didn't know what Henry had been through.

Her breath quickened as she continued forcing her voice to remain gentle and respectful.

"He has more courage in his shaking hands than the entire community does. He watched his friends die defending the freedom that we have here in America. He nearly died himself. He's a decorated soldier." She was proud to say those words out of dialect. "I'm proud of my soldier. I don't think he's done anything wrong."

She didn't know it was what she believed until she said the words out loud. Her words frightened her. What was she saying?

"Henry, please consider what we've talked about," Adam said, without a side glance to Miriam.

Miriam and Henry were silent as they watched Adam return to his buggy and drive away.

"Miriam, why did you say that?"

"Isn't it true?"

Henry sighed. They stood in silence for several long moments before he looked at her and shrugged.

"Ich veiss net." He just didn't know.

Miriam held her breath as she watched him walk down the porch steps and out past the house. While her mind wanted her to panic over their circumstances, her heart was peaceful. After everything, Henry deserved time to consider his future.

She found herself in her room a few minutes later. When the floorboard creaked beneath her foot, she sat down on the floor and opened it. Her soul flooded with emotion as she could feel the life she'd lived through the letters and journals she'd hidden there. She pulled them out and one by one, the words spoke truth to her.

Henry received a draft letter a few days ago. His mother wore black to church. I cried when he said he won't marry me before he leaves. He doesn't feel right about leaving me behind.

We were supposed to be announced in church today, but instead later this week I'll be saying goodbye to Henry, who's leaving for the CPS camp in Hagerstown.

Henry decided to enlist. He said he's following God but I don't understand this. My life will never be the same again. I love him, but I hate what he is doing to me.

Thump and I often sit quietly together and pray. Our prayers comfort me.

Henry said that he and I are on a different journey. He says that God won't travel all of His children through everything in the same way. I'm not angry at his words like I once would have been, but I want to learn what he means by them.

I wish I could understand why God called me to fight. Why would he want me, an Amish carpenter, to leave everything I've ever known and become a soldier? Though I can't understand this, I don't question the strength that I know only He provides.

Ever since I'm learning to be still, I am hearing God's whisper in my heart.

I never thought I'd say this, but I'm starting to see what Henry meant about God's calling. If I could, I would want to go to school to be a midwife.

I know my hope is in the Lord, and if I am to give my life for this cause I pray I will be noble in it.

All that matters is that Henry comes back alive. I know God will take care of the rest.

I promise that I will do whatever I can to return to you.

"Can I join you?" Henry stood in her door frame. His stature looked stronger than she'd recognized before.

She looked around her, letters and journals everywhere. She stacked some together and patted the bare space.

"I suppose we're already in trouble. Being alone in my room together seems to be the least of our problems." She chuckled.

He sat next to her, his knees folded up. He looked younger than he had since she'd seen him at the hospital.

"Your letters were the only things that kept me going," Henry began. "Knowing that you were praying for me. Knowing that you understood more than anyone else here at home what God's whispers meant. Even amidst the explosions and the death and dying around me. It was — well, like I imagine hell would be. I stopped looking for big signs, but just always focused on His whispers to me. They were all I could depend on."

"What would He say?"

"Sometimes he'd just say 'don't lose hope' or 'trust me in all things,' but a lot of the time it felt like this." He reached with shaky hands to her head and brought it to his chest. He breathed in and out. She could hear the warmth of life in his body; she could feel his beating heart and his chest rise and fall. She sat up and looked at him.

"I don't understand."

"The best way I can explain it is like I imagine babies feel when they are nestled in their mother's arms. The only thing they care about in that moment is feeling their mother's heartbeat and breath against them."

He paused as he looked around the room.

"That's what it felt like. Like He was cradling me. Comforting me."

Miriam understood better than she could express.

"Did you mean what you said to Adam?" he asked.

"I said those words without a thought. It was just what flowed out of me. Then I came up here, and I started reading your letters and my journals and I couldn't help but see that at some point in the middle of all of this, I came to understand exactly what you meant. About God's whispering.

About how God takes each of us down our own path. I am learning that our paths just aren't what we expected."

"What does this mean for us?"

"I don't know."

CHAPTER 29

May 1945

Miriam dressed carefully that morning. She was wearing her black dress and her black covering. As she rolled up her stockings, she took care not to snag them. Today would be the day that things would be made right. She couldn't be found in error in any way. Weeks of thought and prayer had gone by and it was time to move on.

She picked up her purse, and with a deep breath she walked down the stairs. The drive was uneventful yet nerve-wracking. No one spoke.

When she arrived and stepped out, she was careful not to dirty her shoes. Everyone was watching her. She smoothed down the waist of her dress, though onlookers pretended to go about their business. She hadn't imagined such a feeling of discomfort in these final moments, but they were there.

Until she saw him. Henry stood there in

the courthouse door, his uniform crisp and decorated and perfect. The smile on his face radiated the love they shared.

She exhaled the breath she had been holding. It didn't matter that strangers were watching. Henry walked to her and with a quaking hand, reached for her. With pride, she took his hand. When their hands touched, all the tension, the nervousness, and the fear receded. He was hers. She was his. This was what she had dreamed of for the last eight years. Today she would marry her soldier. Though the day came in the most difficult way and along a rutted path, still it came laced with God's grace.

"Are you two ready?" Kathryn asked, holding a wiggling Jamie. Nan stood alongside her, proudly wearing a ring of flowers around her head. She called herself the flower girl.

"Yes," Miriam and Henry both said.

Nancy, Ralph, Vic, and Victoria arrived as well. Their small crowd waited just outside the courtroom when the Justice of the Peace approached them. He briefly recounted his time from the First World War and instantly offered to make the event extra special by asking if Miriam wanted to walk down the aisle to her soldier.

"Yes," Miriam said, not knowing how to

say no to so gallant a gesture.

Henry winked at her and squeezed her hand.

"Take a few moments, Miriam. This is your time." Kathryn wrapped her arms around her shoulders and walked through the door into the courtroom with the rest of the group.

She and Henry were alone.

"I'll be right in the front waiting for you." His voice was smooth.

She nodded and smiled at him as he walked into the courtroom. The doors closed behind him and she stood in the hallway, uncomfortable and unsure of the arrangement. She suddenly didn't want to walk down any aisle and least of all, by herself. Then she heard a familiar voice.

"Miriam, Miriam!" Sylvia came running up, her large belly leading the way. "You can't get married."

"Sylvia?" Miriam's anxiety heightened. "I know it's difficult to understand, but —"

"No," she tried to catch her breath, "I mean, you can't get married like that. You need to wear this."

Sylvia opened a paper bag and Miriam saw her royal-blue wedding dress perfectly folded inside. Miriam had never asked for it back after lending it to Sylvia, thinking it wasn't important. Now, in the moments before she was about to get married to Henry, she realized how much it would mean to her to wed in the dress she'd sewn over two years earlier.

Sylvia rushed Miriam into the bathroom and helped her change as quickly as she could.

"And this." Sylvia provided a small strip of blue fabric. "I know it's not yours, but I wanted you to have the silly garter we girls always secretly wear."

"Sylvia, I just can't believe you did all this." She slipped the garter on her leg and hugged Sylvia for her thoughtfulness.

They left the bathroom, and Sylvia pulled her toward the door.

"Just one more thing."

"There's more?"

She pushed her out the door, and Miriam began weeping when she saw her mother standing there next to their hired driver.

"Miriam?" her mother said, her eyes searching for her daughter but not finding her. "I made this for you."

Her mother handed in her direction a perfect white covering. Many in the church would say that it was wrong for Rosemary to be at the courthouse at all. It looked bad. It would give the appearance that she approved of Miriam and Henry's decision. Miriam knew that she would have to answer the questions of her friends and maybe even overhear gossip about herself because of her choice to go to the courthouse to gift Miriam with the white *kapp.* Knowing all of this made Miriam's heart swell with such pride and love for her mother.

"Now, usually you don't wear it until you're officially married, but I thought you might want to wear it now, anyway." Her mother's voice was full of emotion, but the smile on her face remained.

"But, *Mem,* I know I've disappointed you so dreadfully," she said, fighting tears as she took the white covering from her. "How can you —"

"The circumstances have disappointed me, Miriam, not you." Her mother's voice was as sweet as if she spoke to a child. "Of course, I'm sad. Your future has taken a different path than *Dat* and I wanted for you. But, Miriam, I love you, no matter what."

They embraced for several long moments. Then Miriam removed the black covering and her mother helped her put on the white one.

"You look beautiful," her mother said. "Be happy and love your Henry with all your might."

Her mother's expression appeared to settle in resignation to Miriam's choice for her future. They clasped hands for a few moments before Sylvia reminded Miriam that Henry was waiting. Miriam walked to the door, then turned around. Sylvia held Miriam's mother, comforting her, and led her to the car. A lump formed in Miriam's throat.

Lord, I know this is right. Bring peace to my mother.

"Miriam?" Henry's voice brought her back. He was rushing up to her; his eyes weren't panicked, but they were filled with concern. "I waited, but when you didn't come — I thought that —"

"It was Sylvia and *Mem.*" Her voice hitched in her throat. She stepped inside as they spoke.

"Your dress," he said, noticing. His voice softened in awe, warming Miriam's soul. His own unshed tears glistened.

"And a white *kapp.*" She gently touched it. "It's the last of who I am — or was."

"But you're ready? Ready to start a new path, different from where we came from. Start fresh. Who knows where God will take us."

Miriam's eyes looked at the door of the courthouse, then returned to Henry.

"I'm ready. I'll go anywhere with you."

Henry's unsteady hand reached for her face, and he stroked her cheek as best he could. His lips pursed in concentration.

"Let's go." He put an elbow out to her, offering her his arm.

Miriam gladly took Henry's arm and walked with him. As they made their way together down the courtroom aisle, Miriam was reminded of the difficult steps they had taken to get there. She thanked God for His unending faithfulness in their lives and for the enduring love of her soldier.

AMISH PRAYER

Adorn our hearts with the true faith, with a burning love, a living hope.

If Thou art our light, so shine in us; if Thou art our life, so live in us; if Thou art our joy, fill us with rejoicing; if we are temples of Thy Spirit, take full possession of us and make us holy in body, soul, and spirit.

Amen.

A Devoted Christian's Prayer Book
PATHWAY PUBLISHERS

LETTER TO THE READER

The story of Miriam and Henry truly is fictional, though I heard stories in my growing-up years of Amish couples marrying at a courthouse instead of following their customs, and of some who defied their conscientious objector ways and headed for the military, leaving their families crushed and confused. This is merely one scenario of how this may have happened. Please also keep in mind that each Amish district is unique. No two look and do things exactly the same way.

My family is Amish. If there's one thing I've learned growing up among them, it is that they are regular people. They face the same temptations and fight against the same internal struggles as we do. They combat pride, hatefulness, and lust. They fall down and rise up. They sin and plead forgiveness. Life is no easier for them than for us. No additional grace or love is available to them that a non-Amish person cannot attain. They were created by our God with the same need for grace and forgiveness as the rest of us.

I pray you didn't just enjoy this story, but learned that the Amish experienced a unique journey during World War II. Their history is rich with conviction that affected American politics and history. There's nothing *simple* about that. Through this book and the books to follow, I hope you will see that they are more than buggies, uniform dress, and peace. Though their ultimate desire is to live peaceably and serve God in all ways, where there's a group of people, you will find love and hate, peace and war, and grace and justice. If you are interested in learning more about the Amish and their way of life, please go to my website www .elizabethbyleryounts.com. There you will find my contact information. Please don't hesitate to ask me your questions and I will do my best to provide you with answers. Also, please visit NotQuiteAmishLiving .com, where I am a contributing writer. There you will find great stories, recipes, wisdom, and the simplicity many of us long for through this journey of life.

Showers of blessings,
Elizabeth

■ ■ ■ ■

PROMISE TO RETURN

READING GROUP GUIDE

■ ■ ■ ■

INTRODUCTION

Miriam Coblentz and Henry Mast are a young Amish couple in love, yet to be wed, living during the time of World War II. Their dreams of marriage and a family are put on hold when Henry is recruited. Initially Henry serves as a conscientious objector at a Civilian Public Service camp, while Miriam waits longingly for him to return. And he does, except as a changed man. Henry enlists in the army, going against their Amish ways, believing that God has called him to fight in the war.

Miriam is left to decide between loyalty to her church, beliefs, and parents or the young man who holds her heart. A physical war sets a context for a journey of faith, love, and loss as a young Amish woman battles her own internal war for the man she loves.

QUESTIONS AND TOPICS
FOR DISCUSSION

1. Did you grow up in a faith tradition? What are the benefits of being in community, be it faith-based or not? What would you define as your present community?

2. Henry enlists with the army, a decision

that goes against the *Ordnung* and others' expectations of him. Describe a time you made a deciïion that went against others' expectations of you. What led you to make that decision?

3. What presuppositions of Miriam and Henry's Amish culture affected your viewpoint on their demonstrative displays of affection? Did these consistent and romantic interactions surprise you in any way? Explain.

4. Miriam feels like life is passing her by as she waits on Henry during his time of active duty. It was agonizing for her "to watch as everyone around her continued to move ahead while she stood still, stagnated by Henry's leaving" (page 118). Do you identify with the feeling that life is passing you by? What are you waiting on in this present season? How does your posture of waiting resemble Miriam's? How does it differ?

5. How does Henry's response toward Miriam's kissing of Eli parallel God's response to Miriam? How have others in your life shown you grace?

6. In Exodus 20:12, the sixth commandment states, "Honor your father and your mother . . ." Miriam struggles with this commandment, as evident on page 197. What Miriam "really wanted to know was what God said about what to do when the division was between her loyalty to her parents and love for her intended husband." How does Miriam honor or dishonor her parents? How does Miriam's struggle to honor her parents compare and contrast with the struggles for today's generation?

7. When Miriam's mother is burned, Miriam is far away from home with Henry, getting their marriage license. Because of this, she assumes that if she "had just followed the rules, she wouldn't have been burned" (page 247). The "rules" she is referencing are those of her religion. Do you think Christianity is based upon a set of rules, or a relationship? Why?

8. After Miriam stands Henry up for marriage, she boldly stands up to her parents and declares her intentions to be with him. Additionally, she prays aloud for the first time. Discuss what feelings may have

prompted Miriam to take these actions.

9. Why do you think rejection by her family, friends, and church did not propel Miriam faster toward a life with Henry outside of the church? Recall a time when a decision you made brought rejection from your community. Did you seek to please those by whom you had been rejected? Why or why not?

10. Identify the benefits of having an authority figure like the *Aumah Deanuh* and official warnings like the *auh gretahs* in the Amish community.

11. What is the significance of the scene of Miriam's father's death in chapter 20?

12. Describe the second visit from the *Aumah Deanuh* (pages 378-84). In your opinion, did Miriam participate in confession in any way? What are your views of public confession before the church?

13. When Miriam is finally given the chance to go see Henry, their worlds collide. "Saying yes to Henry meant saying no to her confession . . . The peace in her heart, however, told her that God had chosen

for the clashing circumstances to each be part of her life. He found beauty in His plan for her" (page 395). How is this a defining moment of the way Miriam views God? What moments of 'clashing circumstances' have defined your view of God? Explain.

14. How does Miriam's *Mem* travel her own journey of loyalty to her husband and church versus her unyielding love and commitment to her children? How do you view her *Mem* when she gives Miriam the white *kapp* at her wedding but leaves briefly afterward?

15. In what ways does the author demonstrate that war transcends all boundary lines, be it age, culture, religion, wealth, or nationality throughout her novel?

ENHANCE YOUR BOOK CLUB

1. The Amish's willingness toward humility, community, and submission to the will of God is at odds with the individualism rampant in today's society. This anti-individualism is highlighted by the value they place on community and rejection of technologies that could make one less dependent on that community. Select one

of the technology items below that most prevents you from investing in or developing true community. Then, choose to refrain from that item for a set amount of time, ranging from one day, one week, or a month.

- Television
- Mobile Phone
- Facebook, Twitter, or Pinterest
- Texting
- Radio

2. Try a few Amish recipes this week from www.NotQuiteAmishLiving.com where Elizabeth Byler Younts is a contributing writer! If you would like, bring it to your next book club meeting.

- Brown Sugar Dumplings — http://not quiteamishliving.com/2012/09/brown -sugar-dumplings/
- Pumpkin Pie — http://notquiteamish living.com/2012/12/imperfect-paleo -pumpkin-pie/
- Coffee Cake — http://notquiteamish living.com/2012/12/my-favorite-coffee -cake/
- Pineapple Jello Salad — http://not

quiteamishliving.com/2013/01/to-jello
-salad-or-not/

3. Author Elizabeth Byler Younts has also written an Amish memoir titled *Seasons: A Real Story of an Amish Girl.* This is a story of her grandmother Lydia Lee Coblentz, who grew up in an impoverished American family through the Great Depression. Read this memoir and discuss how this book differs from *Promise to Return.*

4. Widespread adoption of the home computer and Internet among the Amish does not exist. In light of this and the prevalence of letter writing in *Promise to Return,* write and send a letter this week to a loved one rather than an email or text.

A CONVERSATION WITH ELIZABETH BYLER YOUNTS

Have you always wanted to write?

I wrote my first novel at age eleven. I was hooked. About this same time I promised my Amish grandma that I would someday write the story of her life. I think I've always thought in story form and "novelized" the real and make believe. It seems I have always had characters in my head telling me their stories.

Describe your favorite writing location or room.

I love a room with a view! I wrote the majority of *Promise to Return* at my parent's house in rural Michigan, while my husband was deployed. They have an amazing three-seasons room facing the wooded area behind their house. Having that natural landscape and all those windows was perfection. But often I find myself in my living room when everyone else in the house is sleeping . . . this means my "view" is usually toys and laundry. I have the TV on for background noise or I can't write. A Starbucks couch also works.

What authors inspire you?

I have been mentored by Allison Pittman for several years. Her voice in Christian fiction and her amazing teaching has been integral in my own writing. I just love her as a writer and as a dear friend. Tricia Goyer has also been a huge inspiration to me. She is a homeschooling mom who still manages to write and encourage other writers. I love her perspectives on how to balance mom-life and writing-life.

What was the inspiration for writing *Promise to Return*?

Really it started with writing *Seasons,* my Amish grandma's memoir. Writing historical fiction fits me but so does Amish fiction . . . so I married the two. My Amish grandpa was drafted in WWII and I always enjoyed hearing his stories about the Civilian Public Service. In exploring this I became infatuated with the amazing stories of conviction and sacrifice that I read in my research. I wanted to bring this history to readers. So, Miriam and Henry's story was born!

Your family was Amish before converting. What are some of the most common misconceptions about the Amish lifestyle that you experience?

The concept of their simple life is true in many ways . . . but that doesn't mean they have simplicity in their relationships. They are so very human and struggle with the same problems non-Amish do: marriage, parenting, finances, etc. Because they deal with these issues or struggles very privately, it can appear that they don't exist at all.

What Amish lessons of simplicity do you incorporate into your own family?

Something that I am very adamant about is that we have family dinners together at the table without electronic distractions. We have home-cooked meals most nights and very little gets in the way of this family time. We also make time for Bible lesson and prayer most evenings with our daughters.

How does your own spiritual journey shape the journey Miriam takes?

Wow, this is a good question. As I wrote Miriam's story my husband and I were living out our first deployment. It was like the historical military world of Miriam and my modern military world collided. As a military wife you know it is your job to hold down the home front while your husband is away serving; knowing this does not make it easy to do, however. My dependence on the Lord grew stronger than it's ever been during the deployment and I could use my emotions to capture some of what Miriam may have experienced.

In *Promise to Return,* you paint realistic

and engaging scenes of family dynamics. Within those scenes, you illustrate that the Amish are equally human, with temptations, joys, internal struggles, and feelings. In what ways is the role of family and its authenticity important to you?

Authenticity is a word I often use. It is very important to me to be real with my husband, children, and friends. Being perfect, or pretending to be, doesn't help anyone. Being real with our own insecurities and failures can. Not only does this make you more relatable but it also eliminates judgment. No one is perfect. We all have our big and small hang-ups. It doesn't mean we have to bare it all for the world to see, but when it is helpful, we should share with each other. This is especially important with children — to show them a graceful way to be real, even in failures and mistakes.

At the end of your book, you note that the history of the Amish is rich with conviction that affected American politics and history. How do you see this even today?

In the climate of our politics today I believe

that the Amish provide a social conscience. I especially recognized this when the Amish suffered the Nickle Mines school shooting in 2006. Their testimony and conviction were visible worldwide. I was so very impressed with their example.

With *Promise to Return* now complete, what are your plans for future writing?

I'm so excited to share Book Two of *The Promise of Sunrise* series. It takes the reader on a journey with Eli Brenneman, from *Promise to Return,* as he serves in the Civilian Public Service at a mental asylum. He will meet a beautiful nurse, Christine, and both will learn more about acceptance, the value of all human life, and love.